BRIEF HOURS

BRIEF HOURS

Stanley Middleton

Chivers Press • Thorndike Press
Bath, England   Thorndike, Maine USA

This Large Print edition is published by Chivers Press, England and by Thorndike Press, USA.

Published in 1998 in the U.K. by arrangement with Random House (UK) Limited.

Published in 1998 in the U.S. by arrangement with Century, one of the publishers in Random House (UK) Ltd.

U.K. Hardcover ISBN 0–7540–3166–7 (Chivers Large Print)
U.K. Softcover   ISBN 0–7540–3210–8 (Camden Large Print)
U.S. Softcover   ISBN 0–7862–1306–X (General Series Edition)

The text of this Large Print edition is unabridged.
Other aspects of the book may vary from the original edition.

Set in 16 pt. New Times Roman.

Printed in Great Britain on acid-free paper.

British Library Cataloguing in Publication Data available

Library of Congress Catalog Card Number : 97-91231
ISBN : 0-7862-1306-X (lg. print : sc)

To Margaret, my wife, with all my love

'Love alters not with his brief hours and weeks.'
William Shakespeare
Sonnet CXVI

CHAPTER ONE

Summer afternoon, at two o'clock.

The boy walked, then ran, then walked again. It had become warm, and the sun cast shadows, though they seemed small, un-black. The road along which he took his uneven progress was wide, and made to appear more spacious by the large, well-kept gardens in front of new council-houses, bright with roses, the margins of the flagged paths staggered with Little Dorrit. One could see rows of potatoes, set on Good Friday and now flourishing. His father approved of this. 'Flowers are wonderful, but there's nothing to touch new potatoes.' 'Don't look so good,' the boy had argued. 'Maybe not, though I can't imagine anything finer than a new-scrubbed spud. It's not meant to attract the bees, only the human beings.' And his father would smile to himself, and stroke his moustache, a fount of unassailable wisdom.

The houses lacked uniformity of shape, even placement, sometimes semi-detached, sometimes in terraces of four. Their roofs sloped rather steeply as if to cope with heavy snow-falls, the front doors often shielded by small covered porches, attractive if cramped. There was nothing violently coloured about these buildings, with pale tiles and bricks, but all was neat, even gracious, unshowy.

Nineteen thirty-eight.

The boy, Frank Stapleton, had almost reached a road branching obliquely off to his right. That was unmade up, runnelled, with pot-holes, but somehow magnificent under old lime-trees, tall and heavily leafy, their roots disturbing the surface of the grassy fringes of the road. It was the Squire's Avenue, down which the family coach had rolled in dignity from the Hall in earlier times. The road must have been in better condition then, for here and there pieces of curb-stone still existed, though coarsely covered with weeds and couch-grass.

Frank Stapleton's head blazed with his thoughts. This was by no means unusual; books, lessons, the cinema, gossip provided a constant, changing kaleidoscope, generally pleasant, in which he appeared as hero, foiling villains modestly, or winning the match with a delicately executed late-cut off the most ferocious of the fast bowler's rising deliveries. The late-cut was his older brother's favourite stroke, often described as played so late that the ball was almost past the stumps before the blade guided it, accurately bisecting the slips for a well-applauded boundary.

Today Frank concerned himself with creation, the Creation.

Again this came as no surprise. The subject was broached often enough in Sunday School,

2

where the omnipotence of God was exhibited for their wonder and praise. The world stretched complex from the bottom of the garden, across the flat lands to the east, or the westward rising hills of Derbyshire, out further to the seas, so contained and shallow by the sand, so dark, loathsomely threatening out in the Atlantic or the North Sea in the adventure stories. Frank knew this but did not exactly connect it with the creation myths. They were simple. God said, and it was so. God cast his eye over it, and behold it was very good, but straightforward, no men in dripping oilskins yet, cursing the weather that doused them with heavy violence.

He was within fifteen yards of the Squire's Avenue junction when he jerked to attention with the thought of what came before God. A blank possessed him. Blind nothing, no-thing. He did not stop his progress forward, but slowed it down as if wading through invisible tar, or an electrical field. It could not be. Fear gripped his spine, then a kind of unconsciousness. He could see and hear and smell but without making connections. It was not possible. How could God need creating, and by whom? He had not arrived at his dilemma by any logical process; it had presented itself.

When he thought about it later in life, and he never forgot this afternoon, he remembered it as if his brain, stumbling pleasantly about among the wonders of the Almighty God, had switched itself off, and at rest had faced him with the unanswerable question. The warmth of the afternoon, the sun, the anticipation of watching a cricket match, the dusty beauty of thick hawthorn hedges, the softness of his sandals on the pavement were wiped away, leaving the icy, wide void. His fear was intense; he was not a bold child at any time, but something of a realist who could face unpleasant situations, look round for ways out, for the possibilities of escape, but here today no such options existed. He had, in some sense, prepared the trap, and fallen into it. He shuddered inside his newly dead universe.

When he came to himself he was fifty yards along the road, had passed the confluence of the streets, the drive to the vicarage and now walked by the hedge, on the unpavemented side of the street, with the farm-fields behind. Frank felt the sun's warmth, heard voices, noticed a wisp of cloud. A man, a small man with protruding teeth and a shapeless cloth cap waited with his back to the hedge, lighting a cigarette. He shook out his match, flicked it into the hedge-bottom and in the pleasure of the first long inhalation of smoke greeted the boy.

'Eh up, kid.'

The child returned the greeting, in a subdued voice. The world was itself again. He knew this man. He kept wicket for one of the

4

minor teams who played round the edge of the cricket field. His name, too, was Frank and he was so keen a player that he would sometimes join in the games the boys indulged in on mid-week evenings, standing ungloved and foolhardy behind the wicket made of wrapped jackets, offering laconic advice, never flinching if the flying compo ball leapt above his hands and into his chest, ribs, face. He wore the cloth cap at all times, even for the real matches when he donned whites.

Frank Stapleton liked it when adults recognized him. Often they did not, passed him by, absorbed in their own preoccupations. Now this man's greeting, the adult smell of sharp smoke in the summer afternoon represented normality, the creation, the existence of God. He moved on, the hollow in his heart not yet healed, but with both feet on holy ground, his eyes peeled for the fine stroke, the quick leg-break, the safe pair of hands under a high-skied ball on the boundary.

People already gathered for the game. The opponents, rough-spoken men from the Derbyshire border and over it, had arrived and prepared themselves for the match, the battle, not by looseners in front of the crowd, batting at dolly-deliveries, but by sitting grasping the wooden seats round the walls of the pavilion with hard hands and staring at the worn, uncleaned cricket boots they had taken from their bags. They exchanged words.

'She wor, I tell yuh.'

'Yo' know best, then.'

These men gave no quarter to their own side, never mind opponents. Saturday afternoon had settled to normality.

* * *

Fifty-six-odd years later Frank Stapleton, retired accountant and a grandfather, mildly considered for the hundredth time that summer's afternoon. It was not a matter of urgency to him, and he had been brought to it by the sight of two grandsons, energetically dribbling a football, away from the park bench where he was sitting. Sailor, his old mongrel, joined them leaping and barking, youth restored by the tackles and swerves, the gasps, the self-congratulatory gestures learnt from television screens. The lads were thirteen and twelve, red of face from exertion on this winter morning, older than he had been, bigger, he supposed, more sophisticated. Were they likely to consider the need for a Creator's creator, or terrify themselves with the absence of a First Cause? He waved to them, certain that they were not. They approached his seat with a rush, the dog bumbling under their feet.

'Ice-cream?' he asked.

'Yes, please.' They were still breathless.

He searched his pockets for a couple of one-pound coins. He handed one to each.

'Will that do?' he asked.

'Oooh, yes. Thanks.'

They set off in a dash, the dog with them.

'Sailor,' he called. 'You come here. You'll do yourself a mischief.' The boys stopped, pointed his master out to the dog, who trotted obediently back. At his command the dog sat at his feet, probably pleased to be temporarily released from further exercise. Stapleton took a biscuit from his pocket and fed it to the animal.

'Just this one now,' he said, scratching the rough head. 'You're getting too fat as it is.'

The boys were at full pelt well away in the hollow.

This was not the same park he had haunted in his youth. That lay three miles away as the crow flies, west-north-west. His grandsons had disappeared. They were making from the dell to a distant gate out to the road and a small shop. He had no anxiety; they had done it often enough before.

He returned to his question. Would these two be troubled as he had been? He thought not. Immediately he wondered what his own father's reaction would have been had he been informed of his son's question. Who would have told him though? Not Frank. He guessed the old man would have been pleased in a weary way that he had sired such a son, but have considered that the problem would be better tackled by doctors of divinity, university professors, not grubby-kneed school children. It might just have crossed his mind that his boy was gifted beyond himself, but the thought would have been dismissed. He did not court hubris or nemesis. In any case a schoolmaster of many years' standing, he was disinclined to overrate young people. Let them learn, and thoroughly, what he had to teach them—most didn't—and then they'd be ready for flights of fancy or scholarship on their own. One of his earliest pupils, it is true, was now a distinguished orientalist, an Arabist, working for or in the Foreign Office. He had been a quiet boy, with glasses; his father had mended Mr Stapleton's shoes, and after a first year in Stapleton's class had later done wonders with Latin and Greek and then had changed to Semitic languages at Oxford University. Horace S. Bramley, that was the name. He had been lively, and quick to learn and answer, but had not raised the matter of God.

Frank Stapleton smiled to himself for thinking his father's thoughts. He was not sure that the old chap would have considered his son, his pupils, Horace Bramley or anything or anybody else in this way. Frank kicked the football for the dog. The ball rolled a few yards; Sailor did not move.

'Don't blame you,' Frank said, scratching the dog's ears. He rose himself, groaning slightly, to retrieve the ball. He sat. 'Time those boys were coming back.'

8

No sign.

'All we're fit for, Sailor. To occupy a bench. Two fat slobs.'

The dog raised its nose in pleasure.

'I'm insulting you,' Frank said, patting. 'And you don't mind. The ragamuffins are coming.' He had caught sight of his grandsons at the top of the slope. Both were running, and whirling their arms.

'Success?' he asked as they skidded to a stop.

'They hadn't,' the younger began.

' . . . got any ice-cream.' His brother finished for him.

'Catastrophe. Why not?'

Sailor had stood, ready for more football.

'He said his freezer had broken down in the night.'

'So what did you buy?'

They showed their treasures, chocolate and chewing gum, and both handed over loose change which the grandfather pocketed.

'Chewing gum?' he said. 'Your mother won't be pleased.'

'She won't know,' Hugh, the younger answered. Ian, the elder, frowned at such naïvety, such artlessness towards adults.

'Unless I tell her.'

'You won't,' Hugh smiled.

'Why not?'

'If you do, she won't let you take us out again.' Again Hugh smiled. 'Grandpa, what's a pox-doctor's clerk?'

9

'Why do you ask me that?'

'The old chap in the shop said the fellow who came to mend the freezer was dressed like a pox-doctor's clerk.'

'Overdressed.'

'Why?' asked Ian.

'A pox-doctor would be somebody who treated sexual diseases. This would be before modern medicine. He'd be an unqualified back-street purveyor of bogus remedies. And so his clerk, his assistant, would be a person of no consequence, but who perhaps tried to improve his appearance so that he'd look important, which he wasn't, but in the end he was so ignorant that he made himself look ridiculous. Thus grossly overdressed. It's an old army expression.'

'Did you use it in the army, Grandpa?'

'I wasn't so rude. Go on now. Ten minutes more dribbling, and then it's home. And don't tell your grandma you've been eating or she'll murder the three of us.'

'We'll finish our dinner,' Ian said, confidently. 'Come on, Hugh.'

He dashed towards the middle of the field, the dog leaping at his side, Hugh trailing. Old Stapleton watched with intense pleasure, shouting an occasional word of encouragement to the younger boy. In answer Ian, the elder, dribbled up to his grandfather's bench and shot past the old man's legs.

'Goal,' he called. 'He's scored. It's in. He's

slotted it home.'

Young Hugh went round the back of the seat to retrieve the ball, not quite content with his subsidiary rôle, but knowing his allotted place, and the unlikelihood of change. A young woman, with a child in a pushchair and a dog on a long lead, spoke to him. The boy answered without embarrassment; Sailor and the stranger animal sniffed each other in a friendly way.

They walked back home, Ian with the ball under his arm, Hugh holding Sailor's lead, grandfather proud to keep up with them.

'Just in time,' his wife called, as they opened the back door. 'Dinner's five minutes from the table. Get washed, you dirty men. And look at your shoes.' All three removed them in the kitchen. 'Your grandpa will clean them.'

The boys rushed upstairs to wash their hands. Frank swilled his at the kitchen sink.

'Is Francesca here?' he asked. His wife nodded, indicating by a toss of the head that their daughter-in-law was in the sitting room. 'How does she seem?'

'As usual.' Thelma Stapleton kept her voice low. 'Get some slippers on and go and talk to her while I take the food in.'

Francesca sat by the window, staring out at her car parked in the drive. She returned his greeting in an abstracted way, but pulled herself together to ask if the boys had behaved themselves.

11

'Full of life,' he answered. 'They run the legs off me and the dog.' He changed his voice. 'How are things at home?'

'Much the same,' she answered flatly.

Francesca and Frank's son Stuart were on the verge of parting. Their marriage was irretrievably broken, they said; nothing could get them back together. The fact that they still lived under the same roof, and talked about separation, offered the father a faint hope, though his wife seemed infinitely more pessimistic.

They heard the boys thundering downstairs even in their stockinged feet and grandma's order to Ian to announce to the others that food was on the table.

The lad pushed at the door of their room.

'It's ready,' Ian said, and disappeared.

'Lunch is served,' grandpa mocked.

Francesca rose, looked hard at him. She was a small, pretty girl with a neatly trimmed bob of dark hair, and large blue eyes. At nearly thirty-five she looked much younger than her years so that she could be easily mistaken for the older sister of her sons. She had a good figure, shapely legs and dressed well. Her hands were beautiful, well cared for, the oval nails manicured. When she smiled, she had barely done so this morning, her teeth were even and white.

'Forward,' Stapleton said, holding open the door. She walked straight past him without acknowledging his courtesy; a faint, delicious perfume and she was away. He allowed her a moment to cross the hall, before he shut the door without a sound. In the dining-room the guests were already seated, and his wife handing out plates and pork chops.

'My favourite,' Ian said.

'Do you like apple with it?' the grandmother asked Hugh.

'Yes, please.'

'From our own trees,' grandfather said. 'They last well.'

The boys helped themselves to vegetables, to gravy. They started to eat.

'I like mint-sauce,' Hugh said.

'Not with pork, surely?'

'We do, sometimes. Don't we, Mum?'

'No.'

One clear, killing word. Frank Stapleton noticed that Francesca had taken very little. Even so, she left some of her meat by the side of her plate. The boys had second helpings.

'You'll fade away,' Frank said.

Francesca smiled faintly, waiting for the rest of them to finish. The first-course plates were cleared, and ginger pudding served with custard.

'Is this your favourite?' Thelma asked.

'Yes,' Hugh answered.

'One of them.' Ian, simultaneously.

'I like a good appetite. Makes a meal worth cooking.'

13

This time Francesca ate the whole of the small piece she had demanded, clearing her plate. The boys finished off the unserved fragments and cleared out the custard-jug.

Francesca stood.

'Thank you for my lunch. It was wonderful. If you don't mind I think I'd better go now. My conference is at two o'clock.' It was now one-twenty, and her office was no more than ten minutes' drive away. 'I'll be home, easily, by five. Do you want me to collect them?'

'No,' Thelma answered. 'We'll deliver them.'

'Don't be a nuisance,' Francesca warned her sons. 'Help your granny if she wants you to.'

'We'll find them something to do. They'll be all right.'

The grandparents accompanied her out to the hall. Frank held her coat. She called goodbyes to her sons who answered casually. They were efficiently clearing the table, and stacking the dishes.

'Haven't you got a dish-washer, Gran?' Hugh asked.

'Yes. Your grandfather.'

They sent the boys out to chase round the garden while the sun was still shining. Thelma warned them not to trample on the flower-beds. They grinned, having heard it all before. They knew exactly which trees they could climb.

At the sink, tea towel in hand, Frank asked his wife if she'd had much conversation with

14

Francesca.

'We had ten minutes. But it wasn't very different. She's seen a lawyer, a young woman. They're going to split up, there's no doubt.'

'And the boys will live with her?'

'Yes. They will. They're both at the secondary school now, she said, and old enough to do a bit for themselves.'

'Keyhole kids.'

'I know. I don't like it any more than you do. Nor can I understand it.'

'The experts say it's better for the children if the parents can't keep the disagreements to themselves. I can see it does no good for them to be living amongst non-stop quarrels. There was no mention of third parties, was there? From her?'

'No,' Thelma answered. 'She just seemed to take it as read that they had reached a point where they see no sense in living together, or even trying to.'

'They've been married fourteen years,' he said.

'I think you should have another word with Stuart.'

'He knows what we think.'

'Well. I often wonder. We've told him, I agree, time and time again, but that's different from his understanding. Speak to him again, Frank. You'll do it better than I do. You'll keep your head. When I think of those boys, I get so angry. I know you believe we can't do anything, but I'd like you to inquire again, at least.'

'Very well,' Frank answered. When Thelma made up her mind there was no gainsaying her. She patted his arm with a wet hand.

CHAPTER TWO

Sunday afternoon shone with winter brightness.

Frank Stapleton and his son Stuart stood together in the kitchen washing the dishes. Father, in shirt sleeves, bent over the bowl, while Stuart flashed a clean, newly-ironed tea towel.

'How are you, then?' Frank asked, gruffly.

'Well enough.'

'I mean between you and Francesca.'

'I know damn' well what you meant. My mother's instructed you to ask a few questions.'

Thelma was sitting in the drawing-room, out of earshot, with her feet up resting after her morning's labour at the meal. Francesca had taken her sons to visit her parents who lived a mile or two away in another suburb.

'Let's have the answer,' the father answered smoothly.

'Much as it ever was.'

Frank clashed his pots unnecessarily loudly.

'You're still thinking of splitting up?'

'We've decided on that. Jenny Townley is looking into the legal position for her.'

'And you're using Duncan Friend?'
'I am.'
'And what's your present thinking? It's like getting blood from a stone talking to you.'

Stuart grinned. He did not mind annoying his father as he knew the old man enjoyed argument. He also knew that his father would be quizzed by Thelma, and that she'd be quick to point out vital questions that he had missed. Thelma was as sharp as her husband, though she appeared not willing to grill her son because she thought he'd be too polite, too bland with her. With his father Stuart could be as rough as he liked, could swear, lose his temper as he pleased, but in the end there'd be more information available.

The two men knew each other well enough. The son after university and professional training with Price Waterhouse, had joined his father's firm, Bell and Stapleton, Accountants. He admired Frank's acumen, realized how carefully and yet brilliantly he had built up the old firm's business, opened new branches, acquired a reputation. The quiet man had formidable qualities, would fight his corner, sort out adversaries, demand the highest standards from his juniors. He never appeared angry, or raised a voice publicly, but had given swift marching orders to two of his young men in the last three years, and had challenged them to take him to a tribunal or before their professional body. Both had gone quietly; both had settled to new positions elsewhere. Frank had told them exactly what he was prepared to write about them in a testimonial. Both saw sense, the strength of his position. One said he was glad to leave. The second claimed he'd sooner work in a church. Frank's mouth had been grim in public for a day or two, but the unpleasant business had done him no harm with his partners and employees or with a wider circle of colleagues and clients. Now the summer before last, he had retired. His son, typically, had not been made senior partner. Stuart had not understood this, though his father had made his intentions clear. When Luke Brailsford retired in two years' time then would be Stuart's opportunity. The young man and the firm would benefit by the period of consolidation. The son could not help feeling disappointment, but realized that his father was both adamant and right. Or so his father hoped. Good old, bright, faithful Brailsford would build the firm solidly up, and then Stuart could expand when he took over. Frank liked to think that it had caused no trouble. Or little. Thelma had not approved of the decision, and said so.

'Fancy not making your own son head of the firm,' she had said bluntly.

'He's not ready yet.'

'Rubbish. He's clever. He's ambitious. It would have put him on his mettle.'

'He'll take over in two or three years.'

18

'You've no telling what the situation will be by then. Luke or some of his cronies might well elbow him out. And there'll be nothing you can do about it.'

'I'm not without influence.' He had kept a substantial financial stake in the firm. 'And if Stuart allows himself to be edged out then he's not the man I think he is, nor the man to lead the firm.'

'What will the others think? Turning your own son down?'

Frank felt certain that his wife would not have kept quiet about her complaint to her son. He did not mind. It was all part of Stuart's trial, his period of testing to prepare him for leadership. He returned to his cross-examination.

'What are the present arrangements or developments?'

'Nothing's certain yet,' Stuart answered.

'Is staying together one of the options?'

'No.'

'What about the boys? Who will they live with?'

'Francesca, during the week. I shall see them at the weekend. But nothing's settled.'

'Will that be satisfactory?'

'As satisfactory as we can make it. I think Francesca's going to have a housekeeper. So meals will be ready for them all.'

'What's the trouble between you?' the father asked.

'Look, Dad, we've been through all this before. We don't get on.'

'Seventy per cent of husbands and wives stick together even these days.'

'And I'd have to be one of the thirty? Just to annoy you?' Stuart juggled a gravy-boat, hand to hand, dangerously confident. Frank knew he'd rattled his son. 'She's not the woman I married. I'm not blaming her. I've changed. We both have jobs, and we're both busy and doing well. She better than I am. That's the top and bottom. And we both feel guilty in a half-hearted way. When you were young and making your way, you had my mother to look after me, and keep your meals warm till you came home at all hours of the day and night. And never a word of complaint.'

'Little do you know.'

'Nothing of any note. It didn't cause you to split up.' Stuart grinned wolfishly. 'It's all very complicated. I tell you this story that we're both wrapped up in our work. And for all I know that's the top and bottom of it. But it's nothing like the truth.'

'Why do you give it to me then?'

'Because,' the son spoke slowly, 'it's the sort of explanation you like.'

'And what do you mean by that?'

'You didn't make me senior partner in the firm because you said I needed a further period of work as a junior member before I was ready to take the firm over. Sounds well, but it's tosh.

20

I'm thirty-five. I won prizes in my professional exams. I've had a wider range of work than Luke Brailsford ever had. All this you know. The reason you didn't allow me to succeed you was that you couldn't bear to see me sitting in your office.'

'I was forty-five before I took over from Tom Bell.'

'And it would have been better if you'd have been in charge ten years earlier.'

'I don't know that.'

'You mean you don't want to know it.'

Frank completed the last of the cutlery, fetched the soiled saucepans over to the draining board, leaned forward, hands on the edge of the sink.

'I didn't realize you felt so strongly about it.'

'There's a great deal you don't realize.'

Frank turned towards his son, slowly, like a very old man.

'Is that part of the cause of the trouble, between you and Francesca?'

'It made me that bit more unreasonable, I expect. At a time when we needed everything going smoothly and exactly as we wanted it.'

'You knew for over a year before I retired that Luke would succeed me. You seemed to accept it.'

'Seemed. Seemed. And it came at a time when Fran was beginning to make big strides in her firm. They've given her chances to show what she can do, and she's taken them.'

'She's not head of the firm.'

'No. That was never likely. But she's a partner. She's spear-heading new work. Her bonuses are incredible. And if she travelled more she'd do even better. She's on the way up.'

'So are you.'

Frank Stapleton received no answer to that. He carefully cleaned and emptied the sink, replaced his cloths and brushes, wiped down the draining-board in a long silence. In the end he spoke. Very subdued.

'That's how it is, then?'

His son squared his tea-towel and hung it up to dry, apparently in good spirits.

'You think about those boys,' Frank said.

'*You* think,' his son replied, and turned on his heel. But he ironically held the scullery-door open to allow his father passage.

Stuart, in spite of his mother's importunity, did not stay for long.

'You can watch football on the telly here as well as at home.'

'No, thanks. I've one or two little jobs to do.'

He left cheerfully enough, kissing his mother, waving to his father.

'Well?' Thelma asked before they were back to their chairs. She sounded grim, as if she'd been disappointed by her son's hurried exit. Frank gave an account of the conversation with his son in the kitchen. When he had finished, Thelma pulled her reading glasses down to the

22

tip of her nose to stare across at him. She licked her lips almost violently.

'You mean he was blaming you?' she asked.

'To some extent.' Frank tried to sound unprejudiced. 'Francesca was getting on faster with her career than he was, and he wasn't prepared to accept this. It altered their way of looking at each other. And one of the reasons he felt at a disadvantage was that I hadn't made him principal at Bell and Stapleton.'

'Is it true, d'you think?'

'Well, it might be a contributory factor.'

Thelma repeated his phrase 'contributory factor', making acid fun of his pretentiousness and then said sharply, to his surprise, 'That's not fair.'

Thelma clasped her hands together as if in an agony of thought. She swayed slightly, almost deliberately across her seat. He watched. 'They're both ambitious, and selfish, but Francesca should have her chance. Why shouldn't she? She's clever. But if they'd a ha'porth of regard for each other they could easily organize things. They could afford to have their house cleaned and their shopping done and somebody to prepare the evening meal and be there when the boys come home from school.'

'Yes. There's talk of a live-in housekeeper for Francesca after they've separated. Presumably he'll help pay.'

'If she needs it. Will she stay in their present

house?'

'I don't know. Nothing much was decided. They've both consulted solicitors . . .

'The same one?'

'No. They can't. She's seeing Tom Townley's girl, and Stu employs Duncan Friend. But nothing's been decided.

'Perhaps they're both recommending reconciliation. They all know each other well. Duncan was in Stuart's class at school.'

'That's not the impression I got,' he said. 'How do you think the boys will take it?'

'Didn't you ask him that?'

'Not in so many words.'

Thelma gave a gasp of exasperation, then relented, gave her view.

'The impression I get from Stu is that now the boys are at the secondary school level they'll be able to cope. I'm not so sure myself.'

'And why not?' he asked.

'If things go wrong, and there are difficulties, say, or snags, they'll need help from their parents to pull them through. That's certain. And if that were the preeminent consideration, it could be arranged. They don't get on for some reason, and are not prepared to make compromises.'

'He'd argue,' Frank said, 'that it might be a lot worse for Ian and Hugh if they continued to live together and were everlastingly quarrelling.'

'He might say that. But they could make it

work. They could keep out of each other's way. I know that both would want to stay late at the office on the housekeeper's night out. That one or both might want to be away frequently. That sort of thing. And it's awkward, galling. I used to hate it, and you, when you didn't come home on time,' Thelma said.

'It's the way to get on.'

'Couldn't you have organized it otherwise?'

'No. I don't think so. Not without loading myself with a whole lot of extra work. Not to mention a bad reputation. I had to do a day at a time, and not let the day's schedule spill over into the next. Even so, it sometimes did. We were expanding, and you don't do that without putting yourself out.'

'You didn't consider me.'

'You knew the man you married, and how I spent my time. I tried to make it up to you, and Stu, in the holidays and at weekends.'

'A fortnight a year. Big deal.'

This was not the first time they'd held this discussion. They used it when they were off colour, or things had not gone easily. It purged them of present petty discomforts, this recounting of ancient ills. Thelma seemed serious enough about it; she'd never forget his treatment of her. But their house and garden, their cruises, her clothes, their bank-account, properties, investments were the results of that former imperfect way of life. Both knew it.

They were surprised to receive a 'phone-call

from Francesca who wanted to visit them. She arranged to come round one afternoon. No, she would not come for lunch, but at two-thirty.

She drew up in her BMW exactly on time, soberly but expensively dressed, quite beautiful. Yes, she would have a cup of weak, sugarless tea, with lemon if they had it, a dash of milk otherwise. While Thelma was out in the kitchen, Francesca smiled at her father-in-law and looked out along a garden dark with rain.

'Wretched weather,' she offered.

'February Fill-Dyke,' he said. Frank could imagine nothing better than sitting with his son's wife, smiling to himself, though he dreaded the message she'd deliver. They exchanged clichés about the comparative mildness of the winter, changing global patterns of weather, greenhouse effects, pollution. Frank talked about his garden.

'It must be pleasant to be able to go out whenever you like.'

'Yes,' he answered. 'Not that I always feel like it. But Thelma and I have ideas. She looks forward to every next bit of the year.'

'Even Winter?'

'Yes. If the garden's done well, she'll photograph it all, and mount the pictures. And she loves to have the ground all sorted out. She draws plans, maps prospective alterations. And you should see her with catalogues.'

'Has she always been a keen gardener?'

'Yes. Like her parents. Her father used to go

26

out to do his bit pretty well to the end of his life. In his eighties.'

'And she doesn't mind you being there all day now you've retired?'

'No. Not that I am there all day and every day. But we've no end of lawn to be dealt with, mown and fertilized and scarified so I'm useful. And it means I can do it when it's most necessary, not the next weekend if and when the weather's fine.'

Thelma appeared, much in command of a large tray.

'I haven't brought biscuits in,' she said to Francesca. 'Is that right?'

'Perfect.'

'You're the only person I know who really can control her diet.'

Francesca acknowledged the compliment with a nod of the head, royally executed. Thelma poured the tea, distributed cups.

'Now, then,' she said, rather harshly. 'If that daft expression means anything.'

Francesca wasted no time.

'I thought I ought to come and say something about this separation between me and Stuart. I owe it to you. You're very good to the boys.' She looked at them. 'And it all must come as a great disappointment to you.'

'Yes,' Frank said, slowly. 'Yes. It does.'

'I don't know if Stuart's spoken to you?'

'Yes, to Frank. His line was that somehow you didn't get on. There was no clear definition of that. That's right, isn't it, Dad?'

'It is.'

'But he put it down to the fact that you both wanted to do well at work. You were rivals for success. And if I understood it properly, you were doing better than he was. This he blamed to some extent on Frank who had obstructed his progress by not making him principal of the firm.'

'I see. Is that it?'

'As far as I can make out. Not that it's very satisfactory.'

Francesca turned towards Frank, put her head on one side interrogatively.

'That's about it,' he answered. 'What we don't understand is this stuff about not getting on. Do you speak to each other? Or fight, physically or verbally? Are you awkward? Do you try to obstruct each other? Deliberately foil his intentions? Mother and I didn't follow him.'

'I'll put it as plainly as I can.'

They waited for her, both faces grim, even formidable.

'Time and time again,' Francesca began slowly, 'I ask myself what I'm doing with this man, why we live together in the same house. I'd sooner be with pretty well any other male I know. And if that seems irrational or exaggerated, it is an exact description. If he asks me to do something, I'm ready to refuse, and rudely, before I've even considered what it is he's asking. Even if it's sensible, or to my

28

advantage, I want to say "No" just because *he's* proposed it.'

'How long has this been going on?' Thelma asked.

'A year or more, in a mild way. This last few months it's become infinitely worse.'

'Sexual relations?' Frank said. His wife looked at him in surprise.

'Next to nothing.' Her face expressed loathing. 'Nothing.'

'There are no outside relationships? Other men or women? He said not.'

'No. Not on my side. I really am very busy, up to my eyes in work.'

'I have never noticed that that stopped adultery,' Frank said. 'The opposite, in fact. It's a kind of reward.'

Both women looked at him in surprise.

'I won't ask you to expand on that,' Francesca said, smiling broadly.

Thelma sat straighter.

'Can you remember what it was like when you were first in love with him?' she asked.

'Yes.'

'Describe it to me.' Thelma sounded implacable. Francesca paused for a moment.

'I wanted to be with him all the time, to be touching and kissing him. He was handsome, and kind, and quick and clever. I felt I wasn't good enough for him by a very long chalk. I couldn't wait to see him the next time.' She spoke without embarrassment.

'Did you never have rows, tiffs?'

'Not much at first. I was jealous once because he seemed to be paying too much attention to a friend of mine. At a dance, it was.'

'And on your wedding day?'

'Absolutely happy.'

'Though,' Frank said, 'I take it a sexual relationship had already begun.'

'It had. But the wedding day was still marvellous, outstandingly so. And the honeymoon.'

Again both women looked at Frank as if to wonder what uncouth question would come next. He sat, eyebrows raised, lower lip jutting.

'Do you never compare the Stuart of that time,' Thelma asked, 'with today's man?'

'It's fourteen years ago, but, yes, I do. Now he's a selfish, self-regarding little . . . '

'Bastard,' Frank supplied.

Thelma smiled, as if thinking of something else.

'You must forgive us all these questions,' she said. 'We don't wish to be either rude or impertinent. But we're very worried about the effect on Ian and Hugh. As you know.'

'I know.' Francesca used the same preoccupied tone as her mother-in-law. 'I think I understand how you feel about this. You'd say that Stuart and I have got it out of kilter. We should subordinate everything to the boys' interest. If, for instance, it was a case of paying

30

their school fees or having a new car, then it's no contest. They come first.'

'And shouldn't that be so?' Thelma asked.

'Oh, yes. In that case certainly. But this is not exactly the same. What good will it do the boys to have parents continually bickering, who can't agree about anything, who've come to hate each other?'

'That situation only arises when you are not putting their interests first,' Frank answered. 'You allow your feelings top priority. They are what count.'

'I can only speak for myself, not for Stuart, but I can't help it.'

'I wonder if that's right,' he said.

'What do you mean?' she asked, flustered.

'Marriages aren't all smooth. But if your main aim was to keep living together for the sake of the boys, then you'd take the necessary precautions. Get into the habit.'

'Live like hypocrites?'

'Yes. Possibly. Yes. There are worse faults than hypocrisy.'

'I don't think I could do it. I'm in such a mess emotionally. And I don't think it's from want of trying. I've said to myself dozens of times, "Keep your mouth shut" or "Get out of the way", and I expect he's done the same. But we're past reason now. Little ploys like that don't work any more.'

'Is work, your respective jobs, the main cause of trouble?'

'I doubt it. Not now. We've so grown away from one another that any subject is a cause of dissension. If he said to one of the boys that the cost of a first-class letter was twenty-six pence, then my hackles would rise, and I'd want to deny it.'

'And would you?'

'No. Because I know it's correct. But it's this surge of feeling.'

'And you can't fight against it?' Thelma asked.

'I've tried often enough.'

'Do your parents know about this? What do they say?'

'They know,' Francesca answered. 'They might wish it otherwise, as you do. But they think Stuart and I are grown-ups and must do as we think best. It's our concern. I guess they judge our kind of marriage more as a temporary contract than a life-long commitment. If divorce were more difficult, then the situation might be different . . . I don't know. They'd prefer us to stay together if it were possible, but they think, rightly in my view, that they can't do anything about it.'

'What do the boys say?' Thelma asked.

'It hasn't been mentioned to them. Not until something more definite has been arranged. We're not looking for trouble, though I know you think we've found it.'

Frank put a peaceable hand briefly on her arm. 'We shall miss you,' he said.

32

'But we're sure to meet. You're welcome at any time to come and see the boys. They're still your grandchildren.'

Thelma shook her head, as if denying this, sadly.

'I remember when Stuart was quite young, I was furiously angry with Frank and I didn't speak to him for a fortnight. Not unless Stuart was in the room. I could easily have left him. There was nothing to be said in favour of our marriage. I used to cry for hours on end when I was left on my own in the house. I didn't want to live, except to hurt him.'

'Was there a good reason?' Francesca asked. The question seemed to demonstrate her sanity, or her care for them.

'I thought he was committing adultery.'

'And was he?' That question sounded over-bright.

'I don't think so. Not now.'

'No, I wasn't,' Frank said. 'I was acting stupidly, I'll admit that. But no adultery.'

'I hung on,' Thelma said. 'I hated him sometimes. I couldn't bear him near me. And it was made worse because he did his best to be pleasant to me. He could see how upset I was.'

'And?' Sarcasm roughened the rise of the syllable.

'I clung on. And gradually it righted itself. I don't know how. When I think back it seems unreal, as if it hadn't happened. But I know it did. It tore me apart.'

33

The three sat in silence. Thelma seemed to blush. Frank knuckled his grim face. Francesca did not move, but it was she who spoke first.

'Some months ago, before things were anything like as bad as they are now, I tried to persuade Stuart to go to Relate with me. He did, but only once. Didn't want to listen, or talk. Said it was no business of theirs.'

'A pity,' Thelma muttered.

Francesca looked up, then back again to the long, spread fingers of her left hand.

'So there's nothing that can be done?' Frank asked.

'No. I'm afraid not.'

'Not even hanging on like Thelma?'

'I don't think so.'

Francesca sighed, deeply, as if the breath was forced out by external pressures.

CHAPTER THREE

At the end of February, Luke Brailsford, the principal of Bell and Stapleton, suffered a massive stroke. Paralyzed and speechless, face distorted, he lay in his hospital bed a caricature of the former solid, rock-like man. The chances of complete recovery were, according to the doctors, remote. His wife blamed the strain of his new position, the additional social burdens, the rich meals he had to eat in the company of his fellow accountants, the long hours he

34

worked and travelled.

According to Stuart, who took over from Brailsford, the man had done little extra in his new eminence. The trouble was that people, mainly subordinates, asked questions, on not very important matters, and these harried the inadequate Luke. He had not been used to quick, off-the-cuff decisions. 'Ask Frank' or 'We must take this up with Frank' had been his stand-by. Now left to himself he tended to say. 'Please yourself' or 'Do what you think best', which caused trouble. 'I'm not saying,' Stuart complained, 'that there should be an overall strategy planned down to the last drawing-pin, but there ought to be somebody about who has some idea of the firm's commitments. There was in your day, Dad. You.'

'And there will be in yours, I see,' Frank answered.

Frank Stapleton found it not quite acceptable that his son said nothing sympathetic about Luke's stroke, nor Mrs Brailsford's subsequent difficulties. Frank drove at once to the hospital where he found his former colleague bedridden and speechless. A daughter, there at the same time, said they were doing their best for her father, giving him all sorts of physiotherapy; she instanced a sponge-ball he held in his left hand which he had to keep squeezing.

'Go on, Dad,' she encouraged. 'Don't stop. He understands every word you say. Don't you,

Dad?'

Brailsford rolled his eyes to look at his visitors, turning Frank's heart over.

Mrs Brailsford, a small energetic woman, rushed from hospital to home, and back, answering the phone, feeding those who came from a distance. She seemed not optimistic about her husband's chances of recovery, but the realization of this galvanized her to more strenuous behaviour, as if she believed that her energy could somehow make up for the immobility of the paralyzed, heavy body. Now she claimed that it had not been a good idea for her husband to take over the leadership of the firm.

'Were you against it?' Frank asked sympathetically. 'At the time?'

'He wanted the position so much. And the status. But he'd had high blood-pressure for years, and the doctor said he mustn't overstrain himself. I said that it would cause stress, and told him that you were pleased to retire. You said so yourself. To me. More than once. And I knew you could stand any amount of hassle. But no. A well-established company like Bell and Stapleton pretty well ran itself, he said, as long as each of the partners and employees did his work properly. But he found out differently.'

'He'll have to go carefully when he gets back,' Frank said, hypocritically.

'He's not likely to get back, even part-time.'

36

'We must hope.'

'That's all I can. But I've got an invalid on my hands for the rest of his life.'

'What do the doctors say?'

'That there's been some slight, early improvement, and that's a good sign.'

Stuart did not move into the principal's office, but made the necessary small arrangements to direct the firm from his own, which was as large and convenient. He used both secretaries, and showed diplomatic tact about their status. His position as *de facto* head of the firm was accepted by everybody, and some of the younger accountants openly said that the change was for the better. The young man seemed thoroughly relaxed, much in command of himself and the office.

'He's much more like the old Stuart,' his mother said.

'Yes, he's doing well,' Frank answered.

'Do you think this will settle his marriage?'

'That's asking a bit much.'

'You never know.'

'No, you don't.'

Francesca had now appointed a housekeeper, a Mrs Daley. The older Stapletons never found out whether their son had been consulted, or whether Francesca, preparing for separation, had alone found a suitable person to care for her family. Miriam Daley, a Scottish divorcee, lived not five minutes' drive from the Stuart Stapletons' house, and had her own room there for the occasions she had to spend the night. She was a cheerful woman, perhaps forty, moderately strict with the boys, but well liked by them. She cooked substantial and delicious meals, did not seem over-burdened or cluttered by her own affairs and so could easily make last-minute arrangements, a necessity with the lifestyle of the Stapletons. She had a daughter of twenty, now away at university, and her ex-husband had returned to Stirling, where he had been brought up. Both Stuart and Francesca seemed to put themselves out to oblige their new treasure, except where their work was concerned.

'How are you getting on with Mrs Daley?' Frank asked his grandsons.

'All right,' Ian replied. 'She's all right.'

'Is she strict?'

'She thinks she is.'

'She makes fantastic apple-puddings,' Hugh offered.

'Suet puddings?'

The boy looked puzzled. Grandpa explained. Hugh nodded agreement and grinning rubbed his tummy.

'She's quite good at football, isn't she, Ian?'

'For a woman.'

Francesca and Stuart never visited the Stapletons as a pair, nor undertook any social activity together except with the boys. Both spoke of the home situation as a kind of

38

bearable stagnation. No further progress had been made towards their separation; they saw no pressing need. Francesca claimed that the presence of Miriam Daley made all the difference.

'Does that mean you're not going to separate?' Frank asked.

'No. It's most likely we shall. But not yet. We're both too busy.'

When Frank reported this to his wife she seemed indignant.

'What about all this stuff about not being able to bear the sight of each other?'

'Perhaps they have to behave themselves when Mrs D.'s about.'

'I can't understand them. I wonder what Francesca's parents make of it all.'

They rarely met the Langs except at the house of their children. Professor Lang taught some sort of engineering at the new University of the North Midlands, the former Poly, while his wife Sarah looked after the paper work of a large car sale-room in the city. 'P.A. to the M.D.,' she announced herself ironically.

'Is it from you or from Jack that Francesca gets her mathematical talent?' Thelma had asked.

'All I can do is arithmetic,' Sarah said.

'And you need plenty of that with that crafty sod you work for,' her husband gibed.

'He's not so bad.'

Thelma met the Langs one morning in the

39

supermarket car-park and tried to question them about their daughter. They appeared affronted, though pleasantly so.

'We're afraid,' Thelma said, 'that a separation will adversely affect the boys.' She received no answer, one way or the other, to her assertion. The Langs stood, he shifting from foot to foot, by their Granada, an expression of serious concern on their faces. They just stood, shaking their heads. Thelma, who expected a professor to have wisdom above her own, was taken aback. 'We talk about it at home,' she said. 'We wonder if there's anything useful we can do.'

'I don't think,' Sarah answered diffidently, 'that they'd brook interference from us. I mean, they're old enough to know their minds.'

'I tell you what I don't understand,' Thelma argued.

'What's that?' Jack spoke with unction, like a keen student, currying favour.

'They give us this story, both of them, that they can't bear sight or sound of each other, and yet as soon as Francesca gets this housekeeper...'

'Mrs Daley,' Professor Lang glossed.

'...Yes, the talk of instant separation disappears.'

'It may be coincidence. Their lawyers might have persuaded them to go easy. The laws on divorce are going to be changed, aren't they? There'll be no quick divorce soon, but a period of at least a year, as I understand it, and encouragement to seek advice about settlement of affairs. Mediation, they call it. So perhaps. . .'

'That's not the impression I have,' Thelma said. 'And I've spoken to both.'

'Together?' Sarah queried.

'No. They never come together to see us. Do they visit you. . . ?'

'They did once. Last week. We were going to take the boys up to the Railway Museum, and they did appear together. I don't know why.'

'They hadn't much to say to each other,' Jack added.

'Well, no. But it didn't seem unnatural,' Sarah said, 'if you know what I mean. You don't need to say much with four extra people in the room, all talking, and arguing.'

Professor Lang again followed his nodding routine.

'We're very fond of Francesca,' Thelma said. 'We shall be sorry to lose touch with her if the marriage breaks up irretrievably.'

'So shall we with Stuart,' Sarah said. 'But it does happen. And I don't see why we should be exempted from the trend. A whole lot of people we know, acquaintances, have had to suffer this experience. Very decent people.'

'Your cousin Daphne,' Jack shyly interrupted, 'for example.'

'Oh, her.' For the first time Sarah Lang sounded angry, perhaps with her husband for

41

raising this family matter. 'Yes.'

'Have you spoken to Francesca? About the separation, the trouble?'

'Yes, we have.' Sarah spoke with exasperation. 'More than once. And without much joy. We're old-fashioned, before the Flood. Things have changed since our day. It's not a matter of life and death now. If people can't get on, they split up. That's that.' Mrs Lang almost stamped her feet. 'I guess she'd speak much more reasonably to you, even if the gist is the same. We're family. She doesn't have to be polite to us.'

'And then there's the upset at EMEG,' Jack said.

'I've not heard anything.'

'They're fighting for their lives. Commercially.'

'I thought Francesca was doing so well. That was one of the reasons why they didn't get on. Stuart was jealous that Francesca was making such headway.'

'I don't doubt,' Lang said, pulling a wry face, 'that she is doing well. She is really gifted with computers. Show her a problem, of whatever sort, and she'll find a solution. But EMEG's snags are not the sort solved by computers. They've failed twice, in the past six months, to clinch big contracts that they fully expected to land and would have kept them in full work for three or four years.'

'Why did they fail?' Thelma asked.

42

'Politicking.'

'I beg your pardon?'

'The biggest contract was for railway carriages. I don't suppose that there was much to choose between the finished products, except that EMEG have had long experience and an outstanding follow-up service. But their main rivals, German, had government backing. They wanted to keep employment there. Result, they subsidize them and they can charge at a lower rate.'

'Can't our government . . . ?' Thelma began.

'Won't.' Lang smacked his lips. 'This German firm are very good, would give EMEG a run for its money in any case, but with some government money behind them will be kept in business all the time. And it won't be a great deal, either.'

'And how does this affect Francesca?'

'Her brigade are chasing work all over the world. They really expected to land this railway contract, were setting themselves to start it, when bang-slap their rivals snatch it away.'

'Jack's very angry,' Sarah said.

'Only because Francesca works there. No, Sal, it happens all the time. And Fran's tied up at this end, trying out means to save a copper or two here, or an hour or two there, or fewer hands. She'll do them proud. The way she solves their engineering problems is a joy to watch. We go over them together sometimes. She'll ask me about some of the technical

43

details. She really is good. But if there's no work, there are no problems for her to look at. It's as simple as that. She's worried to death.'

'She's not mentioned any of this to us.'

'No. She wouldn't. She's just as fond of you as you are of her. She'll be fighting like hell to keep the firm going, but she's not optimistic. She'll make their tenders as low, and efficient, as she can, but she knows she's secondary. She can't argue the way into contracts.'

'Is she likely to be made redundant?'

'She's on the board now. If the firm goes into receivership then there'll be nothing for her.'

'And will that be soon?'

'They've plenty of repair work at present, and that's likely to last for a few months, but they need a really big contract to make the most of themselves.'

'Would she find another job?'

'She's been with EMEG for over five years now. Yes, I think she would, but it would be lower down the order, less well paid.'

'Jack's suggesting,' Sarah said, 'that she does a Ph.D. and goes into academic life.'

'Is that possible?'

Jack shrugged, unlocking the door on his wife's side of the car. Sarah slipped into her seat. The conversation was over, though Lang promised to keep Thelma informed.

'These young people,' he said, 'don't realize how little we know.'

He dived down into his car, sighing deeply.

44

Back at home Thelma discussed the matter with Frank. He said he'd heard that EMEG were struggling, but had no idea how badly. He told his wife that he'd ask Stuart about the business.

'Will this make any difference? To the marriage?'

'Well.'

'Stu's got what he wants now. He's head of the firm, and Francesca's likely to be out of a job.'

'It's not ideal, is it? If Francesca has to go crawling back to him cap in hand, I don't think that would solve anything.'

'Why not?'

'Stu's not very generous, for a start. And she's genuinely frightened him. And she'll be too proud to beg. And that's if they can get over this feeling of detestation they claim to have.'

'Don't you think they do, then?'

'Detest each other. Yes, I genuinely do think so. And it can't be erased on the say-so of one or the other.'

'There won't be so much money.'

'And that's another thing.'

On his wife's importunity Frank Stapleton found an excuse for calling in at the main office of Bell and Stapleton, where his son invited him into his office. Two other of the partners he had seen expressed their pleasure at Stuart's performance.

45

'It's good to get an answer. And when he delegates, he'll leave you to it.' This from one of the older partners. 'Luke wasn't ever too sure. Not of anything.'

When Frank walked into his son's office, he looked round with interest. The room was bare, sparkling, without a book in sight, and no pictures on the elegantly painted oatmeal walls. There were two computers, one on the left of Stuart's large desk, on the top of which were papers, not scattered but giving an appearance of order. Stuart rose, towering above his father, hands deep in his pockets.

'Tea, coffee?' he inquired.

'No, thanks. Norman Grey filled me up. I came in to see him about the Ferguson-John account. Doug Ferguson had spoken to me about it. They weren't altogether satisfied with the way their accounts were being done.'

'By whom?'

'Jardines, Leicester.'

'You surprise me.'

'Norman will ring Doug today. Test the water.'

'That's what I like,' Stuart answered. 'Somebody bringing business in our direction.'

'Are you short, then?'

'The exact opposite. Up to the eyes.' Stuart glanced down. 'As well you know.' He turned on the heel of a well-polished shoe. 'And how do you like the look of this?' He indicated the office.

46

'Excellent. It was a store room, wasn't it? You've made a difference.'

Stuart nodded, seemingly much at ease.

'Now what can I do for you?'

'It's about Francesca.'

The son's eyebrows rose, suddenly, but his lips showed no distaste.

'Is it convenient? Five minutes should cover it.' His father sounded uncertain.

'Unless I argue. Am I right in guessing that my mother's sent you in?'

'Do you know anything about the present position of EMEG? Your mother saw the Langs in the car-park at Sainsbury's.'

'And?'

'They suggested that EMEG were in trouble. They'd failed to get contracts they'd expected to win, and the receivers were not far off.'

'Had they learnt this from Fran?'

'I expect so. Where else?'

'You never know with Jack Lang. He likes to have inside information, and if he hasn't, he makes it up.'

'He's an engineer. He'll have contacts there. They've used him as a consultant.'

'I'm not saying that he knows nothing, only that he tries to make out that he knows more than he does.'

'So you think there's nothing in it?'

'They certainly did fail to land the last two big contracts they were tendering for. But they're an aggressive lot. They'll be after

47

something else.'

'So it's not likely that Francesca will be out of a job?'

'Not really.' Stuart moved effortlessly behind his desk to slide into his chair. He began to finger the papers in front of him. It was a sign of dismissal.

'But if it did happen?'

'I shouldn't leave her destitute. Not that it's likely. She's on a very good line and would easily find another job. And pretty quickly, I'd think. I could use her here.'

'If she were unemployed it wouldn't make any difference to your proposal to separate.'

Stuart sat upright, clasped his hands over the papers. His father noted with appreciation how well-cut his son's suit was.

'I don't see the connection.'

'If Francesca is in trouble, or even just thinks she may be, won't she want somebody at home to talk it over with, somebody who'll support her?'

'You don't know Fran. She's her own woman.' He smiled, as to a simpleton. 'Besides, I never remember you discussing any business crisis with Thelma. You had to trust your own judgement. And that's right. And that's what Fran'll do.'

'The fact that I acted like a bloody fool doesn't mean you should.'

Stuart leaned back, very much the head of the firm.

48

'At present there's a lull. It may be due to the arrival of Mrs Daley. She's efficiency personified; she realizes what it is we want or may need to do, and, best of all, she gets on well enough with the boys. So, things are quiet.'

'Does she know how things stand between you and Francesca?'

'We haven't gone out of our way to tell her. At least, I haven't and I don't suppose Fran has. But she's intelligent, and she'll see it's not all billing and cooing.'

'What I'm driving at,' Frank said, 'is whether the separation is any the less likely because of the advent of this paragon.'

'Paragon, eh?' Stuart smiled, charmingly. 'I don't know. And I'm not trying very hard to find out.'

'Do you want to leave her?'

'I'm extremely busy. I can well do without distractions. We seem to have evolved a system of keeping out of each other's way. I shall do nothing at present to alter this.' Stuart raised his hand to forestall interruption. 'What the consequences will be I can't tell.'

Frank Stapleton turned away.

'How are things here?' He waved a hand round the office.

'Pretty good. We're busy, rushed off our feet. I might even call you in to do a day or two's work for us. Will you mind?'

'Not if it's really necessary. I'll let myself out.'

Stuart rose. Frank made his way through the building to the front door, where he exchanged a few words with one of the secretaries just coming in. She smiled, seemed genuinely glad to see him, but made it clear she had important tasks elsewhere.

CHAPTER FOUR

When Frank reported this visit to Thelma, she looked neither pleased nor sorry, and unusually for her said little, and asked no supplementary questions.

Later as she dashed about with a vacuum cleaner she ventured, 'I should like to meet this Mrs Daley.'

They had the chance on Thelma's birthday, a Saturday, when the housekeeper brought the boys over with their presents. Both parents had sent expensive gifts, but were working away from home. Ian and Hugh kissed their grandmother and shook hands with Frank.

'Aren't you going to introduce us?' the grandfather asked.

'This is Mrs Daley,' the elder said. 'She looks after us.'

'When our Mum's away.'

Mrs Daley made an impression at once. Her fair hair was curly, and smartly trimmed. She wore a dress of Spring-like green with a white collar, and large earrings; her bosom was high

50

and her face handsome. Frank would have placed her in her thirties, for she moved with an elegant energy. Her hands were large and sinewy. She combined a male strength with her femininity. He considered her the exact opposite of his expectations; this was no middle-aged virago. She spoke quietly, with small emphasis. The boys did as she told them, but cheerfully, talking to her without constraint.

After Thelma had unwrapped the presents, they all walked round the garden together. The boys swooped in a game of tag, with its accusatory claims and denials, but never once stepped off the path on to grandma's garden. Thelma suggested that she must visit the corner-shop, on the main road half a mile away, and the boys, anticipating bars of chocolate, volunteered to accompany her.

'Look after your Gran,' Frank called. He noticed that Mrs Daley offered no last-minute advice, merely straightening Hugh's collar with one deft movement of a finger. Frank led her into the drawing-room.

'It's warm here,' he said. 'There aren't too many signs of Spring yet.'

Mrs Daley smiled pleasantly.

'Which is your chair?' she asked.

'You sit where you please.'

'Thank you.'

'We'll have coffee when my wife returns.' Frank cleared his throat. 'I hear very good reports of you.'

A slight inclination of the curly head. Her legs were neatly together.

'You've been with Stuart and Francesca a little time now?'

'Two months.'

'You don't live in, do you?'

'Not unless they're both away, or there is some other good reason. I take the boys to school every morning, and then collect them, and have the evening meal ready by seven.'

'Are the grown-ups regularly home by that time?'

'Not always.' Again the propitiatory smile. 'But they don't mind last minute changes or burnt meals too much. I'm learning my way around.'

'Do you enjoy it?'

'I don't know about enjoy, but I can do it. It suits me. I'm lucky.'

'How did you find the job? Had they advertised?'

'They had. But Francesca had met me at Belshaw's, one of their subsidiaries. I have to have employment, and I worked there in the office. She learnt that I lived not far away from her, and I'd baby-sat for them. The boys and I seemed to get on quite well, and Francesca asked me if I'd act as housekeeper.'

'Were you keen?'

'I'd done it before. Soon after my marriage broke up. For old Mr Willetts, William Willetts.

52

I had to live in there, with my daughter. Mr Willetts was getting feeble. He had a nurse in three times a day. But this is very different.'

'Were there advantages? When Francesca offered you the post?'

'One doesn't move out easily from a regular job these days. But there was a rise in salary, and a saving on petrol and food. And I could even let my flat, and live in.'

'But you don't.'

'No. Emma has to have somewhere when she comes back from college. Or I like to think that's what she wants, a home of sorts. And it makes me feel that bit more independent.'

'And what are the drawbacks?'

'They change their minds.' She laughed. 'That's not quite right. They have quite quickly altered schedules. Called away to meetings. Have to stay overnight after extended conferences. That sort of thing.'

'And it doesn't put you out?'

'No. I don't have a very varied social life. I once had to give a theatre ticket away. But they insisted that I went on another night. The same week. In a more expensive seat. They're very generous in that way.'

'I see.'

'I sometimes think they change their minds just to score off each other.' She looked craftily at him, Frank thought, after this naïve statement. He nodded, understandingly, safely. 'Dinner is always at the same time. Seven o'clock exactly. The boys are allowed half an hour, with a drink and cake when I get them home at a quarter to five or thereabouts, and then it's my job to set them down to homework. They do that on the big table in the small sitting room.'

'Do they do it conscientiously?'

'Yes. They're good, very good, so far. They have the habit. And that's half the battle. And they show me their completed tasks before they are allowed up to their rooms.'

'And they do it well?'

'I'm in no position to judge. I mean, I don't know any chemistry or mediaeval history to speak of. But I look at their past work when it's been marked, and they score well enough. Nine or ten out of ten practically every time, both of them. Their mother inspects their books every week.'

'But not Stuart?'

'Not so far as I know.'

'And they eat with their parents?'

'Yes. All five of us together.'

'They must be hungry by that time?'

'Oh, yes. They've good appetites. They're allowed fruit between meals.'

Far from resenting his inquisition Miriam Daley appeared almost anxious to answer his questions. She would not make any but the mildest criticisms of her employers, who were, it seemed, her benefactors. She spoke with ease, as an equal, in an educated slightly

54

Scottish voice, and Frank would have liked to question her about her ex-husband and her marriage. He did not do so, but approached family affairs obliquely by asking about her daughter. Emma, nineteen now, was studying English at Liverpool University and thoroughly enjoying herself. She was a hard worker, clever, had gained excellent 'A' Levels in English, French and German. Yes, she had been homesick at first, but had not come back at all to Beechnall until the Christmas vacation, and not since. She'd be over for Easter. She had taken four days off at the New Year to visit her father in Scotland.

'Did she have a good time?'

'She said very little. But, yes. I think her father had found himself a new partner, and Emma wasn't sure how I'd receive the news.'

'She's always kept in touch with her father?'

'By letter or 'phone. I encouraged her to go and see him in the school holidays, but it's a long way, and she didn't seem keen.'

'I take it you and your husband parted without acrimony?'

'You're wrong.'

'You are divorced?'

'Yes. Four years now. But we'd been apart for five years before that. He'd gone back to Scotland. That was part of the trouble.'

'She was the only child?'

'Yes. Born inside the first twelve months. I did a preliminary year at an art college, and was

55

going off to Newcastle to do fine art, but got married instead. More fool me.' She sounded only humorously concerned. 'I helped him out in his work.'

'Which was?'

'The rag-trade. Women's clothes.'

Miriam Daley smiled to herself, because, he guessed, he'd asked too many questions, so that he dared go on no longer, even at this interesting juncture.

'I'm sorry,' he said. 'I'm abominably curious. I've no right to quiz you like this.'

'I don't mind. You've every right to find out all you can about the person looking after your grandsons.'

They heard Thelma's key in the door, the subdued shouts of the boys.

'Are you local? Originally?'

'I've lived here most of my life. My parents, both dead now, came from Montrose.'

Thelma bustled in, bag in hand. The boys looked remarkably pleased with themselves.

'Rotted your gnashers yet?' grandfather asked.

'We had gob-stoppers. Enormous.'

'I hope I did right?' Thelma said to Mrs Daley.

'I'll see to it that they clean their teeth.'

They took their mid-morning drinks together, but after half an hour Mrs Daley led her charges away, saying that one needed rest on a birthday.

'What do you think?' Frank asked in the ensuing quiet.

'About what?'

'You know what I'm talking about. Mrs Daley.'

'Yes. Yes.' Thelma's eyes mocked him. 'A very presentable woman. The boys spoke well of her.'

Frank reported his own exchanges with the housekeeper.

'You were favourably impressed. I can see that.'

'She didn't mind my asking questions.'

'You'd be in your element.'

'Did Ian or Hugh say anything about trouble between their parents?'

'No. They were chattering away all the time, but not about that.'

'I wonder if they've any inkling?'

'I don't know. I don't know how we'd find out. I think they look on their parents rather differently from our generation. The family seems less compact. I don't want to overstate the case because I know they are dependent on Stuart and Francesca for food and shelter and holidays and money and transport and all the rest of it, but they seem more detached. Perhaps I don't see things as I did as a child.'

'I should hope not.'

'Somebody's qualifying for a thick ear,' Thelma said cheerfully. 'But we're no further on.'

57

'No.' He pulled a serious face. 'I wish there was something we could do.'

During the next few days Stuart asked if his father would handle a small job for the firm. 'It's Parker's.' A small property company. 'Charles is a friend of mine, and I said I'd ask you. I don't think they'd want one of our youngsters in.'

'Why not?'

'It's the sort of small audit I'd usually send them on. But Charles's Dad is still there, and their auditor has just died aged about ninety, and I think they want to know that it's all been done properly, but they don't want some whippersnapper showing them up. So you sounded ideal. Nobody'll pull the wool over your eyes, but you'll look stately and decently dressed and you'll get on reasonably with Parker senior.'

Grinning at his son's care for old Parker's susceptibilities, a new facet of Stuart the firm's principal, Frank accepted. The job was easy. Accounts had been meticulously kept, and the firm was making a modest profit, forging ahead, investing in the future and paying tax, perhaps rather too much. Frank suggested one or two money-making devices for them, and after he'd finished this, he and the Parkers parted in mutual esteem.

He walked out of their offices and took a bus into town. This he did rarely. He had not even claimed his pensioner's free pass. He enjoyed the ride, and descended at the city's central square. The sun shone, but a north-east wind flicked at the fountains sprinkling the anoraks of passers-by. The place seemed deserted, without unemployed young people, steady pensioners, or alcoholic tramps. Only those with a purpose were out this afternoon, and walking swiftly at that.

Frank called in at the gents' lavatory, running down the steps but holding on to the handrail. The man in charge emerged from his glass-sided cabin, bored perhaps with the lack of interesting customers.

'If this is Spring, give me bloody Winter,' he offered.

'It is nippy,' Frank said, 'but dry.'

'And so's my garden. I'm praying for rain. It's on sand and these winds turn it to dust in no time. And they'll be having a hosepipe ban before you can bat an eyelid. I don't know. The world seems a different place.'

'From when?'

'From when I was a lad.'

'I suppose it is. Not that human nature changes all that much.'

'Yuman nature. You see plenty of that down here. They've got all these steps top to bottom and back up, and the old men don't half grumble. When they've breath. You'd think I was personally responsible for putting 'em there. "Well, at least it's free." And they complain about that. "*You* don't have to work

59

all day cleaning up in a public convenience," I say. And do you know what one of the cheeky boggers said to me, not half an hour ago? "And about as clean as my soddin' dustbin," he says. I ask you. "Thank you very much," I said.' This seemed to cheer the man, who unravelled the dirty cloth in his hand, and whistling set off for his furthest dark corner.

Back at the top of the steps Frank overlooked the square, the pigeons, the neo-classical front of the Council House. That hadn't changed much in the past sixty-seventy years. The golden sword in the pediment gleamed.

'Hello, there. Mr Stapleton.'

He turned, only half-recognizing the voice.

'Mrs Daley.'

'Shopping?'

'No. Time-wasting really. I've just finished a little job for Stuart, and as I'm very rarely here I thought I'd have a ten minutes' walkabout.'

'You've not chosen a very good day for it. I'm frozen.'

'All well with the junior Stapletons?' he asked.

'Yes. As soon as I get back home I'll have to pick up the boys from school.'

'And will the parents be home this evening?'

'Yes. Both.' She took a step towards him. 'Francesca will be going out, straight after dinner. She's very worried.'

'Oh. About what?'

60

'Her friend. Clio Pugh. You know her, I think.'

'She was at school with Fran. I met her at Fran's wedding. I remember her because of the unusual name. I saw her a time or two afterwards. What's wrong with her?'

'You haven't heard?'

'No.'

'Cancer. She's really quite sick.'

'I see.' He didn't. He scratched round in his brain for memories of Clio.

'She's been ill for some time now, but they treated her early. Now she's seriously ill again.'

'Terminally?'

'I don't think anybody's suggested that, but it's what she fears.'

'What's she do for a living?'

'She teaches biology. She's never married, and her only near relative is a brother who works in Gloucester. Both her parents died comparatively young.'

'From cancer?'

'I've no idea. She's a year or two younger than Francesca, looked up to her as one of the big girls in school. She's had an unfortunate life. She was engaged to a man who died in a skiing accident, and then to someone else who broke it off, not long before the actual wedding day. Then this illness. And the deaths of her parents.'

She lives on her own?'

'I believe so. She has a small town house.

Francesca tells me things about her. It's obviously got to her.'

'Were they very friendly?'

'From what I can understand, not really. They were friends in the sixth form though Clio was a year behind, and met occasionally while they were on holiday from university, but Clio went away to teach. Somewhere in Surrey, I think. I don't think they even corresponded. But they met again a few months ago.'

'Yes.'

'I've only these bits and pieces of information. Francesca talks to me about her present trouble. But she seems to think I know a great deal more about her friend than I do. It's upset her, considerably. And it seems to suit her book to tell somebody all about it. I can understand that. I can't make things right, but after you've set some trouble out for somebody else to see or hear, it seems more bearable. That's how I am myself.' She cocked her head, fetchingly, including him in her life. 'Aren't you like that?'

'No, I'm secretive. I run away and hide in my corner. Like a cat.'

She nodded, as if she approved of his wisdom.

'Does she not talk to Stuart about it?'

'She must. She goes out to visit Clio. But do you know, they're like a lot of young couples these days, they don't appear to discuss very much. Or perhaps it's just not in my hearing.

Over dinner they talk to the boys about school-work and holidays and weekends. But if one of them takes the boys out they're as likely as not to ask me to go rather than the other partner. Or they'll suggest it.'

'Do they get on well?'

Miriam Daley looked, for the first time, suspicious.

'Well, they've been married a fair time.'

'Fourteen years.'

'That's longer than mine lasted. We'd been married twelve when Ian went back to Scotland. Emma was eleven. But we'd been at loggerheads well before that. I knew he'd go. He went back home, and I believe he's doing well there. I hope he is. I have nothing against him in that sense. And he supported Emma financially while she was at school. But I was glad to be rid of him. By God, I was.' She suddenly poked a finger at him, jabbing his coat, not hard but surprising him. 'You don't approve of that, do you?' Her voice held no rancour, mocked. The tone of voice, the movement surprised him, as if she'd been jerked into a new persona.

'I've learnt not to judge,' he said pacifically. 'Cases are always complex, so that one shouldn't take sides unless one knows a great deal about them.'

Mrs Daley suddenly looked delighted.

'You know, I spend a great deal of time making things up about Francesca and Stuart.

Fantasizing. My job there is pretty straightforward, ferrying the boys, overseeing the laundry, and preparing the evening meal. It's not difficult; I can manage it and still have time to myself. So I amuse myself thinking about my employers, or imagining their lives.'

'You'll know Francesca better?'

'Yes. She appointed me. And I'd met her before when I worked at Belshaw's.'

'And Stuart?'

'He's new. I'd not known him. I expected them both to be what in fact they are, youngish executives who wanted to be relieved of their domestic chores. But he says very little. To me. Whether that's because he's shy, or he's hanging back to decide whether I do the job properly, or whether he regards me as Francesca's nominee, appointed without reference to him.'

'You prefer Francesca?'

'She's easier to work with. Mark you, she gets tired and irritable and is often preoccupied, but she'll always suggest an answer if I raise some matter.'

'And Stuart won't?'

'I don't exactly say that. Perhaps it'll be different when I get to know him better. But perhaps he's like you, lying low, keeping his head down.' Frank encouraged her with a look. 'But he is like most men. The questions I ask him he considers are not his business. He doesn't want to decide if it's good or even

64

possible for one of the boys to stay the night with a friend.' She glanced first at her watch, and then at the Council House clock. 'I shall have to be on my way. I'll go straight to the school now.'

'Is your car here, in town?'

'Bus station car-park.'

She nodded, brightly, laid a hand on his arm. He noticed that her nails were well-shaped and painted a dark grape-red. She turned and was on her way. Although it was also his way, he made no attempt to accompany her, but stood in the chilling wind watching her cross the square. While she had been talking he had not noticed the cold. She darted into the road at the far end and disappeared among the crowding pedestrians, all dully dressed against inclement weather.

Thelma had heard nothing either of Clio Pugh's illness nor Francesca's concern with it. When Stuart telephoned, mainly to thank his father, his mother questioned him. Yes, Fran visited Clio, once a week now, one evening, and had called in on her more often when she had been in hospital. He knew little of the present state of Clio's health.

'Why not?' his mother asked.

'She's Fran's friend.'

'Is Francesca worried about her?'

'Well, she's sorry she's not well.'

'Stuart, do you know anything at all about this?'

65

'Mother, are you getting on to me?'

'Yes, I am. You make some inquiries.'

'How did you know about this in the first place?' he asked.

'By listening to other people. Something you might start doing.'

'Oh, dear. Oh, dear. I see I'm in trouble.'

He rang off leaving Thelma fuming.

CHAPTER FIVE

Clio Pugh sat by her window. She felt wretchedly ill, weak, nauseated, and ought to have been in bed. She wore a kind of mob-cap, large, like a turban to hide the loss of her hair, even though she was on her own. She bent forward by the window of her pleasant room, eyeing but not enjoying, the early Spring sunshine. She saw Francesca's BMW draw up in the car-park, and her friend, carrying flowers, cross the court yard. She rose from her seat to admit the visitor, but with difficulty, groaning softly.

'Hi,' Francesca said brightly.

'Come in.'

'How are you?' This went unanswered. 'Flowers. Shall I put them in water for you?' Francesca dashed out to the kitchenette to find a vase. Clearly she had done this before. As she ran the taps and arranged the chrysanthemums, she called out, quite loud,

'How are you, then, today?'

'Like death.'

Clio had slumped down with her back to room and visitor, staring listlessly out to the court yard, the green lawns, a small sunlit mountain-ash. Francesca returned with the vase, which she placed without fuss on a small round table.

'Not a drop spilled.' Francesca rubbed her hands. 'How are you then?'

'Bloody awful.'

'When did they let you out?'

'Yesterday. They kept me in for two extra days.'

'This is the last? Of this treatment?'

Clio rubbed her face.

'Can I get you anything? A sandwich?'

'A glass of water with ice.'

'Are you eating?'

'Not much.'

'You should be, you know.'

Clio stared out, her face pure in the pure window-light. By the time Francesca had returned with her drink Clio was in tears. Francesca held the tumbler to her lips as her friend cried quietly.

'What is it, Clio? What's wrong?'

'Everything.' The speaking of the single word seemed to release her inhibitions so that she exploded into a whoop of sobbing. Her shoulders shook as she threw her arms about Fran and clung desperately, fingers biting in.

Francesca made soothing noises, gently rocking the girl, until the outburst began to abate.

'I must look a sight,' Clio said in the end. Francesca held the water to her lips. Certainly the face was smudged with eye-shadow, lipstick, blusher into wet uneven dabs of colour. Tears rolled still from her eyes and her breath trembled between harsh and intermittent croups. Francesca took tissues from the box in her handbag and dabbed at the blubby face.

'I feel so awful,' Clio muttered, voice steadier.

'Never mind.'

'The chemotherapy makes me feel so ill. I'm nauseated, and so weak. And full of pain. I know I'm going to die, Fran. I'm certain.'

'What do the doctors say?'

'What can they? They'll scan me and give me tests and say things that don't mean anything. I hate them. They say that the treatment has been successful and that there are no signs of the growths, and then after a few months I shall hear that it's all returned, as bad as ever. And the consultant will look at me and tell me that he thought we were making big progress and that this is a bit of a set-back, but we mustn't give up.'

'He's a sympathetic sort of man, is he?'

'He does his best, but he must see dozens like me every day of the week. I'm sure he's no idea how wretched I am.Oh, he could put it down on an exam-paper for his students, the pain and the terror, but they're only words to him, words that he's learnt from books not from people like me. He thinks I'm feeble, with no will-power. Some of the others face it and fight it, but I just crumple and scream.'

'I tell you what,' Francesca said, and made her friend wait. 'You go along to the bathroom and straighten your face, and then put yourself to bed. And I'll go to the kitchen and make you something to eat.'

'I couldn't, Fran, I couldn't.'

'Do as you're told and don't grumble.' Francesca felt the comic harshness of her words together with the sense that nothing but such crudity would have any effect. She helped Clio with gentleness to her feet and guided her, hand on back, to the bathroom.

'Clean yourself up, and then get into bed.'

She thought Clio would burst into sobbing again, but the woman straightened her shoulders, and made a strong way into the bathroom. Silence. Then a running tap, and a footstep or two.

Satisfied, she made her way to the kitchen.

When she returned Clio had washed her face, but had not undressed and sat on the side of her bed, weeping. As though dealing with a child Francesca rapidly undressed and settled her.

'I want you to try and eat a bit.'

'I can't. I can't.' She began to sob

desperately.

'I want you to try. Even if it's only a mouthful.'

'I feel so sick.' Her crying intensified.

'I know. But now this spell of treatment's done, you've got to build yourself up.'

Clio tried, chewed and swallowed a mouthful or two of the scrambled egg that Francesca had prepared and sipped at a cup of tea. She began to retch almost immediately, but managed to keep down the morsels. Again she clung to her friend, keening loudly as if she did not realize what was happening. In the end she quietened herself.

'That's good,' Francesca said. 'It's a start. Now I shall have to go, but I'll make a thermos flask for you, and leave a biscuit or two. Don't get up unless you have to or want to. I'll be in later tonight after the boys are in bed.'

'I don't know why you bother with me.'

'We're going to get you better.'

Francesca washed the dishes, prepared a thermos of tea, left biscuits and water by the bedside.

'Keep eating a little,' she wheedled. 'Promise?'

'I don't think I . . .'

'Do as you're told. Is anyone likely to come in this afternoon?'

'My cleaner. She's very good. She'll come to see if I want anything.'

'Good. And I'll be in about nine to get you

70

finally to bed.'

'Thank you, thank you.'

Outside the window in the court yard, Francesca took in a great breath of fresh air in relief. She felt no sense of having done well. Clio was a hopeless case. There seemed no aura of rationality about her, merely childish, resentful awkwardness. An animal would have done better, hiding out of sight to suffer in silence.

Francesca checked herself. How would she have fared? With cancer and the violence of the treatment? She had more to lose than Clio; she had her boys, her parents, Stuart's parents, perhaps even Stu himself. The thought surprised her. Stuart? What would he say if she told him she must put in more time with Clio, to set her on the way to recovery. He'd not be pleased. Charity begins at home. Francesca let herself cautiously into her car, debating within herself, in dubiety.

To her own surprise she explained Clio's condition to Stuart after the evening meal while they stacked the dishwasher. She did it plainly, without exaggeration.

'Have you the time to go up there every day? Twice a day?' he asked mildly.

'Not really.'

'No. Were you thinking of bringing her back and putting her up here?'

'No.'

'It's possible. I guess it depends how quickly

71

she recovers. But if you get a great rush of work away, she'll be left on her own much of the time here, and in a strange house that won't be good. And it'll put more work on Miriam.'

Stuart's eminently reasonable tone cheered her; she had expected either no answer at all or to be told to sort her own problems out. When she called in again on Clio, she found that the initial difficulties had been overcome. A cousin of Clio's, (Francesca had understood that she had no relatives living near), had offered to stay with her for a week, if not more, until she felt stronger. Mrs Weekes, the cousin, Celia, was a widow in her fifties with a grown-up family who lived four miles outside the city in a small flat and no garden. She'd be, she said, glad to do it.

Francesca, relieved that the responsibility had been taken away from her, felt guilty.

'What's she like?' she asked Clio.

'Pretty efficient, I'd guess. Boring. She'll talk me to death. But it means I can stay in bed if I feel ill. And be tempted by meals.'

'She's a good cook, is she?'

'I doubt it. I've no idea. We've had very little to do with each other. I had told her some time ago how things were, and she rang up by chance this lunchtime. Just after you'd left. And almost immediately she offered to come and stay.'

'That's very good.'

'I doubt it.' Clio let her short sentence

72

dribble weakly away. She collected herself. 'I told her that you were coming in this evening, so she said she would start first thing tomorrow. It would give her the chance to organize matters at her end.'

'That's sensible. Have you eaten since I left you?'

'Yes. I've not cooked anything.'

'What would you like now?'

'Could you do me scrambled egg again? I think I could manage to eat that. A little. On toast. I feel less sick. And I'm not so worried now.'

'I'll do it.'

Clio ate a few mouthfuls, drank a cup of coffee, and was led out to the bathroom. She did not ask for a bath, and again Francesca was glad. She feared to look at her friend's mutilated breast, or to try to lift the slippery body out of the scented, deepish water. Straightening the bed while Clio prepared herself, Francesca led the invalid in, tucked her up, left her water, tablets, a huge radio.

'What about the morning?'

'Celia said I was to stop in bed, and she'll get breakfast when she arrives.'

'What time will that be?'

'Between eight-thirty and nine. Depends on the traffic.'

'Are you sure you'll be all right?'

'Yes. And thank you, Francesca. I don't know what I'd have done. Without you.'

73

At home the boys had gone to bed, but were not asleep. She chatted to them for a while, then went downstairs to make herself a drink. Mrs Daley had gone home. Stuart, to her surprise, was waiting in the kitchen. He asked what she wanted, said he would see to it, and ordered her to sit down. She chose a chair in the large sitting-room where he had left the radio playing some music she did not recognize. He returned, carefully procured a mat for her hot chocolate before settling down opposite. The only light in the room was from a small standard lamp by a table near his seat.

'How was she?'

'Pretty weak and sorry for herself.' She gave him a brief account of Clio's medical condition. He listened, cradling his mug in both hands.

'Yes,' he said. 'You should be careful.'

'In what way?' She felt stirrings of ill-temper.

'You're going through a rough patch. At work. I was talking to Bill Watchett only yesterday.' Watchett, an engineer of talent, was a member of her board. 'He said a thing or two. I think he'd have liked to find out what you thought.'

'He could ask me. I see him often enough.'

'Has he said anything about leaving, setting up on his own?'

'It's been in his mind for long enough.'

'Do you think he could do it?'

'He's very gifted, and enterprising. But it takes a good deal of money to set up in our line

74

of business. I don't need to tell you that.'

'If he does make the move, would he take you with him?'

'He's said before now that he'd make me an offer. But I don't know whether he's the will to go. He's not much social ambition, nor has his wife. His children are settled in decent schools. He wouldn't want to uproot himself.'

'Unless circumstances forced it on him.'

'I suppose so,' she conceded.

'Would you go with him?'

'We-ell.'

They sat in silence, amongst the shadows. This was not the sort of conversation she had envisaged as she had waited there for him. She expected talk of marriage, children, home life, not business. She suspected his parents had been at him, and they were expert operators. Stuart was pleased in that he'd now got what he wanted, he was officially principal of the firm with no chance of Luke Brailsford's return, and Frank and Thelma certainly would not lose the opportunity. Francesca wondered if intervention from her own parents would have any effect, but to her outsider's eye, the senior Stapletons were heavyweights compared with her family.

'Venture capital's not easily come by these days,' she said.

'No. But Watchett's full of unusual ideas.'

'Some of which work and some of which won't.'

'I'm sure.' Stuart put down his cup. 'He thinks EMEG will survive. Well, in some form or other. Is that your view?'

'Yes. They might have to cut down the workforce.'

'Is that good or bad?'

'Bad for those who lose their jobs. But it might force us to modernize.'

'Won't that cost money?'

'A great deal. That's why we need a really big contract or two. For the next three years. Something that keeps the cash rolling in, and the banks at bay, and at the same time gives Bill Watchett and one or two others their head.'

'You included?'

She bowed from the neck, a neat inclination which denoted the friendly intimacy between them. This is how they used to talk when first she joined EMEG five years or so ago, when they were both excited by the idea of her working again full-time.

'But it's not ever so likely?' Stuart asked.

'Sam Fitch is out in India and Sri Lanka and Thailand making optimistic noises.'

'Good.'

'If he comes up trumps then we've got enough casual work to keep us going until we make a start on the big contracts.'

They talked for perhaps another half hour, when he said, 'Look at the time.' Within thirty-five minutes of midnight. 'We'll never be up in the morning.'

76

Stuart was a good sleeper, needing his eight hours. She could manage with five, did some of her best work before dawn.

'I've enjoyed talking to you,' she said, laying a hand on his sleeve. 'You go on up to bed; I'll get the things for morning.'

He smiled, patted her shoulders as he passed. He did that sometimes to the boys, indicating that they'd done well.

'Yes,' he murmured. 'Yes.'

Stuart said no more, went upstairs at his usual great rate to his own room. They had slept apart for six months now, after a violent quarrel when he had made up his own bed elsewhere. The boys had asked her first, then him about this move, and she had heard his slick response.

'Your mother likes to put the light on at night.'

'What for?' This from Hugh, the younger. 'Is she frightened?'

'No. She likes to jot things down. Connected with her work.'

'Don't you?'

'I go to bed to sleep.'

She'd allow her husband the gift of tact; he always spoke reasonably, calmly about her to the boys. She swilled their mugs in the old-fashioned way. Perhaps she was reading too much into the evening's exchanges. She could not help feeling optimistic, as long as she did not analyze her thoughts in detail. He had inquired about her health, her state of mind as he had not for some months, and had appeared genuinely concerned. They had taken a step in the right direction. She pondered what else she could do, but decided to leave things as they were. In bed she did not fall asleep immediately, but mulled over their conversation, which seemed more satisfactory by the minute.

The next morning after Mrs Daley, prompt as ever, had taken the boys off to school, Stuart, smartly dressed for the office, held up a detaining finger.

'About work.' He coughed in slight embarrassment. 'If the worst comes to the worst I can always put something in your way. To tide you over. In any case I'm thinking of offering you a consultancy. We're going to have to update our electronics and I'd like you to look into what'll suit us.'

'I'd need to ask a lot of questions.'

'I'm sure you would.'

'Thanks, Stuart.' He grinned widely, perhaps at this use of his name.

She set the alarm, locked the door, and waved to her husband as he drove off.

Clio, after two or three uncertain days, began to show improvement, and ventured out of her house. Weak, tending to be tearful, she had an idea of what was going on in the world, and went with Francesca to the theatre. *What the Butler Saw* pleased her greatly, though she complained that it was 'filthy'. A fortnight later she went on holiday to a hotel in Buxton, where it snowed. She was now, she claimed, normal, and was preparing to return to part-time teaching. Francesca could hardly believe in the improvement in her friend's spirit.

CHAPTER SIX

Frank Stapleton and his wife sat on the chilly Suffolk seafront. Thelma laughed at his insistence that they use the wooden seats, for their holiday weather was still far from clement.

'There's nobody else so daft,' she objected.

'We're the trend-setters. We'll lead the fashion.'

'If I sit here much longer I shall end up in the Northern Cemetery.'

'Don't be so nesh.'

She laughed at his word. Frank's father used it, claiming that it had a long history and traced right back to the Old English, 'hnaesce', soft, crumbling, tender. This was typical of the old man to flash, now and again, a dialect word and then to demonstrate that it had existed longer than more formally accepted words. But should one of his pupils dare to use the word in a composition, then the wrath of God fell.

'You told us, sir,' some argumentative child would object, 'that it was a really ancient word.'

'If I've told you anything about the writing of English composition it is that it is meant, in the examinations you will sit, with results we hope that will change utterly the course of your life, to test the formal expression of thought in standard words. I cannot doubt that occasionally a dialect word might be more vivid, or a grammatical error might add some small element of liveliness to your otherwise dull compositions or narratives, but that is not what your examiners are looking to find. They want a written style, divorced from the colloquial; they need their proportion of words derived from the Latin and Greek; they demand (I am not putting it too strongly) a variation of sentence structure with subordinate clauses and phrases, and a control of presentation by means of suitably chosen paragraphs. That is why you are here. That is why I go red in the face explaining what these learned gentlemen, (and ladies these days for all I know), look for from you illiterate children with your inky fingers and your lack-lustre notions.'

His face would be flushed at the end of his paragraph, and he would have run his beautifully scrubbed fingers at least half-a-dozen times through his thick silver hair. His pupils appreciated these outbursts, did their best to provoke him, and they'd leave his room telling each other that the Old Stapler had it on him this morning.

The old man had been like this at home, a pedant, if self-caricaturing, correcting wife and son, but as he grew old he seemed to lose the gloss of his college education, his degree, and become nearer the boy he'd been seventy-odd years before. In public, or even before guests, he'd speak in complex sentences, with his standard southern pronunciation, though he made an exception of the 'a' in 'bath', 'path', keeping the older short 'bath': 'bæth' in Old English, he said. But on his own, with his wife or near neighbours, something of the local intonation returned, if not the grammatical solecisms of the streets of his childhood. This seemed odd to his son, because his father invariably wore a collar and tie to walk to the shop two streets away to pay for his newspapers or even outdoors in the back garden to mow his lawn. He read less than his son expected, but his eyesight began to fail soon after retirement, so that when he took again to his favourite Dickens or Hardy in the excellent large editions Frank had bought for him he used a stand he had made himself for the book, he was an admirable craftsman, and a large magnifying glass with a tortoiseshell handle and rim.

'You look miles away,' Thelma said to her husband.

'Yes.'

'I thought for a moment you'd been frozen to the seat. A penny for 'em.'

81

'I was thinking about my Dad.'

'He'd have worn a hat, and top coat, and scarf if he'd have been soft enough to sit out here. Let's walk on.'

Frank laughed. Under the overcoat Ernest would have sported a blazer to denote to himself and fellow-diners that he was on holiday. 'Those were the days.'

'Did he ever come here?'

'Not as far as I remember.'

They faced the bracing air of Southwold.

'He was restricted, limited in his ways, wasn't he?' she continued.

'Not unlike the rest of us.'

'But he didn't go abroad much?'

'Well, there's truth in that. He went to Rome, and Venice, and Florence. And he taught himself some Italian so that he could read Dante.'

'Did he talk about it much?'

'Not to me. It was after I'd left home to be married. In any case he thought I was something of a philistine.'

'He was very proud of you, Frank.'

'To himself or to other people. Not to me. I think he couldn't quite come to terms with my earning so much.'

Thelma laughed, stood, made a pretence of pulling her husband to his feet.

'Those were the days,' she repeated as they began to walk.

'People like my father who taught in the

grammar or secondary schools certainly were proud of their status. They taught very clever children, about five per cent of the population, and were paid on a higher scale than the rest of their profession. They knew, on the whole, what they were about.'

'And was that good?'

'It allowed some, a few, working and lower middle-class boys to move up a social step or two. Their schools matched and began to beat the public schools in their own exams. Some few of his pupils fell by the wayside, but most children didn't even reach the starting post. That was the real snag, I guess.'

'Is that what your father thought?'

'Again I don't know. He seemed satisfied. I think he liked his job, and put a great deal of time and effort into it. I looked the other day at the minutes of the sports committee of his school, written out in full in a hard-backed book, detailing amongst other things who said what or what objections were raised to the purchase of three new rugby balls. The meeting must have occupied an hour or two of their spare time, and then this long-hand report would have taken goodness knows how much time.'

'Was it worth it?' Thelma asked.

'I don't think so. But they did. And they spent evenings and Saturday afternoons coaching their pupils. All a waste of time in my view. But...' Frank emphasized the word,

83

stopped. Spluttered. 'I can understand it. It would be about 1934–35, I guess. Sixteen years after a World War in which most of these committee members must have taken part. And in the middle of an economic depression. But the Education Committee gave them preferential treatment, and they felt they had to fulfil their trust. The boys put into their care would be a specially trained élite, academically sound, well-spoken and mannered, good athletically.'

'To be killed in the next war.'

'I don't think they feared that as early as '34. But it was to be so. They trained young men to be fit for air-crew five years later, and to be killed by the hundred.'

'The human race is basically foolish,' she said, pacifically.

'I know, I know.'

They had quickened their pace at this last exchange.

'What do you think,' Thelma began, 'your father would have said about Francesca and Stuart and their goings-on?'

It was some time before her husband answered. He hummed tunelessly to himself, as if to make sure of his ground, to do justice to his father's judgement.

'I don't think he would have understood it. Divorce existed in his day, but at his level of society it was the exception rather than the rule. It wasn't easy. It was a long-drawn out

84

and, to people of his income, relatively expensive procedure. It was, moreover, a sign of moral laxity. So people put up with domestic quarrels and disagreements.'

'My parents were always at each other's throats.'

'Yes. But I would guess they never considered parting.'

'I'm sure they didn't. My father was a bully, and my mother a gifted nagger. But they'd made their choice, and they'd stick by it.'

'Rum,' Frank said. 'I wonder if they were any less happy than people now.'

'No. Their expectations were different. They knew what they could get, and what they couldn't, and they tailored their lives to match. Except for a few who were more neurotic, or more gifted or far-sighted than the rest.'

'Who did what?'

'Ran off. Or abandoned their children.'

They walked on again, inland.

'Do you reckon we've had a good marriage?' he asked.

'Above average,' she answered cheerfully. 'But we haven't changed all that much. You're the decent, handsome man I married. And I'm the quiet, compliant girl you chose.'

'Some hopes,' he said.

Thelma punched him on the arm, harder perhaps than she intended, toppling him slightly from his intended path. She grabbed him by the sleeve.

'Steady,' they said together, and laughed.

Often during this short holiday-week they discussed marriage, and its advantages. In their hotel they picked out a young couple Thelma claimed as on honeymoon.

'Are you sure?' Frank asked.

'Just look at them. He can hardly keep his hands off her. In public.'

'That probably means they've only just met.'

'They're staying in the same room.'

'How do you know?'

'I saw them going in together. And I asked the porter. Mr and Mrs Keys-Smith.'

That evening Francesca's parents, the Langs, phoned to say they were in East Anglia the next day and would like to take the Stapletons out to lunch. That surprised for, though they got on well with the Langs when they met, these contacts were irregular.

'What do you think they want?' Thelma asked. 'Have they come down specially?'

'No. God knows. Nothing probably. They're down for a conference at the University of Essex.'

Professor Lang would call at their hotel for them at eleven and take them on a mystery trip, mysterious in so far that Sarah had not yet made up her mind where they were to lunch.

The weather proved sunny, the Langs arrived on time, and named their destination: Aldeburgh.

'I've ordered our lunch for 1 pm,' Jack said.

'I have to be back in Colchester for a function at seven this evening. What shall we do?'

'Look at the shops,' his wife said.

'Thelma and Frank don't want to do that.'

'Oh, yes, we do,' Thelma said.

'Women,' said the professor. 'Sarah's a compulsive buyer.'

They thoroughly enjoyed the walk down the wide main street. Sarah dropped in to buy two pieces of antique lace, for a collar, she gushed, and three steps on some aids to beauty at a chemist's. Her husband mocked her, and she swung her handbag at him in a short arc. They arrived at the hotel in good time and were shown immediately to their table. It was in an alcove by a window which commanded a view of a cobbled yard where a boy washed down, with a hosepipe, two cars. They ordered sherry which was brought immediately. As they sipped, waiting for soup, Professor Lang said bluntly, once having inquired after their comfort,

'We thought we might just have a word about Francesca and Stuart.'

'Jack.' Sarah, warningly.

'Apart from the pleasure of an hour or two in your company, it might not be. . .'

He left it there. All four put on expressions of seriousness, to such an extent that Frank, grim as the rest, could barely stifle a cackle of satirical laughter. Thelma nodded agreement.

'Jack's in his conference mood,' Sarah said.

'We have not discussed it together.' Lang frowned, lifted and examined his schooner of sherry. 'We get little chance. And in any case, I don't suppose there is much we can do about altering the situation. But we can clear our minds.'

This was received in silence.

'How are things in your estimation?' Lang asked.

'Well, nothing much seems to be happening about their separation. So it can't be all that important to them.' Frank spoke slowly.

'No news is good news,' Sarah said cheerfully.

'Stuart has not recently, well, made any comment?'

'We've spoken to him, both Thelma and I. But we can't get much out of him. He's embarrassed. As he should be. But it's difficult to know where he stands.'

Lang nodded.

'Thelma?'

The soup arrived. They appeared to give it full attention, but Thelma spoke soon enough.

'We were convinced that the separation was imminent a month or two ago.'

'Not so now?'

'Well, no. Not that we've much to go on. It's like getting blood out of a stone talking to our Stu. Frank even went down to the office to beard him. All he'd say was that there was a lull.'

'That's our impression,' Jack Lang said.

'He spoke very highly of Francesca. As a business woman. I think he admires her. And even if her firm's not doing too well, he says she'll never be short of work.'

They finished their soup. Thelma stacked the plates for the waiter.

'We think,' Sarah began, 'that they are now trying to hang on.'

'It's what we'd like,' Jack added. 'That's what we want, so we're a bit careful saying so. I don't mean with them, particularly. We don't want to mislead ourselves. Just because we'd prefer them to stay together.'

'And that's what we want,' Sarah said emphatically.

'They seem ideally suited. And both are doing well in their careers. Or were until recently. And there are the boys to consider.'

The waiter served the main course on scalding-hot plates. Again there followed a pause. Frank had chosen roast beef and Yorkshire pudding. It looked appetizing, and they had been given plenty. They ate in hearty silence. Lang who finished the course first sat back and spoke. He broached his subject without preliminaries, wine-glass in hand.

'If they are getting on better, what's the reason?'

'Is it Mrs Daley?' Thelma asked in return.

'What difference does she make?'

'She's the housekeeper. She feeds them and

takes the boys to school,' Frank answered.

'I know who she is,' Jack said, 'but is it likely she'll be able to make all this difference?'

Mrs Lang stopped her dainty eating, and placed her knife and fork on the sides of her plate. She was far behind the others.

'It was my understanding that they, or rather Francesca, took on this Mrs Daley so that the separation would be all the easier.' She looked round as if pleased to have set them a difficult problem.

'That may have been the case. In fact, I'm sure you're right.' Frank used his accountants' annual conference voice, suitably modified. 'But after a week or two of Mrs Daley's organizing the domestic side of life they suddenly found that they could put up with one another, or at least they weren't at each other's throat all the while.'

'Because she's so efficient?' Jack Lang spoke quietly, as if to sink an over-confident student.

'God knows. Stuart seemed to blame me for their troubles at one time, because I hadn't made him head of the firm.'

'I don't think that was the truth,' said Thelma.

'I don't know,' her husband answered.

'I had a colleague, a very good efficient man who pretty well ruined his family life because he didn't get a chair when he should have done.'

'Why not?' Thelma asked.

'He was unlucky. There was a lull in jobs. And he was a bit selective. And he wasn't the best interviewee in the business. In our line universities want handsome men who look like business-tycoons, or at least that was my impression. And at this time there weren't the number of chairs going that there are now.'

'What happened to him?' Thelma pursued.

'Oh, he managed it in the end. But at a place he didn't particularly want to go to, though he created a first-rate department there.'

'And his family?'

'Well, it was all a bit late. When his children were all out of the way, his wife suddenly left him. She'd be in her early fifties. She found herself a job, and lived adequately as far as one can tell. Quietly but adequately. He's dead, he died almost as soon as he retired. She's still around. Lives in Manchester, I think. Status was important to him. He was producing research that should have made his way easy, but it didn't, and that rankled with him. He could have guessed that he'd get there in the end.'

'Did he want to be a professor at Oxford or Cambridge?' Thelma, questioning again.

'No. He was realist enough, and he knew that with his background that was unlikely. But.'

During this anecdote Sarah Lang had been eating, delicately but desperately, to catch up with the rest who had finished the course.

'Who was that, Jack?' she asked.

'Ted Weston.'

'No,' she said, 'I don't remember him.'

'No, you wouldn't.'

Professor Lang watched his wife, then spoke again. 'I'd guess that when a married couple separate there's not just one reason. There must be dozens. And the break-up depends on personality which depends on genetic inheritance as well as the life they've led. As it is with nervous breakdowns. You see people go through appalling circumstances and retain their sanity, while others buckle at some slight mishap and break down utterly.'

The others listened. Sarah finished her course. Jack seemed rather embarrassed, moodily cleared the half moons on his left hand with the thumb of his right. The waiter appeared, took their order for pudding. The service here was excellent.

'But you think there's some improvement?' Frank asked.

'That's my impression.'

'I hope you're right,' Thelma said. 'Is there anything we can do?'

'That,' Jack answered, laughing drily, 'was what we intended to ask you. You're the senior parents, so to speak.'

'Keep out of the way,' Frank said, slowly.

'But show interest,' Thelma added.

'I'm not so sure about that,' her husband

contradicted her.

'I shall,' Sarah said, quite forcibly. 'I shall ask questions. I shan't be able to help it.'

'We'll act naturally,' Thelma said. 'We must. They're suspicious enough as it is.'

The waiter was back already. Fresh fruit-salad without cream for Jack, plain vanilla ice-cream for Sarah. Black Forest gateau for Thelma, spotted dick with custard for Frank.

'You can see who the greedy-gutses are,' Thelma said.

'You have to indulge yourself sometimes,' Sarah comforted. 'Especially as you're on holiday.'

'That custard looks a funny colour,' Thelma to her husband.

'Tastes good.' Frank smacked his lips, winked at Sarah. Jack chased a cherry round his dish.

They walked down to the shingle beach after the meal, and stared at the dark sea. When Sarah complained of the cold they returned to the car, drove out to the Maltings at Snape, spent an hour walking about the grounds. In one way or another, in mixed duets, they chatted over the ideas that occupied them at lunch, but found they had already said it all. This in no way chilled their optimism, and when at about four o'clock Lang dropped the Stapletons at their hotel they smiled, were thankful, all ready for a nap.

'We should get to know them better,'

Thelma said as the Langs' car disappeared. 'They were kind to contact us. Francesca must have told them we were here.' Then, darting her husband a quick glance she concluded, 'Sarah's not much like her daughter, is she?'

CHAPTER SEVEN

'A good time had by all?' Stuart asked his father. He had called in to see his parents on their return from the seaside.

'A bit too cold. Otherwise fine.'

'Would you go in to talk to Charles Parker again for us?' The property company he had visited a month or so before.

'Why? What's wrong?'

'They're thinking of trying some new project and they want an outside accountant to look at their costing.'

'Property's not my line.'

'Their own accountants will have looked into the technical detail. But old Parker was much impressed by you, as was Charlie. And they're willing to employ you for two or three days just to give them your opinion of the viability of the scheme.'

'I'm an accountant, not a prophet. And my opinion about property has no expertise about it at all. I don't want to waste their money.'

'That's not how they see it.' He turned to Thelma. 'I don't think he wants to work.'

'Why should he? He's retired.'

'Don't you encourage him.'

Thelma quizzed him about Francesca. They were still living together, still talking. They had been to some sort of athletics meeting at the school.

'Keep it up,' Thelma said, lips thin.

Frank made arrangements to call in at the Parkers' offices. The father, George, was there, talked for a quarter of an hour to him about the new project. Frank was not much the wiser, and began to wonder what part the old man played here. He had no answers to any detailed question, and though he seemed enthusiastic about the idea spoke only vaguely of details. They were shown together into Charles Parker's office, much to Frank's relief.

The younger Parker outlined the scheme. It meant buying a large area, more than a mile square, in the centre of a county town not thirty miles off. The land had been sold by the council to a consortium who were to drain the ground, and build a large hotel, sports complex, offices and some 'executive' housing. Almost as soon as the project was under way, the company, after violent struggles, appeals to banks and backers, had gone bankrupt, and the land, fenced off, had been standing derelict for eight years.

'You'll be wondering why this is, if the land is so valuable?' the younger Parker said. He barked out his statements, a contrast to his

95

father's soothing, public-school mumbling. Frank said nothing, waited. 'Well, first of all the Duckmanton Consortium, that's what they called themselves, were in too much of a hurry. They hadn't, for all their bold talk, got themselves on a firm financial footing. Well, it was before the recession began, money was easily available, but even so they were damned careless. Still they might have got away with it, but they didn't employ the right people to do the work for them. The surveyors had clearly outlined all the snags in preparing the land for building, but the contractors they brought in took, he understood, no notice, blazed away, ran themselves deep into trouble, and by the time the consortium, who weren't watching as closely as they might have been, had fetched in somebody else to start setting matters right, money had drained away and they had to call a halt. There again, they were unlucky. Money began to be scarce. Duckmanton became a dirty word. And so it's been a standing eyesore now for eight years.'

Frank listened to the story. He could not see why he had been dragged in. Presumably, it proved to be so, the Parkers had been invited to join a new consortium, but for their expertise and their capital, and were asking his advice. They provided him with an office, small but well furnished, and a thick file and demanded a report on what he read. Puzzled, he set about his task. At ten-thirty a young lady provided him with coffee and biscuits, and invited him out to lunch with Mr Charles at 12.45. He seemed to be situated right away from anyone else. The footsteps of the coffee-girl seemed to clap on for minutes before she went out of ear-shot. He was, however, pleasantly warm, had a convenient loo, and through a sash-window he could see the stone side of a non-conformist chapel on the other side of a not very busy road full of parked cars.

At the suggested time he found his way back to Charles Parker's office, though not without difficulty.

'Would you like a proper meal?' Parker asked. 'Or do you want to join me? I go at the same time every day to a pub for an omelette and a glass of wine.'

'That would suit me fine. I don't like heavy meals.'

Charles asked his secretary to ring the publican and order a second cheese omelette, with salad and a few chips. 'Well worth the walk,' he said, 'though I don't have them every day.' He slapped his paunch, and continued with the papers on his desk until six minutes to one, when he jumped up, pulled a coat from a rack and said, 'Right, sir.'

The secretary came in to open the door for them and ask for last minute instructions.

'If we're not back by one-fifty, go out for lunch and put the 'phone through to Sara.'

'I'm not going out today. Diet and high

thought.'

Charles Parker looked her trim figure over and shook his head.

'How have you got on?' he asked as they walked down the street. 'With the Duckmanton papers?' He adopted a tone of comic portentousness.

'I've read a fair amount of them.'

'And?'

'I don't know what I'm looking for.'

'Guess, then,' Parker said jovially. He wrapped his unbuttoned coat round him. He was a large man in every respect.

'Presumably you've been asked to join a new consortium, either as an employee or an investor. Your father, as well?'

'Both, actually.'

They had reached the door of The Stag and Pheasant, and Parker pushed ahead. The bar was by no means full, but rather noisy while the tables alongside stretched the length of the room, all occupied by diners. Parker led him through the place, up half a dozen steps and into a small alcove, where a table was laid, with starched white cloth. Two chairs stood ready. Parker signalled Frank to a seat.

'Would you advise me to participate?' He had hung up his coat and Frank's.

'My advice is worthless.'

'But I'm paying for it.'

'The scheme seemed strong enough in the first place, but as you say they made careless errors, and took not very sensible decisions. Circumstances ran against them. I can see that. But it's eight years ago. Are the Council anxious to get rid of this eyesore at a price that is pretty favourable to you?'

'That's not far from the truth. But I'm not the prime mover.'

The landlady, none other, came in with the omelette tray. A young man carried a second with subsidiary platters.

'Watch the plates, sir,' the landlady warned Frank. 'They're very hot.' She arranged the table to her liking. 'I'll bring your wine, Mr Parker. Would your friend like a drink?'

'No, thank you.'

'A glass of water, then?'

'If it's no trouble.'

She shooed her helper from the room, and returned within seconds with wine and iced water.

'Will that be all, Mr Parker?'

'Pudding?' Charles asked his guest.

Frank looked at the size of his cheese omelette, and made despairing gestures. It would have filled both him and his Thelma for a whole day. Once they began to eat, Charles began to talk, slowly, with pauses for mastication. He clearly enjoyed the delicious food.

'I invited my father to come in on this. He's just laid his hands on some spare capital and this would make an excellent investment. That is, if it were sound. But he's cautious is my father. He could lose every penny I'm asking him to put into this and still have enough left for Christmas cake every day of the week.' He laughed, and wiped his mouth with the linen napkin the landlady had left. Frank had to wait for a few moments while Charles attacked his lunch again. 'He came in to see me this Monday morning first thing; he'd obviously been chewing it over at the weekend, and said, "I'd like Frank Stapleton to look this over, and if he gives it the go-ahead I'll come in with you." "Right," I said. "You'll pay his fee?" he asked. "I will." Now I understand his point of view, but I couldn't help pulling his leg a bit, even though it might scupper my case. "Look, Dad," said, "Mr Stapleton's an accountant, and a good one, I'll grant, but you've been in property all your life. Why should he be able to advise you about this? You could show him the way about in a matter such as this, surely?" But, no, Stapleton's a shrewd man; he's blest with commonsense, and he may be able to spot something that with all our knowledge of property dealing we may well miss. Of course, I reckon that as soon as I offered to pay your fee he was won over. So, that's how you come in.'

'In answer to a whim of your father's.'

'If you like. This group is much bigger, financially, and more sensible than the last. And we shan't throw our money away on unreliable contractors. And we hope the economic situation will run our way.'

'Is that likely?'

'Can't say. I guess things are more favourable than at the end of the last attempt. Slightly so. But even if they're not I guess we can make something of it.'

'And it will put a fair amount of work in your firm's way.'

'It will.'

They ate seriously for a few minutes in silence.

Then Frank asked, 'You'll want a report on this? In the next day or two?'

'If you please. Though I guess the old man will be on the blower to you tomorrow to ask questions. So if you'll spend this afternoon at it.'

'Right,' Frank said, relieved. 'I'll finish it this weekend. You'd have done better to consult my daughter-in-law. She's a computer expert. And she can set up models for projects that you can feed the snags into so that she'll be able to tell you whether you'd win or lose.'

'Um.' Charles Parker made a sound expressing doubt.

'Don't you believe it?'

'Human beings are the real snag. You'd be amazed at some of the daft things some of the building contractors did last time.'

'Cutting corners or trying to?'

'Yes. Or trying to be clever.'

They finished their lunch and made a

101

cheerful way back to the office.

'You know the ins-and-outs now, so you'll be on the *qui vive*. I didn't want to give you any fixed ideas until you'd had an hour or so on the job.'

Charles Parker led Frank by some back way to his room.

'It's like a rabbit-warren this place,' he said.

'Don't you think of moving to somewhere more modern?'

'No. Never.' He stood by the door. 'Ring the bell if you want anything. We close officially at five-thirty. If you take the file away with you, tell the girl on the outside desk. She'll get you to sign for it.'

Frank glanced at his watch. Five minutes to two. He settled to work, pleased with himself. At four-thirty, he'd worked through the reports again, and knew what he wanted to say. He made a neat, rapid, pencilled note. He stood, walked to his window, satisfied. He had written nine points, numbered, all with subsections, lettered. He examined the unadventurous architecture of the chapel opposite, then rang Charles Parker's secretary to let her know he was about to leave. She replied that she'd be up right away to get him to the front door. As good as her word, she led him out, saw to it that he signed for the file, and thanked him prettily. Mr Parker had greatly enjoyed their lunch together she said. Frank appreciated the V.I.P. treatment.

102

Once home, he realized how tired he was. Thelma seemed to be out, though he'd no idea where she'd gone. He flopped into an armchair, and fell immediately asleep. He had been deeply away for ten minutes or so when the front door bell rang. For the moment he was disoriented, and staggered as he stood up. As he steadied himself by the table the bell pealed again.

A young woman stood by the step, gasping, mouth wide.

'An accident,' she said. 'There's been . . . Can I use your phone?'

He signalled her indoors, showed her the hall telephone. She dialled 999 easily enough, asked for police and ambulance. There was a tinny question from the earpiece.

'What's the name of the street?' she asked him. He told her. She repeated it, and his phone number. She listened, then replaced the instrument. As she turned towards him, her knees buckled and she collapsed, uglily and awkward, to the terrazzo floor. He lifted her trunk, she weighed little, then gently laid her head to the ground and straightened her legs. He rushed to the kitchen for a glass of water, and was holding it to her lips when Thelma returned.

'There's been . . .' she said, and stopped as she made out the two figures on the ground.

Frank moistened the woman's lips. She opened her eyes, large and light blue.

103

'She's fainted,' he said. 'She's rung police and ambulance.' Thelma laid down her parcels on a chair, knelt with him.

'A car has run into Robinsons' wall,' she said.

'Is there anyone there?'

'Yes. Two or three men. They got the driver out. Let's try to move this young woman off this cold floor.' The girl looked about her. 'Can you stand, do you think? We'll ease you up.'

They helped her struggle to her feet, led her to an arm chair, held the glass again to her lips. This time she drank.

'I came up to ring 999,' Thelma said.

'Is he all right?'

'The driver? Yes. He was out of the car, I think he'd hurt his leg.'

'I must go down. To see to him.' The woman's voice trembled.

'I'll go. What's your name? So I can tell him you're all right.'

'Julie.' Feebly. She subsided gratefully into the chair. Thelma with a gesture urged him to hurry. He pulled an anorak from the cloak room and let himself out. The drive seemed unduly long, and he wondered why he hadn't heard the noise of the crash. Too heavily asleep. He made his way out to the road.

A group of eight or ten men and a woman had gathered on the pavement. On a white garden-chair a young man sat slumped, head on chest, face chalky.

'We've rung for the police and ambulance,'

he announced. The people looked grateful. 'Is he hurt?'

'Leg. Chest.' A man said. 'He needs attention.'

Frank moved towards the chair.

'Julie says she's all right,' he said, quietly but with intense clarity. 'We're looking after her.'

The man opened his eyes and nodded thanks, groaning. Another neighbour appeared with a blanket which he wrapped about the seated figure. 'This'll keep you warm until the ambulance comes. It won't be long.'

The ambulance beat the police-car by a few seconds. The paramedics, if that's what they were, worked with thorough efficiency. The police constable took the name and address of the young man, then asked for witnesses. Nobody had seen anything. Frank mentioned Julie indoors.

'Does she need attention?' the ambulance crew asked.

'She says not. She walked up my drive to get help.'

'Better just take a look. Once we've got his nibs aboard.'

They moved the victim with care. The driver seemed to be making a report on the phone or receiving instructions. The policeman told Frank he'd be up to the house in a minute.

He touched the peak of his cap in a subservient but cheerful way. Alec Robinson, next door, made an appearance, late as ever, but well-turned out; he'd put on raincoat and trilby hat to inquire into the fuss. He stared at the damage to his property in silent indignation, not even speaking to Frank.

The ambulance man talked to Julie, made one or two tests, instructed her to report to casualty if she felt the slightest bit off from normal. She said she'd go, in any case, to hospital to see how Terry was. Frank said he'd drive her there.

'Don't be in any hurry,' the man said. 'Get over it a bit. In any case the policeman will be up here any minute to ask what you can remember. And they take a bit of time to process the clients at casualty. So don't you rush anything. Pace yourself. Have a rest.'

He left. There was about the man a kind of rough good will which demanded a more exigent situation than this. Thelma said something complimentary about him to the woman.

The policeman arrived. Julie accepted a second cup of tea, and now looked less agitated. The constable, a husky young man, once indoors, joined her. Yes, he'd have a biscuit. He'd been on since this morning. Still, the nights were beginning to draw out now.

Slowly he elicited Julie's story from her, and then laboriously wrote it down, checking the account sentence by sentence. It moved so ponderously that Frank felt relief when the telephone interrupted the painful process. The older Parker.

He inquired whether this time was convenient, but immediately asked what Frank had made of the Duckmanton file. Frank fetched his notes, read out his nine points, said he would reconsider it all again, and have a typed report ready for Monday morning.

'Would you say it was a good investment?' Parker's voice seemed a parody of an old man's.

Frank explained that he was in no position to give advice of that sort. He outlined such strength and snags he had deduced from the figures.

'That sounds as if it is a good investment?' the voice croaked.

'You must decide that.'

'Would you risk any of your capital on it?'

'I wouldn't be unduly worried, I think.'

Time and time again Parker asked the same question, barely varying his words. Frank found himself, to his surprise, less angry on each hedging answer. In the end he explained about the accident and said he had to drive the young lady to the hospital. Parker cleared his throat, asked again mulishly for the nine points, then ceased the interrogation.

'Never get old,' Frank warned Julie and Thelma who were sitting together.

'Julie's about ready now, Dad,' Thelma said. 'Do you want another cup of tea before you start?'

'She really does look after me,' he told the young woman. He ate a couple of chocolate biscuits. 'Spoil my dinner,' he said.

'How do you know you're getting any?'

At the hospital he found a place in the car-park. The assistant on inquiries at the casualty ward, a middle-aged woman, said that they weren't very busy and if they'd sit down she'd inquire about Mr Naylor. Frank told her that the young woman had also been involved in the same accident and he'd be grateful if an expert would just cast an eye over her.

'Don't worry. I'll mention it.'

'The policeman who took details and the ambulance men made the suggestion.'

'Right, sir. I'll see to it.'

She brought her 'phone into play with a rapid pressing of buttons. Frank sat down with Julie. They'd barely settled when the assistant told them that they could see Mr Naylor in cubicle four. He'd just come back from X-ray. They found the place. Naylor's colour was better, and he grinned widely. He was to be sent down to be plastered any minute. Frank again mentioned that Julie had been in the smash.

The staff worked speedily; a nurse, then a young doctor both inquired after Julie's condition, and offered advice. She said she'd wait for Naylor and take him back by taxi if or when they let him out. Very prettily she thanked Frank for all the trouble he'd taken, and said, no, there was nothing further he could do for her. She already had his telephone number, and said she'd report tomorrow on her partner's condition.

When he arrived home, Thelma said dinner would be on the table in half-an-hour.

'Microwave?' he asked.

'No, good old-fashioned planning.' She went out and returned immediately with a glass of sherry. 'Here,' she said, 'you deserve this.'

'Oh, thanks.'

'You were quite your old self again. At work all day, and then throwing your weight about over this accident.'

'Throwing my. . .'

'Yes, you were. And don't you deny it. But I was pleased. You've seemed a bit lost since you retired. And now here you are large as life and twice as natural. . . A bit like the man I married thirty-eight years ago.'

'Is it that long?'

'It is. Time flies when you're having fun.'

She bounced out of the room, laughing.

The next evening Julie Birch rang at their door. Frank answered since Thelma had gone out to the garden shed with the grandsons and Mrs Daley. They were looking for an old long-bow which Stuart said he'd had as a boy and which Frank thought was tucked away in the roof-beams. Mrs Daley was to pronounce on its safety if they found it.

Julie, well-dressed, had come up in her own

car to let him know that Terry was back in 'the land of the living', hobbling about on two crutches, sore, not best pleased with life. The police had not traced either the car, or its driver, which had caused them to swerve so violently. Even when they eventually did they guessed it would be no help. It would be proved to have been driven by some fourteen-year-old lunatic who'd stolen it for a joy-ride. Frank and she were sorting out methods of dealing with such anti-social children, when the garden-shed party returned, the boys rushing into the room first.

They had not found the bow.

'Did you see the flowers Julie brought you?' Frank asked Thelma. 'I put them in a bucket in the kitchen.'

Thelma thanked the girl, who blushed.

'Hello, Julie,' Mrs Daley said. 'Long time, no see.'

'Miriam.'

Explanations were forthcoming. Both had worked in the offices at Belshaws' together.

'These are Mrs Stapleton's boys,' Mrs Daley said. The boys, ushered forward, shook hands with Julie, as they'd been taught at school. Julie asked them a sensible question or two which they answered without embarrassment, and then announced, 'Your mother was my boss.'

'I think she's beautiful,' Hugh, the twelve-year-old, answered. This surprised everybody,

110

not excluding the boy.

'So she is,' said Julie, then quickly to Frank, 'I had just wondered if there was any connection between you and Mrs Stapleton. It's not an uncommon name.'

Frank offered a couple of minutes of family history, before Mrs Daley swept the boys and their grandparents towards the front door. When Frank returned, Julie still stood where he had left her.

'That's quite a coincidence,' he began.

'I'd heard somewhere, that she'd taken over Francesca Stapleton's children.'

'Were you surprised?'

'I suppose I was, really. I'd left Belshaws' about six months, so I'd no idea how things were there. But she's seemed rather a senior person, head of the pool. Secretary to the M.D., and all the rest of it. And it was rumoured that she and Mr Cranbrook were getting on well together.'

'Cranbrook?'

'He was the other partner, a widower, in his fifties.'

'You thought they might marry?'

'Well, you must know what office gossip is. A little bit suggestive?' She glanced up at him, and reddened again. She blushed easily. 'They were certainly seen out together.'

'Do they still? Commingle?' He laughed at his word. His Dad would have looked down his nose at it.

'I've no idea. I've not seen her since I moved to Star Refrigeration. Nor have I seen many of the girls. I met Angie Williams at a disco. She told me about Miriam.'

'Did you like her?'

'Sure. She knew what she was doing. And could always sort you out if there was a problem.'

'And did she and Mr Cranbrook make a good pair in your eyes?'

Julie laughed outright.

'He seemed a dusty old stick to me, though he patted our bums in a half-hearted way.'

'You didn't approve of him, then?'

'I didn't think about him. He wasn't worth it. He was said to be a very clever engineer of some sort.'

'That wasn't the reason why Mrs Daley left?'

'Angie didn't say so.'

Thelma had been standing in the open door listening for some minutes without the other two being aware of it. Now she stepped forward.

'He asks too many questions,' she told Julie. 'He's always been the same.'

'I don't mind; it gives you something to answer.'

'We've formed a rather favourable impression of Mrs Daley,' Frank said. 'She seems very efficient, and she gets on well with the boys. She has a daughter, I believe.'

112

'A clever girl,' Julie answered. 'At university.'
'Did you know Francesca well?' Thelma asked.

'No. She used to call in. But she was EMEG, whereas we were just a small concern. John Belshaw and Mr Cranbrook used to hover about her. She had nothing to do with us. Whipped straight past the typists, like royalty, and into the M.D.'s office.'

'Why did you leave Belshaws'?' Frank asked. 'Aren't they good employers?'

'Star is much closer to home. And the pay's better. Slightly.'

Julie talked freely to them, but, as Thelma said later, grew less interesting with every word. She described Terry Naylor in his rôle as invalid, hopping about on crutches. She gave them a demonstration, and said he'd do his best to make advantage for himself out of his disability. He complained a great deal, and even wanted her to sprinkle sugar on his cornflakes. She'd have to ferry him around once he started to go out, and he'd not be thankful in the slightest. He'd criticize her driving. 'He's a baby, a great big mother's darling.'

'Like all men,' Frank said pacifically.

Julie looked at Thelma.

'You think I've not made a very good choice, don't you?' she asked.

'No, I just thought you were under pressure for the present.'

'It'll be the same when he's better. I have

113

thought of leaving him.'

'What stopped you?' Frank demanded.

'Well, he's nice sometimes. And good company. He makes me laugh. And there's sex. We enjoy that.' She looked up at them, uncertain of their reaction. She it was who blushed. 'And we're getting used to each other. Bit by bit.'

'You don't think about marrying?' Thelma asked.

'I think about it. There doesn't seem much advantage.'

'And what about children?'

'I'm in no sort of hurry. I'd like to see a bit of life.'

'In what way?'

'Holidays. Nights out.'

'Concerts?' Frank interrupted.

'Pop concerts. Musicals. That sort of thing.'

'Gilbert and Sullivan?'

'Well, we haven't. Not so far.' She grinned, making fun of their pretentious pleasures.

They talked for half an hour, mostly about Julie's next holiday and the possibility of Terry's fitness for the coming cricket season. She chattered, obviously liking them, willing to amuse the old people as she was unwilling to try with her parents who 'weren't old really, but boring'. The Birches never did anything of interest, would stop in the house twenty-four hours a day if they were given half a chance.

'But they're happy?' Thelma asked.

114

'I wouldn't say so.'

When Julie had gone, shown out by Frank, he returned and found his wife sitting where she had sat five minutes before at the table. She touched, tentatively, the lace square under a vase of cut-down chrysanthemums. Thelma did not speak, did not even look up.

'Well?' he asked, dragging the singleton word up and out.

She shook her head.

'Young people,' she said.

'What about them?'

'We were never like that, were we?'

'We were better educated than she is.'

'But what does she do? Or think about? Except present pleasures? And pains when somebody forces them to run into a stone wall?'

Frank stroked his face.

'Well, she holds a job down, and is obviously well-qualified and presentable enough to move to somewhere more convenient when the opportunity arises. That's something these days.'

'But that's about all she is.'

'So were we at her age. Most of our working hours were taken up with jobs and studying and making money.'

'But Saturdays and Sundays?' Thelma asked.

'I spent mine worshipping you.'

'A pity it didn't last.'

CHAPTER EIGHT

The older Stapletons spent the first fortnight of May in Egypt. They enjoyed themselves, but decided that it was not their ideal holiday. The hotel had looked after them, and the expeditions had been beyond expectation, but it was all too hot and the importunity of the beggars had frightened and distressed Thelma.

'It reminded you of England?' her son Stuart asked.

'It was so much worse. And the dust and the heat. Our hotel, it was called the Metropole, was air-conditioned, and we used to come back and lie on our beds for an hour and a half to recover and prepare ourselves for the evening meal.'

'Was that good?'

'Some of it. We're too old for very exotic food. But there was a choice.'

'But you won't be in any hurry to go again? Or Dad won't?'

'No, I don't suppose so. But he soon recovers.'

Thelma inquired after Stuart's marriage, not beating about the bush.

'As it was,' her son answered.

'Oh, come on. Let's hear a bit more than that.'

Stuart looked quizzically at his mother. He never quite made her out; her bluntness needed careful handling.

'We have meals together with the boys. Breakfast is always a bit of a rush, but we all chat away when we're in together at dinner.'

'How often is that?'

'Three or four times a week, including Saturday and Sunday.'

'Do you ever go out together, all four of you, at the weekend?'

'It hasn't happened.'

'It hasn't happened.' She mocked him. 'You mean you haven't tried to make it happen.'

'No. That's right. But I don't want to tempt providence. We speak naturally to each other, especially when the boys are there. We don't bare our souls.'

'Can you remember what it was like, how you felt about Francesca, when you first decided you loved her?'

'As a matter of fact I can.'

'But it's not like that now?'

'No. But I wouldn't expect it.'

Thelma did not give up easily.

'Is she busy at work?'

'Yes. There's plenty for her to do, though they haven't landed any of these big contracts they're angling for. She doesn't say too much about it. She's done several consultancy jobs outside EMEG and you can draw what conclusions you like about that.'

'What conclusions do you draw?'

'She's not altogether sure that EMEG will come through this present phase intact. So

117

she's getting herself known, as well as making some money. We're going to use her.'

'At Bell and Stapleton's?'

'No less. She's not sitting at home brooding, if that's what you fear. And she visits this friend of hers, the one with cancer.'

'How is she?'

'Not doing too well. Pretty bad, I guess. But she has help. You hear about the NHS doing nothing for all sorts of desperately ill people, but everybody has done plenty for her. She has a nurse regularly, and she's visited by a counsellor. And there are two cousins, retired maiden ladies, no, one's been married, school-teachers I think, who take turns to come in for six days, Sundays off. I gathered for a start that there were no relatives at all, but these two turn up, and are prepared to put themselves at her service for one week in every two.'

'What's the woman's name? It's unusual, isn't it?'

'Clio Pugh. Clio's the Muse of History, spelt with an "i". We looked it up.'

'Is she getting better?'

'I don't know. I doubt it. Fran doesn't issue bulletins. But I don't think they've cured her. Or at least that was the first impression I had. I gathered it was terminal, but I don't know how long she's got to live.'

'Is she Welsh?'

'Not so far as I know. What difference does that make?'

'None. Has her illness upset Francesca?'

'It's not done her any good. They were at school together, so they're roughly of an age.' He wagged a forefinger at Thelma. 'We none of us like to be reminded that we shall die.'

'And how is it at B and S? Now you're the king-pin?'

'We've plenty of work, and I'm beginning on one or two reorganizations I've had in mind for some time.'

'Have you consulted your father about them?'

'No. Not really. He wouldn't expect it. But he comes into the office and talks to people. He did a little job for us the other day. So he can see for himself what's going on.'

'He's made no comment, then?' Thelma asked.

'Not to me.'

'What's that mean?'

'Nothing. He's made no comment to me. Full stop. Nor to anyone else. Or if he has it's not reached my ears. Has he said anything to you?'

'No. I think he enjoyed the work. He's too young to retire.'

'He's sixty-five. He can go off with you to Egypt or the Caribbean whenever he likes. Or go to a Test Match or the Chelsea Flower Show or railway exhibitions with the kids. He can have a good time if only he'll set his mind to it.'

'He's not that sort of man. As well you ought

119

to know. He can only enjoy going out to please himself if he knows he's got five good, solid days of work behind him, and five more starting on Monday next. He looks at the Sphinx or the Taj Mahal or the Sea of Galilee, and says the right things. But he's not moved as I am. And this is unexpected to me because he reads a lot more than I do, and knows more history. In short, he realizes what he ought to say, but can't bring himself to feel it.'

'Why is that?'

'It's not that he lacks imagination. He doesn't. But his accountancy and his family seem more real and important than ancient kingdoms.'

'And you're the opposite?'

'No. But to stand somewhere and see just the same shape of hills that Jesus or Alexander the Great stared at seems a kind of miracle.'

'They could see the moon.'

'I know. And now we've had men actually walking on the moon's surface. It spoils it, somehow.'

Stuart enjoyed these sessions with his mother. She'd have made a good lawyer. His father had been called to account for his every action, but had never, as far as the son could make out, resented these interrogations or condemnations. He vividly remembered his father giving him a sharp slap across the head for trampling over some freshly-set broad beans. The blow had shocked him, because his

120

father rarely had recourse to corporal punishment. Seeing the one or two broken plants Stuart at once understood his father's anger, but he sulked over the assault and withdrew to his bedroom. A little later he heard his father, now indoors, ask, 'Where's Stuart gone?'

'He's in his bedroom, I think.' Then a pause. Thelma could fashion these silences like steel scaffolding holding the time, the participants in a fixed place, allowing nothing or no-one to move on. Perhaps it was the grim expression of her mouth, the fish-wife set of shoulders and elbows which precluded change or escape. 'There was no need to hit him, Frank.'

'He ran straight over the rows of beans I'd just put in.'

'I didn't say he'd not done wrong or hadn't acted thoughtlessly. I said there was no need to strike him.'

'He's not blind. He could see what he was doing.'

'So he deliberately walked all over your plants?'

'I'm not saying that.'

'So if I burnt your toast or failed to iron your shirt properly you'd feel entitled to hit me, would you?'

'No. You're not a child.'

'What difference does that make?'

'He's a boy. I'm in some sense responsible for his upbringing. He's to be taught the

121

difference between right and wrong. If he's careless or thoughtless then he can expect to be punished, especially if he does damage. I'm not responsible for you. We'll, not in that way.'

'You clouted him because you were angry.'

'Well?'

'You'd no thought of teaching him anything. You saw where he'd trampled on your beans, and you just hit out.'

'It'll do him no harm. He'll think twice next time.'

'That's no excuse. You used your superior strength on him because you were wild.'

'What should I have done, then?'

'Spoken to him. Pointed the damage out.'

'He could see for himself what he'd done. He's not daft.'

'And you'd plenty of replacements.

'But suppose I hadn't?'

'You had.'

'You do the talking to him then.'

'It's too late now.'

They moved away, his father first. Stuart heard the door close. The argument would now be complete. There might be an atmosphere of constraint for an hour or so, but after that they'd return to normality. Except. That was it. Except. Even the child knew. Neither would forget. They might or might not raise the matter again, but his father would realize that he'd done wrong in Thelma's eyes, though she would wonder if she had gone too far with that

122

good man her husband, weighed down with the responsibility of work and money, who'd had his hour of pleasure spoilt first by a careless, rumbustious lad and then by a shrew.

In fact Thelma had asked Stuart if he'd apologized for the damage.

'No. It was only three beans.'

'You say you're sorry.'

'He hit me.'

'You say you're sorry.'

'It hurt.'

'I hope it did. If it had been my grandfather he'd have taken his belt off to you.'

Stuart apologized. The look of twisted pain and embarrassment on his father's face made it worth it. They were rivals for Thelma's approval.

Now, head of B and S in his father's chair, Stuart remembered these incidents and learnt his strengths. Such as they were. This incident, remembered so long, did not fundamentally cause him to be as he was. His father's decision to promote Luke Brailsford, a stick-in-the-mud, over his head rankled more, but now that was out of his way so that Stuart Stapleton knew exactly what he must do at work, and did it. He could generously hand a bit of patronage out to his father, but he certainly would never consult him on any important matter, because he knew (he thought) what his father would say. Unlike the opinion of Charles Parker, or the Charles

Parker of Frank's brief account, his father's views did not carry much weight in the modern, cut-throat world. Old Parker had financial gravitas, heavy money to invest. Frank still kept a fairly substantial financial stake in Bell and Stapleton, but was unlikely to increase it.

Stuart talked easily enough to Thelma, enjoying the arguments with her, dodging her questions, but that was because he considered her to be basically ignorant about his business. Not unintelligent but ignorant. She knew what accountants did; she had been married to one for thirty-eight years, had often listened to his complaints and self-congratulations, but she had no idea why the firm preferred one contract to another, or to work for one firm while rebuffing a second. Thus he could talk to his mother, as he could not to Frank or Francesca. He shared with Frank an honesty that was apparent in all his concerns, and with Fran the idea that technology would smarten or straighten old indirect or long-winded methods. He'd use the old man for jobs that needed tact, and his wife to bring to bear her expertise on her marvellous machines to his everyday work.

When, this lunch-time, he left his mother's house, he whistled as they walked down the long drive together.

'Don't do that. You sound like the milkman.'

In the leafy street he had parked in front of a red Fiesta. They noticed that its windscreen had been shattered.

'Whose car is that?' he asked.

'Dorothy Lloyd-Jones's. My neighbour.'

'I don't suppose you can remember her 'phone number, can you?'

She could. He called Mrs Lloyd-Jones on his car 'phone. Soon she, a small, elderly woman with a large, moustachio'd husband, appeared. They cleared the glass from the front of the seat with some care, Thelma going back to the house for a waste-bin and brush. Nothing was missing; radio, cassettes and player were all in place. A small, interestingly beaded bag lay unopened on the back seat. A brief-case leaned against the hand-brake. The search completed, Lloyd-Jones complained.

'This used to be a respectable street. Now, look. The Robinsons' wall's demolished by joy riders. My car window smashed in out of pure, unadulterated envy.' The adjectives seemed to Thelma oddly chosen.

'You'd say hardly anyone used this street,' Dorothy Lloyd-Jones said.

'Must do,' her husband answered. 'I mean, it can't be the neighbours. Though I wouldn't write enthusiastic testimonials for some of them. No, it must have been some unemployed yobbo wandering the streets on the look out for mischief to do.'

Stuart drove off, leaving his elders deep in conversation. They seemed in no hurry either to contact the police or the garage. They'd hang about in the street, and wring what entertainment they could from the incident.

'At one time,' Dorothy said, 'you could leave your car in the street for twenty-four hours and nobody touched it. Not now. When I was a girl you could go out to do your shopping and leave the doors unlocked.'

'And have a good meal in a restaurant with wine and a woman afterwards and still have change from half-a-crown.' No glimmer of humour lit her husband's face.

'George.' His wife rebuked him. The man grinned, then winked at Thelma, who paid no attention. Mrs Lloyd-Jones began again. 'It doesn't seem the same world.'

'I wonder,' Thelma murmured. Her neighbours looked at her in sorrow.

'I know what I'd do with vandals like this,' Dorothy ground out.

'They used to hang people for stealing sheep,' her husband answered mildly, 'but it didn't stop them. If you're hungry you'll rob and pillage.'

'You're as bad as they are,' Dorothy told him.

'I know. Well, I'll get hold of the police and the garage and the insurance people.'

He set off up the path, wiggling fingers facetiously at Thelma.

'Will it upset him?' Thelma inquired.

'I don't know. I don't think so. To tell you the honest truth it gives him something to

126

occupy himself with. When he first retired, and that's more than ten years ago he was full of life and ideas and projects. But now he just seems to be waiting for something to happen to him. I sometimes say to him, "George, what are you hanging about for?" and he says, "The Grim Reaper."'

'How old is he? If you don't mind my asking you.'

'Seventy-eight.'

'He looks fit.'

'Yes. We can't grumble. But he can't occupy himself. He's always been busy. He started life as a joiner and cabinet maker, and then made his own reproduction furniture and opened three shops, retail outlets, you know. He had his own little factory-workshop, employed half-a-dozen craftsmen. I managed the smallest shop; it was in Oakham. We did pretty well, and sold off at a good price. Just at the right time. But he doesn't know what to do. So if you break a leg off a Chippendale chair, don't run round the antiques people; bring it next door. He'd be in his element.'

'Has he still got his tools?'

'And more. Drills and lathes and God knows what. His father was a bank manager in Wrexham. George went to the grammar-school, but he'd no time for it. For formal education, that is. He wanted to use his hands. Left at sixteen.'

'Did his father enjoy his retirement?'

127

'He never had time. He died soon after we started up in Beechnall. Still at work. Wouldn't lend George anything to start his business. He wanted his son to be B.Sc and Ph.D. and all that. He saw no sense in manual work. But George'll leave a lot more in his will than ever his father did.'

'I see.'

'We've never had a chat like this before. Takes some vandal to break our ice.' Thelma thought that quite witty, but wasn't sure it was intentional. 'You come in and have a cup of tea one morning, or afternoon, if that suits you better. I can talk to you. You're not like some people.' Mrs Lloyd-Jones had lost some of her gentility, but there was no trace of Welsh in her accent. 'I'll have to go in now. He'll be losing his hair. What bit he's got. "Where did you put the insurance papers?" Where did I put them? I ask you. Husbands. But I expect yours is the same.'

She scurried off up the long, shrub-bordered drive which cut her off from the conversation she craved for. She would have been happier, Thelma thought, with a front-door that opened straight on to the street, so she could have stuck her head out and exchanged greetings at any time of the day.

Later that afternoon Thelma received a 'phone call from her neighbour asking her to walk round for tea and a biscuit if it was convenient. Thelma, on her way to the shops—

128

she had forgotten Frank's Earl Grey—had to refuse.

'Have they replaced your windscreen?' she asked.

'They have. George knows the right people. But it's all a nuisance, and getting worse. Oh, God. There he is shouting out again about something. He's like a great baby.'

CHAPTER NINE

Stuart Stapleton knocked unexpectedly on his mother's door one Saturday morning. From his appearance she could tell something had gone seriously awry. His face seemed set; his hands and head twitched.

'I've some bad news,' he said, quietly enough. Thelma led him to the kitchen. 'Is Dad in?'

'No. He's driven over to Mansfield. To an old friend's. Jim Lewis's. What's wrong?'

Stuart straightened himself in his chair.

'It's Hugh,' he said. 'He's in hospital.' He allowed her time to come to grips with this.

'Has he had an accident?'

'No. We found him delirious in bed this morning.'

'What is it?'

'They think it's meningitis.'

'Has he been ill? Have you had any warnings?'

'No. Not at all. Not till last night, when he said he'd a headache. He went to bed a bit earlier than usual, but he'd been overdoing it. Physically at sports. And they'd had school exams. But he didn't complain much. That's like him.'

'Is he very bad?'

'They don't say too much as yet. But it's serious. They're testing him and giving him drugs. He's young and strong, and that's on his side.'

'Is his mother with him?'

'Yes. She went with him in the ambulance. I've just come back from there.'

'How did he seem?'

'Hot. Delirious. In and out of consciousness. Poorly. It didn't look like him.'

Hugh, the younger of his boys, seemed the sturdier of the two, less likely to be affected, knocked over by disease.

'Will he have caught it from somebody?'

'They don't know of other cases, they said. And an epidemic's usually earlier in the year than this.'

'It's serious, isn't it?'

'He's the right sort of age to fight it, one of the young doctors told me. Very small children and old people are more likely to die.'

'Hugh won't die, will he?'

'We, they hope not.' His voice faltered.

Thelma fiddled the kettle on, and placed a mug of tea in front of her son.

'Have you let Francesca's parents know?'

'No. I can't get hold of them. He's away at some external examiners' meeting in London. She's staying with friends. Near his conference. They went down together. I haven't got, can't find her number. I've left Jack a message to ring home or to ring you if he can't contact us. Mrs Daley will be staying at the house most of the day, looking after Ian. He's upset.'

'He's shown no signs? Of it?'

'No. Miriam Daley will be on the watch.'

'What are the symptoms?'

'Something like bad 'flu. Headaches. High temperature. A rash. Delirium. Shrinking from light. But Ian seems normal. She's taken him somewhere. She's always full of ideas. They really like her. She's very sensible.'

Stuart sipped at his tea, spat his words and sentences out as if he was trying newly-learned snippets in a foreign language. He did not sit still, although he never left his stool, but wriggled, jabbed at the air with his feet, picked up and put down his mug, which he then would fractionally shift and reposition, again and again. His eyes searched the clock, and when his mother's 'phone rang he leapt clumsily to his feet. Thelma answered it.

'Francesca,' she said. 'Yes, he's here.' She held out the 'phone.

He ran the three or four steps, stumbling, almost drunkenly. Francesca spoke, not quickly, but Thelma could not make out what

131

was said. It could not have been the worst. Then the intonation would have been different. She stood, propping herself by the sink, mouth agape.

'Right, right,' Stuart was saying. 'I'll see to it.' He seemed to be ringing off, but there had been a gap, a chasm in her consciousness.

The son moved away from the 'phone.

'She's coming home to collect things, and then going back to stay there. She'll take a taxi.'

'How's Hugh?'

'Much the same.'

'No worse?'

'I suppose not.' He seemed loath to say the words, as if his slight show of optimism tempted providence.

'And what are you going to do?'

'I shall go back home first so I'm there when she arrives. And then I'll take her back to the hospital. And if there's nothing to be done then, I'll spend an hour in the office.'

'That's sensible,' she said.

Stuart finished his tea, set his mug carefully on the draining board.

'I'll be on my way.'

'Keep me posted, won't you?'

'Yes. I will. And I guess Miriam will be at the house any time you care to ring up.'

Thelma approached him and threw out her arms. He clasped her to him, squeezed her hard, then kissed her forehead.

'He's young, remember. That's in his favour,'

132

she said.

'Right.'

'And don't forget to eat, yourself.'

'I won't.'

'Look after Francesca.'

He waved, stepped with normality down the drive. She watched from the kitchen window until he was out of sight. Thelma washed the two tea-mugs, hooked them on the tree, and sat down. Her daily list hung by her face. As it was Saturday she intended not to shop; Frank would be home mid-afternoon so needed no lunch. She had decided on, prepared for tomorrow's main meal. She tapped the work surface, without satisfaction. The rest of the day was her own, to spend as she wished. How could she say such a thing?

A clawing gulp of grief heaved irresistibly up from her chest; the sound frightened her. Like croup it tore at her flesh. Tears splashed from her eyes. A moment previously she had been occupied, reckoning things up, in command of herself. Now she sat devastated at the thought of Hugh flat on his back, fighting death off, in a strange place. She had no clear picture, either of bed, of nurses, of equipment, of the child's dear face, distorted perhaps, of the involuntary groans, rough breathings drugs, encouragement, footsteps.

She stood, leaning forward, propped on her hands. Weakness emptied the strength from her limbs so that she was forced again to sit.

133

Sobbing she laid her head on her folded forearms as her body shivered and collapsed, racked with her helpless sorrow. She squealed. The noise shattered her. Her lungs gasped; her lower lip, her chin shook like thin leaves.

'Hugh.' She made herself say the word. 'Hugh. My little Hugh.' Even as she muttered this, she knew with no extenuation of the weeping, of the surrender of her body to appalling distress, that she would not have called him 'little' in ordinary conversation. He would have resented it or despised her for it. Ian would have laughed at the pair of them. The time had appeared close when she could no longer kiss the boys in public, only shake hands. They might allow that; at school they shook hands with one of the masters on duty when they had been dismissed at the end of the afternoon. 'My little Hugh,' she said again, striving to steady her voice. The phrase did not comfort, but tossed her into another paroxysm of grief. Now she made no attempt to staunch it, but let her shaking body dictate behaviour to her.

In perhaps five minutes she became calmer, sitting upright now, her paralysis of grief ripped intermittently by a single hiccough of a sob. 'My little Hugh,' she whispered once more, a test of her emotional equilibrium. Tears wet her cheeks, but she could stand. She forced herself over to the sink, picked up one of the washed mugs, and turned on the tap. She

134

drank, a lip-wetting smidgin, and returned her pot to the board; she walked as far as the door and passage out to the hall. Her legs obeyed her, but small, involuntary squeals of distress, as from a hurt animal, escaped her. These surprised, but she had no control; it was as if she had been taken over, occupied by an incubus of grief. She put up a hand on the cool paintwork of the upright of the door frame, stood swaying there until she finally chose to rest her head on the back of her hand.

'My little Hugh.'

This time the words did not defeat her. She trembled, but knew that momentarily she was herself again.

She wished Frank was here. Something of her old argumentative temperament revived. Men were always the same; never there when they were wanted. When the six-year-old Stuart had broken his arm on holiday Frank had just gone off to buy the morning paper, and had spent a little time poking round for treats, chocolate figurines, a fishing-net, a cheap. pretty brooch which she had still, a leaping dragon. This meant he had taken a quarter of an hour, twenty minutes longer than she expected, and the delay had seemed endless as she comforted the child.

'Get the car out,' she'd shouted. 'Where in hell have you been?'

'What's wrong?'

'Stuart's had a bad fall. He needs to go to

hospital.'

Frank had the old Vauxhall on the road in no time. It wasn't more than five minutes' drive to the hospital. As she had comforted her child. she could not help reminding her husband that they would have already been there and the treatment under way had he not chosen this morning to laze about the shops. Frank didn't answer, efficiently parked his car, swiftly carried the child into the Casualty Ward, but once they were inside and waiting it was the mother that Stuart wanted, her softly compliant body, the light comforting voice. She knew she was being unfair to her husband. Frank looked to the holiday to provide him with opportunities to spoil both her and the boy, and this morning had been no different. What would have raised smiles and murmurs of joy became a cause of complaint. She wasn't reasonable. She knew it.

This interlude had momentarily taken her mind away from Hugh.

Stuart's broken arm, though a mischance and probably his own fault, was understandable. Hugh's meningitis, snatched from the air, afflicted some part of the brain and then grappling, shearing outward deafened him, paralysed those supple limbs. How had this happened? Why Hugh and no-one else?

Miriam Daley rang soon after lunch to report little change. Francesca would stay the night. Stuart would ring after his evening visit.

There was nothing further anybody could do. They must wait.

'How's Ian?' Thelma asked, prolonging the conversation.

'He's all right. He's upset about Hugh, but I don't think he knows how serious it is.'

'He's not been to see him.'

'No. No visitors except parents.'

'When shall we know? One way or the other?'

'They don't seem certain. Or won't say. Or haven't been asked.' That was the first sign of frustration on Mrs Daley's part.

'Will there be permanent damage? That is, if, that is, if he recovers?'

'I suppose it's possible. I don't know enough about it. There could be.' Miriam paused. 'We'll keep in touch. If there's any change, one way or the other, I'll let you know at once.'

Thelma was relieved to hear Frank's car on the drive, but waited for him to come in before wiping the smiling satisfaction from his face with her news. As she expected he questioned her closely, repeating himself in his anxiety to such an extent that she became angry.

'I don't know,' she snapped in answer to a further variation on a query. 'I've told you all I know. You don't want me to start making it up, do you?'

'No, but I want to be sure. You might have forgotten something.'

'And why should I do that?'

137

'You're upset, so you might not see it quite straight.'

'Don't be so bloody daft,' she said, and rushed out of the room.

Ten minutes later he joined her in the kitchen, put an arm round her shoulder. She allowed it, rather woodenly.

'I'm sorry,' he said.

'No, it's me. I think of that boy lying there.'

'How did Stuart seem?'

'Coping. He was shocked. You could see that.'

'And Francesca.'

'He didn't say much. Just you think: going into the bedroom and finding him in that state.' Thelma's voice did not rise above a mutter.

'Yes. I don't know if it's good or bad. It might have meant he'd been suffering some time. If he'd been awake they could have called the doctor earlier.'

'I don't know. He seemed such a strong, robust little chap. Always dashing about.'

Later in the evening Stuart rang, reporting that there'd not been any great alteration, that Hugh was holding his own. She asked her few questions, then insisted that he spoke to Frank, who listened to the same story, nodding his head.

'How's Francesca?' the father asked.

'She's very good,' Stuart answered. 'Women seem better at dealing with these things than we are.'

'Hear, hear,' Thelma interrupted. She had parked herself upstairs at the second 'phone to monitor the men's exchanges. Her intervention made them all laugh, if briefly, nervously.

Stuart explained that they had provided Francesca with a room and bed. The hospital authorities seemed keen for her to stay.

'I thought it was only with very small children they invited parents.'

'Twelve's not all that old.'

'No. Perhaps not.'

The son promised that he'd ring from the hospital when he'd visited the ward, or from home if Francesca had been in touch.

'She'll ring, I guess. She might want me to take something up. I don't think there's much difference in hospitals between Sundays and any other days.'

'No matron's inspection,' Frank said.

'No matrons.'

They had begun to recover. Thelma invited Stuart and his wife for Sunday lunch, if they saw fit to come away from the hospital for an hour's break.

'I don't know if she will,' the son said.

'It'll depend anyway on how Hugh's shaping.'

'Ask her, will you? Let us know in the morning. I'll cook plenty, and if you don't come your Dad can eat it cold.'

Next morning Stuart rang from the hospital with good news. Hugh had had a better night, was responding well to the treatment. He was ill, but he could talk to them, hear them, knew them. Francesca would come for lunch, not he. She would go home, have a bath, put her Sunday best on (they recognized his optimism from the phrase), and be at their house exactly at one o'clock.

'It'll be on the table, ready for her,' said Thelma, uplifted.

'We'll let you know if there's any change.' Caution had returned.

'What about you? Shall we save you something?'

'No, thanks. Doing without a meal will do me more good than eating. I'm putting weight on.'

'Since you took the firm over?'

'Before that.'

He rang off, said he had one or two errands to do.

At five minutes to one Francesca arrived, bright as a new pin, Frank thought. She wore a summer frock, high-heeled shoes; one would guess she had just emerged from the hairdresser's. She refused all wine, claiming she was driving. Hugh seemed, yes, much better. She could hardly believe it.

'Has he eaten anything?' Thelma asked.

'He did have a little breakfast. Not much, but yesterday he wouldn't have been capable of opening his mouth, even. Now he seems conscious, with it. Of course he's sleeping a lot,

140

but he understands what we're saying and can answer back.'

'The treatment's working?'

'It seems to be.'

'They're very good,' Frank said, to be part of the recovery.

'Yes. It was strange to me. The doctors seemed to know exactly what was wrong. They did confirming, confirmatory tests. And then treated him, saying they were already on the right course.'

'That wasn't odd, was it?' Thelma asked. They were now eating delicious soup, with home-made brown rolls.

'Well, for a time they didn't seem exactly certain. They'd diagnosed the condition, and treated it according to the text books, but then they had to wait. "He should be all right." ' Should be. That had hardly seemed like science to her. Her mind careered uneasily still.

The parents-in-law saw how deeply she had been troubled, and how, now the prognosis, the evidence was good, she was able to voice her distress of yesterday. Francesca ate heartily, not a huge amount, but clearing her plate each time. Roast pork and apple sauce. Gooseberry fool. Then even Cheddar Cheese and biscuits, much praised.

'Our cheese never tastes as good as this,' she said. 'Do you buy a whole cheese?'

'No, we buy our pound lumps from a man who has whole cheeses, and a quick turn-over.'

They walked briefly round the garden. Early summer, late spring promised much in the sunshine.

'Another month it'll be at its best,' Frank said.

'He says that all the year round,' Thelma mocked.

The older Stapletons could see that Francesca was anxious to hurry back to the ward, and made no attempt to delay her.

'Let us know if there's anything we can do,' Frank said.

'And tell Stuart that if he feels like a meal later in the day, we'll knock something together for him.' Thelma, the practical.

Francesca thanked them, but her mind was already on the next stage, at the hospital, sitting with Hugh, his one sign of the status quo.

'She's a good girl,' Thelma said, at the closed front door.

'Very.'

'Our Stu's lucky.'

In the early evening Miriam Daley telephoned, then called round with Ian. The news from hospital continued to improve. Stuart had consulted his wife, and had decided to attend a conference in Buxton on Monday: Miriam and Ian had not been to visit Hugh, as he was still poorly, but perhaps they'd go tomorrow. Both Francesca and Stuart carried mobile 'phones so that it was easy to make contact. Francesca didn't like anybody

142

'phoning the ward.

'Could you get through?'

'I imagine so.' Stuart had used his, but he'd gone outside in deference to his wife's wishes.

'Francesca won't be at work tomorrow?'

'She will not.' There sounded a kind of moral compliment in the strength of those three words.

The grandparents fussed over Ian. Thelma raided the freezer, and provided him with two ice-cream Mars bars. Mrs Daley watched with amusement. He handed one to her.

'You think we're spoiling him,' Thelma said.

'I'm sure you are.'

'And why not?' Frank argued.

Ian enjoyed himself, said that Hugh was lucky to have completed his school exams. His own form were going through their papers, and 'Knocker' Adams, the Latin teacher, was making them learn daft Latin poems by Horace, Quintus Horatius Flaccus. Ian spoke of this as typical of the kind of lunacy to be expected of ancient classics masters, but was quite proud of his achievement.

'Can you give us a bit?' Frank asked.

'Diffugere nives, redeunt iam gramina campis Arboribusque comae.'

'Do you know what it means?' Thelma, the schoolma'am.

'Something about the snows disappearing, and the grasses coming back to the fields and leaves to the trees. It's a bit hard for us. Old

143

Adams keeps saying, "You don't know that construction yet." '

'Why do you have to learn it?'

'We asked him. He said it was probably the best lyric poem ever written in Latin, and we might just as well get this masterpiece by heart, when we are young and it comes easy to us, as learn the names of a string of international football players. "They'll all be forgotten in five years' time," he says. "This has lasted for two thousand." '

'Is he popular?'

'Who?'

'Mr Adams?'

'He's all right. Old-fashioned. Still living with the Greeks and Romans. But, yes, he's all right.'

'How old is he?' Frank asked.

'We know that. He told us. He's thirty-seven.'

'That's young,' Thelma said. 'Compared with us.'

'The teachers never told us how old they were when I was at school. I thought they were all about ninety.'

'Oh, Frank.'

'And when I look now at some of those old school photographs, they all look so young.'

'Ian's sent a very nice card to Hugh,' Miriam said.

'Was it comic?' Grandfather asked.

'No. Study of flowers and insects by Jan van

144

Kessal,' the boy answered. 'Beautiful butterflies. And I changed the Jan to Ian. Miriam chose it.'

'Good for you,' Thelma said.

The visitors left the old people much cheered.

'It's no wonder people pay good money to have their children educated privately,' Thelma began.

'What makes you say that?' Frank asked.

'There's no fooling about. The boys have to learn their Latin poetry.'

'Did you?'

'Not till we got into the sixth form.'

'And it's done you good?'

'I'm not saying that.'

'But?'

'But rubbish. If you do two or three years of Latin you'll understand the grammar of your own language. And children, young children learn so easily. That's what Ian's teacher said. It's worth it.'

'I don't know that our Stuart did Latin?'

'Oh, Frank. He did it for a year, and then he dropped it. I tried to encourage him to keep it up, but he wouldn't.'

'I'd like everybody to know something about science,' Frank argued. 'We all ought to know about physics, the universe, medicine, biochemistry, chemistry. Electricity and nuclear power. You know what I mean. When I see an aeroplane, with four hundred people

145

aboard and hardly any wing-span to speak of, taking off, it seems the very opposite of common-sense. It oughtn't be so, and so I'd like to know exactly why it's possible.'

'*You* don't know all these things, then?'

'No.'

'But you'd make the children learn them.'

'You've just told me that that's when you learn quickly. Not like me.'

Thelma kissed him and dodged matronly away. He aimed a slap at her buttocks, missing on purpose.

On the next day when they visited Hugh in hospital their hearts lifted, but less frivolously. The boy sat in a chair by his bed, and looked pale, thinner, stiller than they remembered. The doctors had expressed their satisfaction, in hope of complete recovery.

'He could have been deaf, or lost his balance, or his nerve, but as far as they can see he'll be normal.'

'Play football and cricket?' Grandfather gruff.

'As far as we know.'

Hugh talked to them, with the same easy but distant familiarity he had shown before his illness. He explained the difficulties of a Lego model, a small ship, he had just completed, and showed them plans and pictures. He had been reading a book about inter-galactic travel. The grandparents could not make out whether this was a novel or a technical description of the

146

difficulties of such a flight; the child's bias seemed to swerve towards science. Magic did not exist for him, merely marvels derived from equations.

'Do you ever read school-stories?' Thelma asked. 'About boys of your own age?'

'No.' Hugh smiled sweetly at her, like an invalid.

'Aren't you interested?'

He knitted his brows, as if the question veered outside understanding.

'Quite interested. But there are others I like better.' He took a lurid, fire-red paperback from his shelf. *The Lair of Unvola* proclaimed itself in yellow letters, while underneath wraith-like monsters writhed in shocking green.

'I'd be terrified to read that,' Thelma said.

'You wouldn't.' Hugh laughed. 'There's nothing to it.'

'Don't wear yourself out,' his mother warned.

On the way to their cars Thelma said, 'He's doing really well.'

'Yes,' Francesca answered. 'He's come on extraordinarily in the last three days.'

'It's marvellous,'Grandpa concluded.

They stepped out with pleasure.

'I can't help thinking of those who don't recover,' Francesca brought out, leadenly.

'We were very lucky,' Thelma answered.

The three completed the short two hundred

147

yards in silence, only brightening to exchange kisses in the car-park.

'It's knocked her about,' Thelma said, once they were on their way. Frank nodded, added nothing more, but asked her to provide him with a barley-sugar.

'You'll never get any thinner,' she said, complying with his request, unwrapping the sweet, pushing it into his skilled mouth. He touched the horn for no reason she could see.

CHAPTER TEN

Hugh was sent home from the hospital, and Miriam Daley immediately moved into the house for a week or two to look after him. There were no setbacks, though Mrs Daley kept a close watch on the boy to see that he did not overtire himself. His recuperation had for her as for the parents a kind of miraculous quality. 'When you see the boys together,' Stuart asserted, 'you'd be hard put to it to say which 'em had been ill.'

During the next month Francesca dropped in four times to visit her parents-in-law. She did not bring the boys, (that was Stuart's job or Miriam's), but called in on Thursdays for an hour in the evening. She drank a cup of coffee, did not refuse a biscuit, walked the length of the garden if the weather permitted, and talked to them, rather like a neighbour or a friend of their own age.

'I wonder,' Thelma inquired from Frank after the second visit, 'why she comes round. To see us? On her own?'

'Ask me,' Frank, awkwardly.

'I think she thinks . . .'

Frank guffawed.

'. . . that she owes us something.'

'Such as?'

'Well, we supported them when Hugh was so ill.'

'Supported?' Frank rubbed his chin. 'Supported in what way?'

'When people have been in difficulty and have come out of it they feel grateful. To all and sundry. It's not surprising, is it?'

On Francesca's third visit the Stapletons inquired after Clio Pugh, and discovered that she was again in hospital undergoing a violent bout of chemotherapy. She seemed hardly alive, unwilling to talk, ghastly in appearance though her consultant spoke of the excellent progress they were making in dispersing the cancer.

'She might just as well be dead,' Francesca said. 'When you remember how lively she was, how gifted as an actress and a talker, how beautiful she was only a couple of years ago, it makes me hate life. It's so unfair.'

'Those cousins of hers have been very good to her?'

'Yes. Incredibly. It's not as if they had been

149

close. They were both teachers, and they both retired in their mid-fifties because they had enough of the hassle in schools.'

'Do they live together?'

'No. One in Ilkeston, the other in Retford.'

'Do they go on holiday together? That sort of thing?'

'Not as far as I know. And to tell you the truth I don't quite understand how they arrived at their arrangement to care for Clio. They come in alternate weeks. I guess that Celia, Mrs Weekes, made the first suggestion. She's a very positive woman, an ex-headmistress. And she'd been helping a neighbour's family out. They had a badly brain damaged child. A young couple with four children, this little girl the youngest. She was a year or so old. Couldn't suck or eat, was blind and deaf, had discomfort and pain without hope of improvement. Celia used to go in for two hours or more every single morning to give the mother a break. The other older children were all at school or nursery.'

'What could she do for the child?'

'She'd hold it, and cuddle it, and clean it up. The doctors said the baby had a certain amount of feeling or awareness, so that she'd enjoy this love, especially if they had managed to dull the other pains.'

'Did the child show any signs of responding?'

'I don't think she could. But I'm not sure. Celia told Clio that the baby had the most beautiful eyes she'd ever seen. You couldn't believe there was no sight in them. Emma, the baby, would open them. Wide as wide.'

'What happened?'

'She died. About a month before Celia suggested that she'd come and help Clio out.'

'It must be terribly hard work for them. They'll be my age,' Thelma said. 'And I've barely energy to look after Frank, never mind a desperate invalid.'

'Thousands of old people have to do so, caring at home for spouses or mothers or relatives with all sorts of dementia or physical incapacities. I don't know how they manage it. It's unthinkable. They must be near to despair.'

'But this Mrs Weekes chose to spend the time with that dying baby and then almost immediately with her cousin.'

'It's more typical of your generation than mine,' Francesca said.

'Do you think so?' Frank butting in.

'Certain. Younger people think that if their parents have paid their national health insurance then they should be covered for care. I know taxpayers can't afford it. The medical profession's been too successful, kept too many old bodies alive, and needing looking after.'

'Us,' Frank said.

'Speak for yourself,' his wife countered.

'I never really understood how Celia persuaded her cousin to join this scheme.'

'Had she any experience?'

'Not so far as I know. She had rather an old

151

mother who went gaga, but Jean just put her into a nursing home. She wouldn't give up her job, though she didn't like that very much. But Celia somehow got round her. Perhaps Jean had developed a conscience now she thought she was getting on a bit herself. I don't know. But there they are.'

'But is Jean any good at it?' Frank asked.

'I believe so. She's a little, well-organized body, practical and a very good cook.'

'Could make a four-course meal with wine out of two potatoes and a carrot,' Frank said. Francesca frowned slightly as if she'd been caught out paying only half attention.

'Don't listen to him,' Thelma, to the rescue. 'He's always like that.'

'Of course they get nurses in to give her a bath and fetch her out of bed, even to take her to the sitting-room. They don't want her to develop bed sores.'

'And they're both on holiday now their cousin's in dock?' Frank said.

'Yes, they are.'

'Have they gone away together?'

'No. I don't think so. Celia likes the sun so she's gone to the Algarve. Jean has made for Scotland on a walking holiday.'

'She's not Scottish, is she? With her name and so forth?' Frank, again.

'Not as far as I know.'

'Frank's thoroughly nosey,' Thelma said. 'He's always asking questions about every little detail.'

'That's the way to learn,' he objected.

' "Ask no questions, you hear no lies." '

Francesca described the way the cousins managed to have Sunday off. Celia claimed that this encouraged Clio to look forward to the next week's carer when she arrived on Monday. Francesca did not believe this story.

'I think myself that it was Celia adding a needless complication just to show that she could solve it.'

'Perhaps she wanted to go to divine service every single Sunday.' Frank.

'I never thought of that.'

'Does she go to church? Do either of them?' Frank again.

'I've no idea.'

'They sound a bit like Major's communicants,' Thelma said. 'Cycling Anglicans.'

They all laughed as if they realized that they could not keep up this serious conversation even at a trivial level. After each visit the older Stapletons re-examined the evening's conversation with their daughter-in-law.

'She's got her head screwed on the right way,' Thelma concluded.

'I enjoy her visits, every minute of them.'

'That's because you like pretty young ladies. You're like your son.'

'She doesn't mention him.'

'No. If she turns up again I might just ask her

153

about that. What do you say?'

Frank shrugged, venturing nothing.

'Come on,' Thelma pressed. 'I'll do the inquiring. I shan't leave it to you.'

'She's gone through enough these last weeks without being bothered by us and our vulgar curiosity. And that's all it is. We can't do anything about it, even if things aren't right.'

'She might like to talk about it.'

'She might not.'

'You never know. And it would be a pity to miss the opportunity, if that were so.'

Again Frank half turned away.

'I see you're going to ask,' he answered, 'whatever I say.'

Thelma pulled an ugly face at him, but admitted to herself that he spoke somewhere near the truth.

Francesca called in, on her own, on Saturday of the same week. She brought presents, an unusual rose in a pot for Thelma, a CD, Mahler's Fourth, for Frank. All went well at home; Hugh rattled round the house, she claimed, like a tank these days.

'How's work?' Frank asked.

'Well, it's the slack time. We shall close the first fortnight in August for holidays.'

'And these big orders?'

'They haven't arrived.'

'Does that mean you've failed to clinch them?'

'I don't think so. I've no first-hand

knowledge, but oriental governments seem not to function in the way we do. That's not exactly true. Some of the business communities in this country act in the oddest way. Just because we're trying to sell them something, they lose all sense of decency or even polite behaviour.'

'Is it the risk?'

'That comes into it, certainly. But there's a lack of confidence. They feel that whatever they do they'll hit obstacles.'

She gave them an example or two.

'Do you feel much the same?' he asked.

'No. Not quite. I am sure that we'll provide them with a first-rate product. Our trouble is keeping going. Money. The stuff you knew all about. The banks do not afford the steadying influence they ought.'

'What's their trouble?'

'They need very large profits.'

'And make 'em.'

'But they don't know who to support, and who to step back from. How can they? They have to guess.'

'Yes,' Frank argued, 'but your firm's been established—is it a hundred years now?—and has an international reputation.'

'The banks think,' here Thelma interrupted for the first time, 'that if you really need to borrow from them then you're not worth lending to.'

The other two looked at her in amazement.

'Yes. It is something like that,' Francesca

155

said. 'You'd be surprised.'

Over a cup of coffee, and in the middle of a discussion of greenhouse-culture, during which Frank grew eloquent over the virtues of his favourite cherry-tomatoes, Thelma suddenly said, 'I don't know if this is the time and place to ask, but how are things between you and Stuart now?'

Silence toppled. The question dropped reckless, tactless, feckless, infantile even. Thelma blushed, drew breath quickly in, clenched her plump fists on the arm of her chair. Frank noticed the brown liver-spots on the backs of her hands, important for the first time.

'Perhaps I shouldn't have interrupted your important talk.' Thelma's jest fell flat, as the silence stretched stronger. The older people awaited a signal from Francesca, who sat staring, wooden-faced, at the wall opposite. It seemed to Frank that she never would speak, that she'd rudely sit wordless until they started a new, acceptable topic.

Francesca suddenly smiled, to herself, making a small contact not with them but with something inside herself.

'Has he not said anything to you?' she asked.

Thelma and Frank hesitated together as to who'd answer 'No'. In the end they shook their heads, not speaking. Francesca's eyebrows rose, stagily.

'He's still seeing her,' she said.

That set them back.

'We didn't know,' Thelma said.

'No.' Frank, heavily.

'"Ye ken noo".' Neither understood the reference. Perhaps this momentarily strengthened Francesca, made up in some small way for her confession.

'We've heard nothing about this at all,' said Thelma, very businesslike. 'In fact as far as I remember you both denied that there were third parties involved.'

'Um.' A short, dismissive sound.

'Do we know her?' Frank asked gently.

'I don't think so.'

'It just crossed my mind that it might be somebody we'd met.'

'Such as?' Francesca's voice scratched.

'Oh, I don't know. Mrs Daley, perhaps.'

'He'd certainly be seeing her still,' Thelma said.

'I took it "seeing" meant something other than merely "casting eyes on".' Frank did not know why he had been shocked into this pedantry.

Francesca looked from one to the other.

'Her name's Clare Cooke,' she said.

'Oh, she doesn't work at his office then,' Frank asserted confidently.

'No.'

'Francesca never said she did,' Thelma offered pacifically. In spite of his trouble, Frank approved of his wife's mild intervention

157

on Francesca's behalf. It momentarily supported her in her difficulty.

'It's been going on for some time. The Cookes were my friends rather than his. We met at a party.'

'She's married, then?' Thelma asked.

'Yes. Her husband is a junior manager at EMEG.'

'Have they any children?'

'No. They've not been married very long. She works. She teaches art.'

'Is it serious?' Frank asked.

Francesca stared at him, in scorn or disbelief. The older Stapletons waited for her to answer.

'What do you mean by that?'

Frank felt a pulse of anger.

'Is he likely to leave you? Does he think that he wants to spend the rest of his life with her? Would he like children by her?'

'I see.' Francesca appeared to consider. 'I take it he has sexual intercourse with her, though I haven't inquired. But perhaps that isn't serious these days.'

'Do you want to get rid of him?'

'I'm too mixed up in my mind to answer a simple question like that. If I wanted anything, it would be to live as we did three years ago. Plenty of work coming in, the boys healthy, Stuart doing well.'

'When I recommended Luke Brailsford to be principal, do you think that affected Stuart,

158

and thus your marriage?'

'It shook him, for certain.' Francesca spoke without hurry. 'He thought he'd be promoted on merit. It never crossed his mind that you'd opt for the old order.'

'And what did you think?'

'I took it for granted that he'd get what he wanted. After all you were his father, and there was no comparison between him and Luke Brailsford.'

Thelma who had been quietly listening interrupted without force.

'But he's got the position now. And yet he starts this affair.'

'It came too late.' Francesca tossed her head, writhed into a more comfortable position in her wide chair. 'I'm never sure that these single big traumas cause shattering life changes. I suppose they do often enough. But in this case, I'm uncertain. I suppose you discussed it with Stuart at the time?'

'Yes,' Frank answered.

'And more,' Thelma added. 'Stuart acted like a madman.'

'Oh.'

'He was very disappointed,' Frank said. 'I don't think he'll ever forgive me. I'd let him down. In his view he'd worked hard to qualify himself to succeed me, but this didn't carry any weight with me. I followed some sentimental principle and appointed an old dunderhead on grounds of long service.'

159

'Was that right?'

'In his eyes, yes. Luke Brailsford had been a faithful, hardworking partner in the firm for many years. He'd retire after two or three more, full of honour, pension slightly enhanced and then Stuart would succeed. That was my view. It would do Stuart no harm to wait for a couple of years or so.'

'Hadn't you discussed this with him? It seemed to come as a slap in the face.'

'It shouldn't have. I thought I had made it clear. Perhaps he didn't want to know. When I told him officially, he shrugged, like a child, said not a word and walked straight out of the room.'

'Somebody got something wrong somewhere, that's obvious.' Francesca spoke in the direction of her mother-in-law.

'Stuart and his father don't think alike,' Thelma said.

'That's clear enough.'

'If you could go back,' Thelma this time to her husband, 'would you make the same decision again?'

'Probably not. With hindsight. Luke had this stroke. He'd seemed fit enough before. But, then, if he'd not been appointed, I might have put the illness down to fretting over his disappointment.'

'Do such things worry you?' Francesca asked.

'Yes. They do. Especially as there are no

plain answers. As you say.'

Francesca picked up her empty cup. Thelma offered her a second. She accepted. Looking down into the black liquid she said very steadily, her voice clear as glass.'

'This has been a digression. That's what you think, isn't it? A diversion so that I don't have to answer questions about Clare Cooke. To tell you the truth, I don't know much about her or her affair with Stuart.' She sipped the coffee, put the cup and saucer safely on the table. 'For the past year or two we've been growing apart. That's not quite right. It's not that we hadn't much in common to hold us together. We did talk about the boys and their progress at school, and holidays, and how we could fit in my schedules with his. But in this last eighteen months or so, this boredom, if that's the word, this lack of shared interests has seemed more like outright hostility. At least, on my part. We were in one another's way. We were positive obstacles to each other. Then you didn't make him principal.'

'It wasn't altogether my decision.'

'He doesn't believe that.' Then more coldly. 'Nor do I. You could have worked it for him, had you wished. He perhaps blamed me. I don't know. I was really beginning to get ahead. I was promoted to the board. I had to spend a great deal of my time even at home, thinking schemes out. This was just before our present setback. It threw more responsibility on him,

161

fetching and carrying for the boys.'

'But if he took up with another woman it would occupy even more of his time.'

'Yes. But I don't think that counted for much with him.' She lifted her head, looked first Frank, then Thelma straight in the eyes. 'Stuart has had two short affairs that I know about in the last five years.'

'And you don't mind.'

'Of course I bloody mind. What do you think?' Exasperation rasped in her voice. 'He's always had something of a roving eye.'

The conversation collapsed there. None wished to take it further. Thelma, now the soul of tact, left the room on some errand to give the other two chance to pursue the topic. Neither took the opportunity. Francesca toyed with her cup, sadly smiling to herself. Frank, in desperation, said that he and Thelma were going to see the gardens at Sheldon House, and then he invited her to accompany them.

'What day would that be?' she asked. He told her. She took a diary from her handbag, consulted it, then shook her head.

'Sorry,' she said. 'I should have enjoyed that, though I'm no gardener.'

She packed away her diary and pen.

'I don't know,' he said. His sentence sounded like a sigh. 'We oughtn't to have raised this with you. You've enough on your plate. We were trying to help.'

'Yes,' she said, tight-lipped.

'Has Hughie's illness not ... ?' He paused, uncertain how to express Stuart's immorality. 'Not stopped his meetings,' (that seemed wrong) 'with Mrs Cooke?'

'No. It might have in the first day or two, but once we, he knew there was a good chance of recovery ...'

'I see.'

'I don't want you to think that Stuart doesn't care for his children. He does. But as with most fathers it's only one of several important matters. He spends some time with the boys; he's good with them, generous, lively. They like him.'

'But doesn't he see that if he goes off with this other woman, it will affect them, perhaps adversely?'

'Why "perhaps"?'

'I thought that if you quarrelled openly at home that wouldn't do them any good either.'

'I see.' She placed fingers to her mouth. 'My guess is that he'd hope to keep this affair out of sight, my sight, like his other little flings.' Scorn corroded her voice to a huskiness. She coughed it back to normality. 'I know precious little about this business. I've kept it at arm's length, perhaps wrongly.'

'I'm sorry.'

'Thanks,' she said. 'It's rotten for you. And Thelma.'

'Yes. But I seem in some measure to blame.'

'That's marginal. If it made any difference at

163

all. Which I doubt.'

Thelma came back carrying a large biscuit-tin. She looked from one to the other, then brightened her face.

'I've packed a few coffee-kisses for the boys,' she said, handing them over. Francesca delicately removed the lid, looked in.

'A few,' she said. 'My.'

'Well, they've good appetites at their age. And you can help them out.'

'Thanks.' Francesca stood, placing the closed tin on the table. 'I shall have to be on my way.'

Thelma mentioned Clio once again, and asked that Francesca take their love to her.

'I can't get her out of my mind,' she said.

'Makes me think that I've nothing much to complain about,' Francesca said in a flat voice.

'Yes.' Thelma walked across to the girl, and put her arms round her. 'You look after yourself, Francesca. And if the worst comes to the worst, you'll still come and see us, won't you?'

Francesca gravely nodded.

'I'll do that,' she promised.

'You and Frank and I and the boys are related by blood,' Thelma said.

'Well, not quite,' Frank answered.

'You know what I mean.'

'I do. And a very good meaning it is.'

He carried the coffee-kisses as they walked out to Francesca's car.

CHAPTER ELEVEN

In early August Ian and Hugh spent three days with their grandparents. Frank took them, with football, to two parks. They did not seem keen to spend the day at the County Cricket Ground, but walked instead for an hour along the embankment near by, watching the fishermen, making no big demands on their elders. They asked questions, suggested their own answers, skipped about, accepted ice-cream. Both in their spare-time seemed to be readers, insofar that in the evening they sat with books which they then took up to bed. Ian in the morning invariably asked permission to look at his grandfather's newspaper, and occasionally passed on items of information to his brother. They caused no trouble, were polite, could occupy themselves but when they went back home the grandparents enjoyed a slower tempo of life.

'We did try to keep up with them,' Thelma said.

'I didn't. I know my limitations.'

'How do you think Hugh seemed?'

'Very fit. But I did imagine sometimes that he was a little bit hesitant.' Frank paused to consider. 'I'd never noticed it before. He'd always been headstrong, dashing at every thing, but not now. Or that's how I saw it. He's got a marvellous lot of energy, especially after all he's been through, but I couldn't help thinking

165

that the illness had made him that bit more timid.'

'Will he get over it?' she asked.

'I should think so. He seems strong enough. In fact, from time to time I couldn't help wondering whether this change, if change it is, wasn't, . . . well, just me. What I'm saying is that perhaps I imagined it, that it didn't exist. I know what he's suffered, what a close call it was, and so I'm on the look-out for some scar or symptom, and if it's not there I make it up.'

'That wouldn't be like you, Frank.'

'I'm not so sure about that.'

'Ian's good with him, isn't he? Spends time on him.'

'Yes. He's suddenly grown up,' Frank said. 'Here he is, only fourteen, and yet he acts more sensibly than I did at twenty, and God knows I was no fly-by-night.' Frank rasped his hand under a cheek bone. 'He seems to have a damn' sight more sense than his father.'

'I wonder.'

'They don't have girl-friends.'

'They do,' Thelma said. 'Both of them. Ian's is called Helen.'

'Did they tell you this?' Frank sounded slightly aggrieved.

'Yes. They talked about it, quite openly. Not embarrassed. Quite unlike the way we used to be at their age. As if they were speaking of marbles or a new tennis-racket, say. I think they were waiting for me to giggle, or be silly

166

about it.'

'When do they meet?'

'Hugh gets off the bus at the same place as his. I've forgotten her name. It couldn't have been Evangeline now, could it? Ian meets his in town now and then at weekends. They sit about and talk.'

'And visit each other's homes?'

'As far as I can make out.'

'Does Francesca approve?'

'I think so. And Mrs Daley.'

'She's still in favour, is she?'

'Yes. She'll go on holiday with them to France soon, after the boys have had next week under canvas in the Yorkshire Dales with their father.'

'Are they looking forward to it?'

'Is Stuart any good at it? He never had much interest in cooking when he was young.'

'He turns sausage on their barbecue,' Frank mocked. 'That's men's work nowadays. And if enthusiasm runs short he can always drive 'em somewhere for a pub-lunch.'

'Did they say anything to you about the holiday with their mother?' she asked.

'Not much.'

The French holiday, for Francesca had luckily booked a cottage, took place in the last fortnight of August. Miriam Daley and Emma, her daughter, accompanied the three. The weather scorched; they came back looking like Red Indians: all had practised their French; all

167

were enthusiastic.

'Did you talk to the locals?' Frank asked.

'The boys went every morning to the shops in the village, and across to the farm to fetch milk.'

'Could they understand you?'

'Yes. Sometimes Emma went with us, and she could rattle away,' Ian said.

'We could always point,' Hugh added.

'What about restaurants?'

'We managed,' Hugh said.

'*Qu'est-ce que je vous sers?*' Ian, handkerchief over his arm.

'*Un poulet rôti avec une salade verte. S'il vous plaît.*'

This for some reason made them laugh. Grandparents could not resist joining in. Tears coursed inexplicably down Frank's face; Thelma choked.

'What are we laughing at?' she asked.

'The talking Frogs,' said Hugh.

'What's French for "frog"?' Frank asked.

Nobody knew, but Hugh took a small dictionary from his trouser-pocket. He looked it carefully up. He frowned. 'How do you say that?' he asked his brother.

'*La grenouille,*' Ian pronounced. Hugh repeated it.

'Now, all together,' Ian said in a strange accent. '*Tous ensemble. La grenouille.*'

That set them off again.

'Who's that meant to be?' Thelma inquired,

168

'Your French teacher?'

'Yes,' Hugh answered. 'Monsieur Williams.'
The boys laughed loudly.

'A Welsh Frenchman,' Frank said. 'Or a French Welshman?'

'You racist.' At this the boys glanced up suspiciously at their grandmother.

'And what did you do all day?'

'We went on trips. Or there was a caravan park nearby and we played with some of the boys there. And we went down to the beach every day. And Mum and Miriam and Emma liked to sit at the table outside and drink glasses of wine. They tried to do a crossword. Miriam always takes a book of them, she says. They joked a lot.'

'That wasn't the crossword, it was the wine,' Ian said, knowingly.

'And no quarrels.'

'Not one,' Hugh answered. 'Mum and Mrs Daley are big friends. Emma just now and then went off on her own, and we used to ask her if she'd found any boys or Frenchmen.'

'And had she?'

'Hundreds, she said.'

The boys declared themselves ready for school, though they could put up with another week at home. They had their new forms and gym-kit. Next year Ian would be able to wear a grey suit instead of a blazer and flannels. He looked forward to it. The suits seemed old-fashioned to Thelma, the sort her husband

169

wouldn't wear even on high days and holidays, but she said nothing.

'We soon grow out of things,' Hugh, grumblingly adult.

'You can have mine.' Ian.

'Thanks very much. For nothing.'

A few days later Professor Lang telephoned. After inquiries to Frank about weather and health he sobered his voice.

'Sarah thought I ought to ring you,' he said. 'It's about Francesca's friend, Clio Pugh. She's died.'

'I see. Was it unexpected? I'd heard she was very ill.'

'It was, rather. We all knew, she included, that her cancer was terminal. She'd just finished a bout of chemotherapy that had made her dreadfully sick, but she seemed to be recovering. She'd come home, and had with help got out into the garden and sat in the sunshine.'

'She had cousins or relatives of some sort helping out, hadn't she?'

'Yes. They'd been on holiday, and had started their rounds again with her. It was Celia's duty week. I don't know her, never met her, but she seemed the senior partner, the organizer. She found Clio dead in bed last Friday morning.'

'Had she been all right last thing?'

'As far as I can make out. The evening nurses had been in to make her comfortable. And

Celia had looked round the door sometime during the small hours.'

'Oh. Do they know the cause of death yet?'

'If they do, I don't. There'll have to be a post-mortem. We'll hear the result any time now.'

'And how's it affecting Francesca?'

'That's what I'm ringing about. It only happened a few days ago, and she seemed to take it steadily enough. Very quietly. She talked to her mother about it, sensibly. So Sarah says. Thought it better to die than to be clinging on to life with all that pain and squalor and distress.'

'Yes,' Frank said. 'I see.'

'But,' Jack Lang lengthened the word. One could imagine him on his dais, pausing before making some crucial point to his students. 'Once it's sunk in, you never know what difference it will make. I had a sort of feeling that she looked on this Clio as a kind of alter ego, another self; if Clio had it right, it would all go well for Francesca. A talisman. A totem, if you see what I mean. Rank superstition, I know, but we get these ideas in our heads and they take some shifting. Clio was quite ill at the time when things started going awry at EMEG. Well . . .' He drawled out his word.

'And you want Thelma and me to look at her?'

'Exactly. Try to get her talking. She thinks rather highly of you two, rates you above her own parents, I can tell you, in spite of the recent trouble between her and Stuart.'

'How's that going?'

'I thought you'd know better than we do. She's more likely to confide in you rather than in us. But my impression is that it's still not good. There was a lull in hostilities while Hugh was so very ill, but now he's recovered, well, they're back where they were. To tell you the truth, I don't quite make out what they expect. From marriage.'

'Stuart has a mistress.' Frank did not know if he did right in confessing this outright, but felt he must reciprocate, pay back confidence with confidence. 'Or so Francesca believes.'

'A Clare Cooke, according to Sarah. I've never met her, but she's the wife of one of the managers at EMEG. We know nothing about her. Do you?'

'No. She's just a name. Stuart has never mentioned her to us.'

'Keep an eye on Francesca, Frank.' Lang rarely used the Christian name. 'We'd be grateful. It's our job, really, but we seem to have ruled ourselves out of the reckoning somehow.'

Professor Lang soon rang off. He sounded embarrassed, convulsively clearing his throat, but he had fulfilled his mission efficiently enough. When Frank told Thelma about the conversation, she nodded, and laughed to herself.

172

'He's a decent man,' she explained her mirth. 'But he reminds me of a great big schoolboy. A sixth-former. A prefect. Always with some ready-made scheme of his own for the improvement of the world.'

'Why do you say that? He seemed genuinely concerned.'

'I don't say he's not. In fact I'm sure he is. But he has to have his own little nostrum to hand to apply to the injured part. I suppose that's what a professor has to do. It's his job. Or yours as head of Bell and Stapleton. You make some decision and then call on some subordinate to carry it out. We housewives have never had that privilege.'

'You wouldn't have a nanny.'

'I won't keep a dog when I want to bark.' Sailor, the mongrel, waddled in at this point, and sat at her feet, staring up. She stroked his head. 'If things go wrong, now all I can do is put my arms round this beast, and stroke him, and talk idiotic phrases to him. But it works. Doesn't it, Sailor, my beauty?'

The dog rested his jaw on her thighs, gazing in admiration.

It was not until after the inquest and Clio's funeral that Francesca asked if she might call round. She spoke cheerfully, said she was lucky in that she had been 'on loan' to some firm in Derbyshire to instruct them in the use of computers.

'Is it interesting?' Frank asked.

173

'No, not very. It's all rather elementary. But I've been supervising the change-over for them for some months, and now the machines are set up I've had to produce instructional schemes for employees, to get the most out of the new stuff. From managers to secretaries, even shop-floor personnel.'

'What do they make?' Thelma asked.

'High-class underwear, men's and women's, and similar products. They mostly market for themselves, but they also produce very large numbers for firms like Marks and John Lewis. It sounds a rather small concern, but it isn't. You'd think there wouldn't be the money about for such luxuries, but you'd be wrong. And they decided to bring their administrative machinery up to date, and called me in to advise them. This month, when I spend all my time with them, is the end of the package.'

'EMEG are slack enough to let you go, then?' Frank asked.

'Yes and no. We're beginning to get encouraging, very encouraging noises from the Far East. We shall soon know for certain; perhaps by the time I've finished at Kaylux. I've got the instructional course so planned out that I could send in my personal assistant to complete my part, if EMEG suddenly wanted me full-time. But they won't. And I'm glad. I've another fortnight to do with Kaylux, and it occupies me, and tires me, bores and stretches me in quite a different way from my usual work. I'm having to think out all sorts of dodges and tricks to make people use their computers to the full.'

'Isn't it all cut and dried at the lower end?'

'Of course. But even there you might just as well learn some of the hundred and one humdrum uses they wouldn't, they don't seem able to, work out for themselves.'

'Thank goodness it's not me,' Thelma said.

'No. You'd manage. It's like giving someone a pencil. One man doesn't even sharpen it, but he can, like most people, leave an efficient message for the milk-man with it. At the other end of the scale, a mathematician can write, work out some important mathematical equation that helps us to understand the universe, or a writer can scribble down a poem, or if you're a Picasso you can knock off a wonderful drawing. But it's the same old HB. A computer may seem a bit more complicated than a pencil stub, but it's there as an instrument to help you do a job; it's as simple as that.'

'I'm still glad it's not me,' Thelma said.

'Oh, many of 'em think like that. "It's beyond me" or "It's nothing to do with what I'm doing". Even the managers. They know all about the product and the machines, and the marketing, and the publicity, and they think that's it.'

'But it isn't?'

'No. I'm afraid not. Because nothing's static.

And a computer can help you change your mind quickly. There are new situations to be faced week after week, and a computer can help try models out to see which will give the best results.'

'You need to know what you're about,' Frank said.

'So you do with my lead-pencil. You need to know which language to use, and how to spell in that language, and how to make sentences in it. And if you don't know how to do these and dozens of other tricks, your pencil won't help you, however expensive it is.'

Francesca spoke both pleasantly and with authority as if her time spent in instruction had unearthed or developed new, pedagogic gifts in her. Her expression was alert, suggesting that whatever the objections they raised she had a smart answer.

Thelma, tactfully in time, mentioned Clio's death. Francesca said it had come as a shock, because, though the therapy had made her friend very ill, the doctors felt it had successfully checked the cancer.

'They didn't expect her to die when she did. No.' Francesca's voice sounded utterly steady, controlled in answer to a plain question. 'It mentioned carcinoma on the death certificate, but cardiac arrest was the reason. She'd been through one long ordeal after another, and her heart just couldn't function properly any more, I guess.'

'Had she had heart-trouble before?'

'Not to the best of my knowledge.'

'She wasn't very old, was she?'

'My age. Fifteen months in it. Just a bit junior.'

'Not old, then. Young.'

'The doctors were optimistic, were they?'

'Their tests showed that the cancer had been cleared. Or checked. That's what they told her. I don't know whether we can believe them but that's what they said.'

'And they'd speak the truth?'

'Well ... My impression is that her death came as a surprise to them, even. In some ways I'm glad. She'd been reduced to a living corpse. She was brave enough, and stoical enough, but she wasn't anything like the person she was before she was ill. She had been a marvel, really.'

'How?'

'She seemed so full of vigour. She acted, sang in the operatic society, did all sorts of physical activities. She made me feel like a lump of putty.'

'But you had children and a demanding job.'

'That's what she used to tell me. She'd poke a finger at me and say, "You've a family and a job which affects hundreds of people", and then, "*I* flit about filling my time in as best I can".'

'She was modest?'

'Very. That's what was so attractive about

177

her. She could do so much, and so effortlessly, but she'd never boast. She'd act, but not praise herself.'

'Did she see herself as successful?'

'I don't believe she did. It's hard to judge.'

Francesca left them without their putting questions to her about her relationship with Stuart. As they reached the front door together she turned to them and said with a bright voice, 'There's nothing further to report from the marriage front.'

They were slightly taken aback. Thelma recovered first. 'Stuart's still at home, is he?' she asked.

'Oh, yes. We're keeping appearances up. Or he's hanging on to his comforts.'

'Is there anything we can do?' Frank said, subdued.

'I shouldn't think so.'

She smiled brilliantly, hitched her bag higher on her shoulder, strode down the drive, wiggling comical fingers at them in farewell.

CHAPTER TWELVE

Frank and Thelma saw little of the younger Stapletons during September. Stuart put three pieces of work in his father's way, but did not make the overtures himself, left his secretary to fix times and terms. Frank did all three, but he and his wife often discussed why Stuart took

178

the trouble.

'He could easily get somebody in the firm to do it. There's nothing out of the way or difficult.'

'Doesn't he say that these are assignments that need tactful handling?'

'He might say so, but there's not much truth in it.'

'Perhaps the businesses he sends you to will be flattered that their bits and pieces are being handled by so senior a figure.'

'I doubt it. They won't know me.'

'Won't they inquire?'

'Not they. If they connect me with the firm, they might think I'm some aged relative who's failed to make the best of my connections. That's if they've bothered to learn, and remembered, my name. Young people these days aren't very concerned with hierarchies. As long as I do my job properly, and don't get under their feet, that's all they want to know. Not who I am or what I was.'

'Why does Stuart keep offering you this work?' Thelma asked.

'Perhaps he's trying to provide me with spending money.'

'We don't need it, Frank. As he knows. Is it to show you he's boss now?'

'Maybe there's something in that.'

'Why do you accept the work?'

'It gives *me* something to do. It might just be helping out.'

179

'It might,' Thelma said, 'be his excuse for not coming round here himself to see us.'

'A bit far-fetched, that.'

'Why doesn't he come, then? You tell me that.'

'He's occupied. As far as he can tell, we're in good health, and in no need of assistance of any kind, therefore he keeps away. He sees to it that Mrs Daley brings the boys round now and then, and so he's done his duty by us. He'll be very busy, ferreting out work for himself if I know him. I'd also guess that Hughie's illness shocked him rigid, and he's making up lost time.'

'And what about his Clare Cooke?'

'She'll brighten his leisure, I expect. Though how much I just don't know. She's a bit of a mystery.'

'Do you think her husband has any inkling of what's going on?' Thelma asked.

Frank shrugged, pulled wry faces, made exaggerated gestures of doubt with his arms.

At the end of the month Francesca rang to ask them to a dinner-dance for the higher powers of EMEG and their friends. Professor and Mrs Lang had already accepted the invitation.

'So there'll be somebody you know to talk to,' she encouraged.

'I'll have to ask Thelma,' he objected. His wife was out at a class on Rembrandt.

'I realize that,' she said. 'She'll want to come,

180

I'm sure.'

'Is it a party to celebrate this Far Eastern railway contract?'

'I wish it was. No, that's still dragging on. Our man says officials know our tender is the best option by a long, long chalk, but they're deliberately making him cool his heels. He's not quite greased enough of the right palms. Or made enough promises.'

'Will he be here, at the dinner?'

'No. He was over last week, and now he's in America, and then back to the final stages of argument.'

'Is he hopeful?'

'Yes. Yes and no. It's dragged on a lot longer than he expected. I think he's fed up. He's done enough to sell them our product a dozen times over.'

'Isn't he used to this sort of protracted negotiation?'

'I'd have thought so. He's been at it long enough. I just don't know enough about it. We've had an answer well before this in all the contracts I've heard about since I joined EMEG, five years ago. This one's probably political and so there's nothing we can do about it at our end.'

Thelma expressed delight at the invitation, made it an excuse for shopping expeditions and the purchase of a new evening gown. She also sent his dress-suit to the cleaners, and without consulting him bought a new frilly-fronted

181

shirt.

The dance did not take place on the firm's premises, though EMEG owned plenty of leisure spaces, including a hall with a very suitable floor. The chosen venue was a room at The Senate, a modernish hotel by one of the city exits from the motorway. Francesca, an eye on the door, immediately welcomed them, and sat them by her parents. Jack appeared extremely smart, his wife rather uncomfortable and dowdy.

Guests were welcomed from the dais by the managing director, a stout middle-aged man with hair that went backwards from a peak on his forehead in small, tight waves. He did not speak well, but shook his jowls and pressed the table ferociously with extended fingers. He appeared a caricature of a business man, awkward, not fluent, promoted well beyond his capabilities, but Francesca had often told them how clever, and cunning, and knowledgeable he was.

Dinner was efficiently served. Francesca did not eat with them, but at the high table. Stuart had not made an appearance. The Stapleton-Lang table was made up by two pleasant youngish couples whose name Frank did not catch and whose cards he could not read. One spoke about the Promenade concerts, claiming always to go down for two or three. In their youth, (not so far back, Frank opined), they had queued and stood. No, they no longer tried to get in at the last night. They offered easy reminiscences of their experiences there.

'What do you think of all this modern stuff they've put in this year?' Lang queried.

'I think it's enterprising,' the man answered.

'Modern works,' his wife said pacifically, 'are a lot easier to listen to in the concert-hall than on the radio or TV.'

'Why should that be?' Lang, the genial examiner.

'Speakers seem to take the nature out of sounds somehow, however good your equipment is. I'm not saying that you can't tell an oboe from a clarinet, you can, but there's a kind of merging, a melting together you don't get when you're actually there.'

The second couple, slightly older, seemed envious of the first, but they had grandchildren who needed attention.

'We're lucky,' the woman said. 'We have three daughters, all married, and all living within a radius of ten miles. That's unusual. But we're called on to baby-sit.' She seemed satisfied with her lot.

'Are you a musician by training?' Jack Lang asked the Promenade woman.

'No. I'm an amateur.'

'Do you play any instrument?'

'The piano. Badly.'

'She paints,' her husband said, dismissing her modesty.

'Oil? Water-colour?' Lang kept the

questioning alive.

'You name it.' The husband's voice, overloud, rang. All four couples were now listening to the exchange.

'Does it occupy a great deal of your spare time?' Lang asked.

'I wouldn't say so.' She smiled, ready to retreat. Sarah Lang drew in the second couple, who embarked on an interminable story about trying to find a late-opening chemist for a prescription, and after the vicissitudes of the chase discovering that the place had run out of the medicine required. The often interrupted story had not been completed by the time dinner had been eaten, and they broke up to give time for the dance floor to be prepared.

Thelma grasped Frank's sleeve.

'Did you ever hear such a rigmarole? Every time we made any sort of pause she was off again. She's the sort of woman who, if you met her in three months' time, would take the story up again exactly where she broke off.'

'Some of it was interesting.'

'Frank. I sometimes think you like being bored. I wanted to hear more from the painting woman.'

Waiters rushed about moving tables; for a few moments Frank and Jack Lang, returned from the urinals, stood together, backs to the wall in the chaos, the scrape of chair legs, hoarse orders, temporary uncertainty. Francesca made her way towards them. Their wives had not yet returned.

'I'm sorry,' Francesca said, face black as thunder. 'It never crossed my mind that it could happen.'

Frank and Lang kept their expression of polite interest.

'It's absolute coincidence. Damned unfortunate for me.'

'What are you talking about?' Jack Lang asked, after an awkward pause.

'You're on the same table as the Cookes.'

Nothing registered on the fathers' faces.

'Trevor and Clare Cooke.'

The penny dropped. Clare Cooke.

'Which were they?' Frank asked. 'I couldn't make names out.'

'She wore a deep-red silk dress.' Francesca, in a near-whisper of disgust.

'Short, dark, bobbed hair?'

'Yes.'

'They're the couple who go to the Promenade concerts,' Lang said, amicably. 'She's a painter.'

'There are all these tables,' Francesca continued, 'and by the purest mischance somebody has to put you with them. I hadn't noticed anything amiss on the seating-plan. It had never crossed my mind.'

'You couldn't have done anything about it without drawing unwelcome attention to yourself,' Lang said.

'Just think,' she said, vehemently.

185

'There's no harm done,' her father comforted. 'We didn't know who they were, and I don't suppose they had any idea who we were.'

'I wouldn't bet on that. She'd be poking round. She'd find out soon enough.'

'Well, that's that,' Frank said. 'Nothing we can do.'

'I'm very sorry. That's all I can say. I just don't know how it happened.'

'Ignorance. Coincidence,' Lang said. 'Don't you bother yourself.' Francesca left abruptly.

On the wives' return, Lang broke the news.

'Which one was she?' Sarah asked.

'The Promenade concert woman, the painter.'

'I rather liked the look of her.'

'Well, don't tell Fran so. That's all I can say.' Her husband appeared unruffled.

The waiters efficiently restored order to the room, and a band assembled on stage. The MC welcomed them to Part Two, more at ease than the MD, and announced the first dance, a quick-step. The Langs and the Stapletons sat this out.

'I'll save my strength,' Jack said, 'for later.'

'Will it all be ball-room dancing?' his wife queried.

'I guess so. In fact, I'm pretty sure Francesca said so. Ball-room and old-time.'

'Spelt with an "e" and a "y"?' Frank asked.

'Absolutely.'

186

The four did not talk about Mrs Cooke, though the women, Frank guessed, would have liked to; they preserved the proprieties. Later Frank found himself standing by her in the bar, and she nodded pleasantly, then volunteered information about a forthcoming concert.

'Will it be difficult to get tickets?' he asked.

'I shouldn't think so. There are two modern pieces on the programme. Webern and Berio.'

'What else?'

'Rossini and Beethoven's First Symphony.'

She waited, ironically pleased, for an answer which she did not get.

'I'm sorry,' she said. 'I didn't catch your name at the dinner-table.'

'Stapleton. Frank Stapleton.'

'Thank you. Mine's Clare Cooke.'

He thought that the end of the exchange, for Mrs Cooke stood silent, concentrating, as if, say, recalling a tune. When she did speak it was hesitantly.

'Are you connected in any way with Francesca Stapleton?'

'My daughter-in-law. The other two at table with us were the Langs, her parents.'

'He's a professor of engineering, isn't he?'

'Yes.'

'So you'll be the father of Stuart Stapleton, the accountant?'

'I am.'

'He's not here tonight?'

'No. He's away, I believe.'

Again there was a pause at the end of which he was surprised to find she had laid a hand on his arm.

'Do go to the Birmingham Symphony concert,' she said. 'They're such marvellous players that they make even difficult modern works clear. And interesting.' She looked at him. 'At least that's what I've found.'

'I'll see,' he answered. 'Thanks.'

She removed her hand. It had been a friendly gesture, sexless, an encouraging signal from a teacher to a favourite pupil. Mrs Cooke smiled, moved away. He did not know what to make of the exchange.

He returned to his wife and the Langs and immediately reported the meeting. He could remember every word; Thelma made him repeat the conversation.

'That's all she said about Stuart?'

'Yes. That he was an accountant, and not here tonight.'

'And that's all?'

'Yes. It seemed quite, well, natural. She seemed more interested in getting me to go to this concert.'

'Do you think she knew all the time who you were?' Sarah Lang questioned.

'Why do you ask that?' Jack, her husband.

'Some women are crafty. She may have been trying to worm her way into Frank's favour.'

They considered that in silence, then exchanged useless brevities. To Frank they

188

appeared like a junior school-yard group drawing close to hear some risky story. They had even moved their chairs. Later, when Francesca came over, they said not a word about Clare Cooke. After she had gone, Jack Lang said.'

'She seemed more upset that she was on our table than I'd have expected.'

'You can't expect her to be pleased,' Sarah answered.

'I said "more upset", nothing about "pleased".'

'Oh, did you?'

Francesca, it seemed, was not alone in her distress.

They spent the evening quietly, occasionally dancing. They enjoyed a display by a team of formation dancers, and a quarter of an hour's lunacy by a clever, clownish comedian. They left, together, just before midnight. Francesca was not to be seen. Once, the Cookes had walked past and Clare had smiled at Frank. Sarah made a sound of disapproval. In the car-park they shook hands, none of your new-fangled kissing, and said they must meet again.

'I'll tell you what,' Sarah had gushed. 'We'll go out for a pub lunch together.'

'Some of us have to work, y'know,' her husband objected.

'Just you. And you can skive off. Any time. I love pub lunches.'

'We never have them.'

'That doesn't mean to say I don't.'

As they drove home Thelma said, 'They're a funny couple. I don't make them out.'

'Why not?'

'They never seem to agree very much.'

'Now,' Frank answered, like a pedagogue, 'I think they do basically. It's only the marginal detail they argue about. A bit like us.'

'Do you think I'm like Sarah?'

'She's younger than you.'

She punched him, but not hard enough to interfere with his driving. She gave him a moment, then continued, earnestly.

'Francesca did seem very angry that that Clare Cooke sat at our table. From what you said.'

'Yes, she did.'

'And Jack noticed it.'

'He did.

'Why was that, do you think?'

'It was an unpleasant surprise. There'd be what, twenty tables? And we and the Langs, she'd have issued orders that we four should sit together, found ourselves on the same table as the Cookes.'

'Do you think it was deliberate?'

'Not for a minute. Coincidence. But Francesca's a big noise here, she's on the board, and she didn't expect her evening to be marred by this little, unfortunate mischance. It's very unlikely that anybody connected us with Mrs Cooke even if they knew there was anything between her and Stuart.'

'She could find out who did the arrangements?'

'I guess she knows that already.'

'And?' Thelma's eyes were wide.

'And nothing. Fran won't kick up a fuss unless there's something to be gained. If she thinks some underling has done this deliberately, she'll make him, her suffer for it. But I think it was purely fortuitous.'

'Good word.'

There followed another pause for thought, before Thelma started again.

'You quite liked her, didn't you?'

'All old men like it,' Frank said, 'when young women spend a little time on them. And she didn't waste it on fulsome compliments; she tried to get me interested in something she thought highly of.'

'Why should she do that?'

'Presumably she thought I should profit from attendance at this concert.'

'Why should she think that?'

'I don't know.'

The plan for a pub lunch with the Langs came to nothing, but towards the end of October Jack rang the Stapletons to ask a favour of them. The university were sending him to some conference in America: this was unusual so near the beginning of term and he didn't particularly want to go, but he supposed he had to do his duty. It left a snag.

191

'At this time of year on Wednesdays and Saturdays I usually take Sarah out to see her mother. She's in a nursing home. Has been for three or four years now. She's well into her eighties, and suffers from senile dementia.' Frank already knew this. 'Now I did wonder, and this is a bit of an imposition, I know, if Thelma or both of you could run Sarah out to Rawston to the home while I'm away. It's usually in the afternoon she pays her visits in summer and autumn. She could go and come back in a taxi or her own car easily enough, but she hasn't got used to her mother's condition yet, though the old girl started going gaga in her seventies. It upsets her, and so she needs a bit of company there and on the way back. I'd ask Francesca but she's got enough on her plate, and seems touchy, might say something out of place. Now don't be afraid to say you can't do this. Sarah said I wasn't to ask you, that it was imposing on you.'

'We'll manage something,' Frank said. 'Do you want us both to go, or just Thelma?'

'I don't mind. Whichever's more convenient to you. I know Sarah will be pleased. She won't ask anybody to do this for her. The poor old dear can't help the way she is, but Sarah seems, well, ashamed of it all. As if somebody's let the side down. I tell her, it's an illness. As if she'd been the victim of an accident or a virus, but it doesn't seem to register with her.'

Frank consulted with Thelma who

192

telephoned Sarah and arranged that all three should go the following Wednesday.

He could tell that his wife felt uncertain because she inquired from him how she was to dress.

'As if you were going to church.'

'I never do.'

'Well, as if you were invited to a Lord Mayor's function at the Council House.'

'I don't do that, either.'

Thelma pulled comical faces at him, but dressed neatly and soberly in twin-set without pearls. She looked old-fashioned and efficient. Any beauty she retained from her youth had disappeared with this outfit. Sarah had similarly adorned herself, and both appeared stiffish, well-to-do, oldish, not to be put upon. Sarah seemed in no way upset, chatted freely, especially about Ian and Hugh who had visited her, in the company of Mrs Daley, the previous Saturday.

'How were they?' Thelma asked. 'We didn't see them because we were away at a wedding. My youngest brother's son. In the Lake District. Lovely church.'

'Oh, fine. Full of go. Hugh had been picked for his year's rugby team. He was very pleased with himself.'

'Doesn't Ian?'

'What?'

'Play for his team?'

'Yes. But he says he's more interested in

soccer, and wished the school played that.'

The nursing home, a red-brick house at the end of the old village had ample parking space in what had been a large back garden. Two ancient hawthorns in height and girth as large as trees and an enormous sycamore in the furthest corner were all that remained of horticulture; white lines divided the area of tarmacadam. This afternoon visitors seemed few.

'Just come in for a moment,' Sarah said to Frank. 'Just so you know what's what. Then you can go out and walk round. It's a lovely afternoon.'

They pushed through a wide door into a highly polished hall-way, where two potted plants which Frank did not recognize droopingly obstructed easy passage.

'Makes a change from Swiss Cheese plants,' he said nervously pointing. The women did not answer. He did not like the smell of the place: it looked clean, exceptionally so, but the air seemed barren, mechanically produced, dull, stale. Sarah led them at a good pace up an oaken staircase, Frank bringing up the rear carrying her parcels. She pushed through a fire-door and then a second into a long rectangular room, the result of joining three, perhaps four bedrooms.

Sarah looked about. A uniformed young woman waved to her and pointed downwards. The three in her direction stopped in front of a figure slumped in a chair.

'How is she?' Sarah asked.

'About as usual. She's eating not too badly.'

'Any signs of animation?'

'Not really.' The nurse turned her attention to the old woman in the chair. 'Look who's come to see you, Anne,' she called out in a public voice. 'It's your daughter.' She attempted to straighten the scarecrow figure, without success.

'Hello, mother,' Sarah Lang said, trying the nurse's loud manner. 'I've brought you some visitors. Mr and Mrs Stapleton. They're Francesca's parents-in-law.'

The old lady fractionally raised her head. The face, deeply lined, channelled, was sallow, and had, like the untidy, thin hair, something of death about it. The eyes met Frank's: colourless, washed-out, red lids barely apart, made a brief meaningless contact, dropped, drifted away. She emitted a little sound: he could not tell whether it was a murmur of greeting or a small groan.

Sarah was unwrapping parcels.

'I've brought your favourite,' she said, as to a child. 'Chocolate cake,' to the other two. 'I'll fetch a plate.' She marched confidently off.

Thelma glanced at Frank, then gingerly took the old woman's left hand.

'How are you, Mrs Jordan?' she whispered. No answer. 'Sarah's just gone out to get a plate for you.' She signalled to her husband to take

195

the other hand. He did so. It seemed almost weightless, a skeleton, withered skin barely covering the bones, but it was faintly warm, still alive. 'Are you better today? You've not been very well. A bad cold and cough.' This went unanswered. The old lady did not move. 'Sarah's going to bring you something to eat.' Thelma signed to Frank to contribute to the conversation. He squeezed the bony hand.

'Are you comfortable, Mrs Jordan?' he asked. The old woman moved an inch at most in his direction, as if the depth of his voice had caught her attention. 'It seems very pleasant in here. Warm. And these are very good chairs.' The last statement approached the truth. The chairs, though old and scuffed, were large, well-made, too wide if anything for the wasted hams of the inmates. 'Are there any men in here?' he asked. Thelma appeared slightly shocked that he should ask such a question.

A nurse-attendant deliberately stopped in front of them broadly smiling.

'That's it, Anne,' she said. 'You enjoy your visitors.' She turned, a thick-set young woman with legs wide apart. 'They do, you know,' she informed Thelma. 'We don't fathom all that goes on in their heads, do we, my duck? But a change, a new face, a new voice acts as a stimulant.' She beamed her approval at the group; Thelma massaged the old woman's hand more vigorously.

'Does she show any reaction?' Frank asked.

'Well. Sometimes. She'll be pleased with a sweet or a cake. You can tell.'

'Is she worse than most?' he persisted.

'Oh, yes. But she's no trouble. She tries to cooperate even when she's ill, as she was last week. She'd a dreadful cold. Sneezing. Eyes and nose running, temperature.'

'Did you leave her in bed?'

'No. We think she's better off up and in here. She feels at home.'

Again the young woman smiled in approbation apparently of Thelma's ministrations on the hand. The attendant nodded. 'I'll love you and leave you,' she said, wheeling away. Thelma wiped the social smirk from her face and looked to Frank for comment. He said nothing, watched the movement of the nurse's broad buttocks as she proceeded along the row of unvisited patients.

'Sarah won't be long now,' Thelma said to Mrs Jordan. Frank joined her with sounds of agreement. The room settled to its barren silence. Outside all flashed and dazzled in brightness.

'It's a fine, big room,' Thelma said, betraying her unease.

'Yes,' he answered in a whisper. 'It will take some heating.'

'I like the plaster work.' She tried again, pointing upwards. He looked at the squares on the ceiling, to the leaves and flowers, and the highly decorative circles round the candelabra.

197

'They took a great deal of trouble in those days.' He could see from the plaster patterns on the ceiling where one room had been divided from another.

'Do you think they could get it repaired?' she asked. 'If they had, let's say, an accident?'

'Yes. Not easily. But there'll be ersatz stuff. Polystyrene or something of the sort. I don't know whether you'd get bits to match. If you had the money.'

Again Thelma pointed upwards, where they could see that a plaster division and more than half of a large flower had broken away and been left unmended. The damage was not obvious.

'It wouldn't be worth while getting a man in just to repair those bits,' she pronounced.

'No,' he purred. 'No, it wouldn't.'

With relief they noticed that Sarah Lang was coming in at the far door. In no hurry, she sought out and drew up a small table and placed on it the plate and spoons before fetching out a wrapped rectangle from one of her three bags.

'Now, mother,' she called. 'Time for cake.' No reaction. 'Cakey.'

Sarah began to unwrap the small parcel.

'You go for a stroll round,' she instructed Frank. 'It's a lovely day and it's quite pleasant either way out at the front. I don't know if you've been here before. If I were you I'd turn left at the main gate, where you came in, and down towards the village. It's getting on for a quarter past three now. Be back for a quarter to four. We shall be ready for you then. They feed the animals officially, tea and biscuits, soon after four.'

'Thelma?' he asked.

'Thelma'll stop and help me.'

'Anything I can get either of you while I'm out?'

'No, thanks.'

She had opened the container, extracted the cake and put it almost formally, but on its side, in the middle of the plate. She now rummaged in another bag, came up with a large towelled napkin.

'Off you go,' she ordered, 'and don't be late back. Right, mother, let's have this round you.' She flourished the bib.

Frank scrambled to his feet and made for the door.

'Quarter to,' Sarah called.

'Synchronize watches.' Thelma, quietly, a whisper of sarcastic, comforting reason.

He walked out at speed, but even the shadowed back garden path offered no relief, as dry and stuffy as the house, so that it was not until he had almost reached the end of the gravel drive that he realized that a breeze tempered the warmth of the sun. The main road passed one or two large houses, Edwardian or Victorian, though nothing like the size of the nursing home, and then on to the

199

more haphazardly placed dwellings in the village, mostly cottages, but with here and there a modern bungalow built into a larger garden. The pub, The Barleycorn, looked roomy, up-to-date with its newly decorated sign on a golden post, but closed. The church stood back from the road and the lych-gate; only the tower and spire could be seen, graceful in sunlight. 'Crocketed,' he told himself. 'Fifteenth century.' These snippets of knowledge surprised and pleased him. He had no means of checking them. 'Crocket'; the curling ornamentation along the spire. The upper windows of the vicarage were to be seen further along the road behind a beech hedge. A lime tree was heavy still with green leaves.

A little further on the road swerved at ninety degrees to the right. It had been widened on the corner and plastered with warning arrows in black and white, sign posts, bold restrictions, directions. He could see no reason for the original turn in the road; the houses stood well back; no trees interrupted; the ground was flat; streams cut no ditches. Seventy yards further on, much marked, the road turned again, left this time, resuming its original direction. Cottages and new executive housing continued; a small Methodist chapel, 1843, cowered slily behind iron railings. The information about it he took from a stone square high above the front entrance; no modern, wooden notice-boards were to be seen, and yet the windows looked cleanly black in the sunlight. Perhaps the place had been sold off and was now a dwelling-house. In that case each of the windows would have had curtains. He stared. The glass was frosted, shaped by narrow, crossed diagonal lead spars, with here and there a yellow or green diamond. If this were a house now surely there'd be a place for parking cars, but he saw none. The grass between the front wall and railings was lush and green, not exactly short, but by no means neglected. A rowan, still leaved and berried, half-blocked the grassy space to the right of the church between it and the wood-pannelled fence of the next house, a recently-built double-fronted miniature mansion aping the style of Lutyens. The villagers used the chapel as a meeting hall, perhaps, and had found no need for notice-boards. He grasped two spear-like tops on the uprights of the iron-railings, and examined the paint. Retouched during the last three years, he guessed. He moved to the unpadlocked front gate, turned the knob. The gate swung easily, without a squeak. No rust disfigured the joints. He closed it, quietly.

All this time cars had been passing on the road, yet he had seen not a single pedestrian. A huge lorry and trailer now viciously shook the ground, battered his ears. It was immediately followed by another almost as big, with a German name proud across its shuttered sides. In the calm after the departure Frank saw a man emerge from one of the cottages and walk in his direction. They exchanged greetings, and the villager, middle-aged, hatless, with strands of hair plastered across a bald pate, stopped.

'Are you lost?' he asked. It seemed a curious question in so small, open a spot.

'Not really. I was just wondering ... Idle curiosity ...'

'Oh?' The man drew the one syllable out, giving it colour, expressing interest, even approval.

'I was puzzled by the chapel. It looks in pretty good order; paint-work and so on. And yet it lacks the notice-boards a place of worship would have, and I can't see any signs of its being a private dwelling-house.'

'Ah,' said the man, again at length, this time with relish. 'Well.' He seemed a master of the expressive monosyllable. 'You're right. It's a private house. Has been for some years now. The couple who lived there were elderly. Well, late middle-age these days. In their sixties. And it's too big for them. The ceilings are high, even in these little places, though the conversion was very nicely done by a firm from Newark. So the old people handed it over to their eldest son. He lives in the next village. They bought a cottage, oh, the other side, up by The Bull. They've been out now about a month. The son and his family are supposed to be moving in at any time, but we've seen nothing of them yet. Well, that's not quite right. He's been up a few times. Stopped for an hour or two. Doing the odd job, I'd guess. And there you are.'

'Thanks,' Frank said. 'Mystery solved.'

'Ah.'

The man waved a hand in solemn farewell, and turned back, disappearing into the front door of his own cottage. Neighbourhood watch. The man had checked up on him. Am I my brother's keeper? It appeared so, in this village. Frank grinned, broadly, delighted with the development. He glanced at his watch; he'd been out twenty minutes, but would easily make it back to the nursing home inside the allotted time. He set off at a smart pace, arms swinging, still grinning. Children, from the school, spattered the street. He'd no idea where the school building was. Perhaps they had come off buses; he had not noticed. Both boys and girls wore uniform and all carried satchels, containers, brief cases, lunch boxes and paid not the slightest attention to him.

Back on time, he let himself in to the nursing home. It seemed hardly right to walk straight in and upstairs without challenge into a house on his first visit. Nobody showed up. He heard a clash of piling or unstacking crockery in the distance.

Sarah and Thelma were ready for him, coats buttoned, hand-bags zipped. The old lady slumped stonily untidy in the chair, hands in her lap, veins faintly purple against the sallow skin.

203

'Well, 'bye then, mother,' Sarah called, and swooped to kiss the bony cheekbones.

'Good-bye, Mrs Jordan,' Thelma said, lifting the old woman's hand an inch or two.

'Good-bye,' Frank echoed.

The old woman stirred, they could not be certain, and Sarah led them away. They did not look back.

Outside the door, as they descended the stairs, Sarah called to Frank over her shoulder, 'You were dead on time.'

'Oh, yes.'

'He respects punctuality,' Thelma said. 'That's one thing he learnt on National Service.'

'It's one that young people don't understand these days,' Sarah answered. 'Any time within a couple of hours will do.'

As they crossed the car-park he inquired of Sarah how she had found her mother.

'Just as usual. There's no change. She'd no idea who we were.'

'Are you certain?' Thelma asked.

'Yes. Any other three people would have done. I think she enjoys the cake and the sweets, but I can't be sure. It stimulates her. Slightly.'

'Did her condition come on her suddenly?' Thelma, again.

'No. Well. She became forgetful in her later seventies. Vague. And by the time she was eighty-odd it wasn't safe to leave her on her own. She's become much worse since she came in here four years ago. She's eighty-seven now. It's a big age. Even these days.'

They were seated comfortably in the car, black seats hot with the afternoon's sun. They wound down windows. Thelma insisted that Sarah rode in front with Frank. As he drove he offered observations on the beauty of the autumn weather.

'It's soon dark, though,' Sarah said.

'What time will Jack be home?' Frank asked.

'Let's see. Today's Tuesday. Six o'clock. It varies.'

'Does he come up with you to see your mother?' asked Thelma from the rear of the car.

'Yes. Especially in the holidays. Then he'll come twice a week. He's very good. Otherwise just the once, Wednesday. This week's the exception. He's away from home.'

'Does Francesca ever come with you?'

A pause followed. Hedges flashed by. Thelma suspected she'd hit on the wrong question. Sarah answered in a flat voice.

'No. Not now. She came a time or two when mother first was in. But she has a job and a family.' She perked up, spoke more strongly. 'Besides she takes a more logical, sensible view than I do. Always has done. Gran doesn't know her now from Adam, or Eve. I can't tell whether she wants to be bothered with visitors, or prefers to be ordered about by the nurses. I work on the assumption that it gives her a bit of pleasure, but that may not be right.'

'Does Francesca argue her case?' Frank asked, rather brutally.

'No. She sees it's between my conscience and myself.'

'Did she get on well with her grandmother when she was young?' Thelma inquired.

'Oh, yes. When Fran was little my mother was only in her fifties, an energetic woman. My father was still alive. She knew her mind then. She wasn't keen on my marrying for instance. I'd just finished at university, and Jack was doing his Ph.D. What was the hurry? We'd only been married thirteen months when Fran was born. Jack had just got a job, in industry, not as an academic, in South Wales. She used to come to our little house in Port Talbot and lay the law down. "I was thirty when I had you," she used to say. 'You should have given yourself a bit of elbow room, enjoyed yourself, worked or something, not saddled yourself with nappies and bottles at this young age.' Mark you, I breastfed Fran. I was into natural childbirth, Dick Read, and Spock and all the rest of it. My mother used to laugh at me, and we'd argue. "You're making a rod for your own back." But she and Fran got on like a house on fire. Fran could twist her round her finger.'

They all laughed.

'And to see her now.' That sobered them quickly enough. 'She doesn't even look the same. She was a broad, well-set up woman, strong. Jack used to say when she'd got across him: "Your mother would make an ideal washerwoman." Now she's quite different, like a skeleton. I wouldn't recognize her.'

They drove along in sunlit silence. Sarah coughed, spoke again.

'It hardly seems ten minutes ago. Fran bobbing about the house and my mother following her round telling her things, showing her, explaining to the child. They seemed a bit alike. Stiff and know-alls. Fran's not like that now. She's more laid back as if it didn't matter one way or the other. But she was a little madam, then, with her elbows going, and her face bright.'

'It does you good to think about it,' Thelma said.

'It's thirty-one, thirty-two years ago since Francesca started school. In thirty-two years I shall be older than my mother is now. I hope I don't live that long. Good God.'

They delivered her home, and by that time she had cheered herself up, was chattering on about some baking she had done that morning. She insisted that they come inside to collect a bag of buns she'd made especially for them.

'Was your mother a good cook?' Thelma asked.

'Wonderful.'

'And she showed you?'

'She did.'

207

'And Fran?'

Sarah burst out laughing, remembering how the child had emptied the whole currant jar into gran's cake mixture. 'I could tell she was exasperated. If it had been me as a child I'd have got a slap, real smart, no messing. But she helped Fran pick them out, a spoon each. And the girl's face. It was a picture.'

CHAPTER THIRTEEN

The younger Stapletons held early in November a firework party to which the grandparents were invited. The grandsons with a dozen or so children, boys and girls, rushed round an enormous bonfire as Stuart and one other father took charge of the lighting of fireworks. The rest of the adults sipped punch or red wine and exclaimed at the ingenious beauty, length and warmth of the spectacle.

'I don't like bangers,' Sarah told Frank.

'Nor I. Tonight's are a marvellously civilized selection.'

'Fran, I reckon. She'd make a good choice. And no argument.'

In the interval for roasted potatoes and thick slices of quiche (Francesca again) Hugh told his grandfather that they were going abroad for Christmas.

'Where?' Frank asked.

'Italy.' Ian, passing, added detail. 'Tuscany.'

'Who's going?'

'Mum and Dad, Ian and me.'

'Not Mrs Daley?'

'Don't think so.'

'Are you looking forward to it?'

'I don't know. We shan't get all our presents out there.'

Mrs Daley, questioned, said it would be advantageous for her and the boys to have a respite from each other.

'Emma and I can spend the holiday together. That is, if she comes home. I'm not sure of that. Money's the guiding factor with students these days. She might have landed a little Christmas job up there, and then she'll stay put. If she does, I'll lounge and shop for a fortnight, and clean the whole house out.'

'It'll be a break for you.'

'I'll say.'

Frank asked Francesca about the Italian holiday.

'We were lucky, really. It seemed too good a chance to miss. I don't think you know the Buckleys. He was MD at Stansley Engineering, and retired a year or more ago. They live out there now. We've kept in touch. Maria and I have. And they have to go over for a wedding of a grand-daughter in Los Angeles just before Christmas and they're stopping for a couple of weeks, making a holiday of it. And so they offered us their house. Only last week. Don't know why. We're not as friendly as all that. But

209

offer it they did, and it seemed too good to turn down.'

'What's the weather like there?'

'Mixed, Maria said. It's winter, but you can have beautiful days.'

'Frost?'

'Possible. They even had snow, not much, last Christmas Eve, but that was unusual. Windy and wet sometimes. But George Buckley will have made sure his house is warm. He likes his home comforts.'

Francesca talked to her father-in-law as if she'd all the time in the world. Hostess to forty-fifty people she seemed in no way fazed. She had delegated jobs, so that guests were helped to ample food. The noise grew, extraordinarily comforting, controlled but ebullient.

'Will the boys enjoy it?' he asked.

'It seemed an opportunity. I expect they will.'

His eye caught Stuart, in teen-age mufti, cheerful and extrovert, shouting some loud instruction to a heavily-bearded man in hectic charge of the wine-bottles.

'Is Stuart going?' he asked.

'That's the plan so far.'

She smiled at him as if they shared some ravishing secret. 'Don't forget to eat?' she warned, moving and waving.

'No fear.'

The Langs had only just learnt of the Italian holiday.

'Christmas is one break I like to spend at home,' Jack said.

'You're an old stick-in-the-mud,' his wife gibed.

'Besides, I've no rich friends who offer me their foreign villas.'

'I understand Stuart's going,' Frank said.

'So we hear,' Sarah answered, grimly enough.

'Is that good news?' Frank asked.

'I've no idea. None at all.'

Thelma thrust her head forward, an aggressive cleft between eyebrows.

'That's the thing I can't get used to. Here are these two on the edge of a breakdown of their marriage, and yet we've no idea what they feel, think, or are doing about it. Nearest and dearest.'

'I couldn't agree more,' Sarah said. 'When we ask Fran, and I'm not backward in coming forward in that department, I can tell, she gives us some idea of the situation. But she might be a solicitor summarizing somebody else's troubles, not her own.'

'And?' her husband asked.

'And? And what?' Sarah sounded angry. 'She's your own daughter. You don't think she's happy, do you?'

'I do not. But I'm at a loss to see what I can do to improve matters.'

'You can start by not asking me bloody-fool questions.'

Lang's face set hard so that for a second Frank feared he might slap blindly out at Sarah. Jack then, almost comically, blubbered his lower lip, and nodded as if a serious objection had been raised, and he had taken full cognizance of it. He tapped at a kitchen chair with a fingernail.

'I've just about got used to the idea that there's nothing much we can do,' he answered, slowly and mildly. 'They're outside our influence.'

'You can try to argue with them,' Thelma said.

'We have done this. Sarah particularly strongly. She, Francesca, knows what we think. There's no doubt about that. But our opinion has no effect, none whatsoever. Not that I can see. I think I've told you, Frank, that she pays more attention to your views than ours.'

He spoke in a quiet voice. The four stood now, behind a trestle-table on which stood square cardboard boxes, presumably of food; they seemed separated from the other guests, physically and in mind. Sarah had sat down on the wooden chair, and strained her head upwards.

'We've told both Francesca and Stuart,' Thelma said, 'that the welfare of the boys should be their main concern. They agree. Even snap at us as if we're reminding them of something they know better than we do.'

'I suppose they do,' Frank said.

212

'It's no use knowing something if you do nothing about it,' Sarah said, from below.

'I imagine,' Jack Lang interrupted, without heat, 'that they think they are doing something, paying attention to the interest of the boys, but it doesn't alter their own hurt.'

'It should,' Sarah almost shouted.

'Well, no. If you're badly bruised, you feel the pain, whatever the outside distractions. They're emotionally damaged, and they're sore. They'll make out, to themselves, that they're acting sensibly, and within limits they are, but the quarrels cripple them, and determine the direction of their lives.'

'It sounds like a college lecture,' Sarah said bitterly.

'I'm trying to be rational,' Jack said.

'Don't try too hard,' a cheerful voice shouted, and a flat hand slapped the top of one of the boxes. Stuart, grinning all over his face, leaned across the table. 'And what's the upper house discussing just now?'

'You, amongst other things,' his mother answered.

'No wonder you look so cheerful.'

'You're spending Christmas in Italy, I understand?' Jack Lang asked, drily.

'We are indeed.'

'Whereabouts?' Sarah asked.

'Tuscany. Somewhere near Fiesole. Do you know it?'

'We've been there,' Sarah said.

213

'Good?'

'It's high up. You can look down on Florence.'

'We'll look down on everybody.' He beamed at his mother-in-law. 'Have you got plenty to eat and drink?' He spread his arms, foreign-waiter fashion. 'Food for thought?' They smiled, not answering. 'Try to enjoy yourselves. That's the idea of these parties.'

Stuart backed away, joking with the people he jostled.

'He's pleased with himself,' Thelma said.

'Let's hope he is,' Jack answered.

They attended for a few moments to their plates and cups.

'I sometimes wonder,' Jack Lang began, brushing crumbs from his waistcoat, 'what it was like in the days when parents had a powerful influence over their families.'

'What do you wonder?' Thelma asked.

'Whether it made much difference. I don't doubt it set up frustrations, but they'd only be different from today's in that our old people aren't responsible for the situation.'

'I was, it appears,' Frank said, unemphatically.

'How was that?'

'According to Francesca one of the reasons she and Stuart are at loggerheads is that I didn't make him principal of the firm when I retired. This hit him very hard. Had the nasty effect, apparently, of making him envious of

214

Francesca who at the time was doing so well at work.'

'It wouldn't apply now to the poor girl,' Sarah said. 'She's driving herself crazy about what's going to happen to the firm.'

'No good news yet?' Frank asked.

'No,' Jack answered.

'They're hanging on by a thread,' Sarah said. 'Just enough casual work coming in to keep them solvent. Jack says they've been lucky there. They could easily have run into a slack period while they were waiting for these big orders. And that would have meant closures, and redundancies, if not the receivers.'

'And if they get these orders, the bright young men who've cut their teeth on them, will be looking round elsewhere. They won't want to soldier on in a place that has run so close to ruin.' Jack rubbed his chin, head shaking.

'Do you mind if I ask you something?' Sarah spoke softly to Frank.

'No. Go ahead.'

'If you had known then what you know now would you have made Stuart principal straight away?'

Frank stepped a little further from the questioner as if backing away from her question, but he smiled when he finally answered.

'Yes, I suppose I would.'

Sarah nodded, puppet-like.

'I wouldn't have risked it,' Frank continued.

'It didn't do Luke Brailsford any good, for a start. He had a stroke after a few months as principal. You could say it all proved too much for him. On the other hand if I hadn't promoted him he might well have had the same stroke out of disappointment and stress. As to Stuart, well, I can hardly bring myself to believe that his anger solely brought about the rift between the two of them.'

'You mean you won't blame yourself?' Sarah asked.

'That's right. I'll admit my decision might have been a minor cause of the trouble, a last straw, dropped on at an awkward time, but that's all. Stuart, or perhaps both of them, was beginning to tire of his life-style. If he'd had, oh, a superior stimulation at work it might have satisfied him for the moment, left him too busy for matrimonial foolery.'

'So you wouldn't have taken the decision you did?' Sarah again.

'No. With hindsight, no.'

They shuffled, each one an inch or two, biting into buns, all uncomfortable.

'And yet you were sure at the time?' Sarah, unwilling to let it go.

'Frank's never sure of anything,' Thelma said. 'He sees all sides far too easily in my estimation.'

'You surprise me,' Sarah answered. 'Jack's a bit of a ditherer, but I thought Frank would weigh it all up and then come down on one side

216

or the other. Isn't that the way accountants think?'

'By no means,' Frank answered. 'We have to try our hand at prophecy from time to time, but ours is only a guess.'

'An informed guess,' Jack suggested.

'We try to apply such facts that we have.'

The grandsons arrived to stand the other side of the table to greet the old people. They and their companions had tins of coke and wedges of stodge, currant cake, burgers, treacle flap-jack in their none-too-clean hands.

'Are you enjoying the fire?' Thelma asked.

'Fine,' Ian answered, 'but we're chasing about in that wood over the back fence.'

'Doing what?'

'Running and shouting,' young Hugh replied.

'And cuddling the girls.' One of the hangers-on spoke up with brash clarity, force even, his face keen with mischief.

'You are, you mean,' Hugh said. 'Sexy Sam.'

'Oh, dear,' Sarah said. 'Oh, dearie dear.'

An awkward, brief embarrassment possessed and silenced the whole group, on both sides of the table. Sexy Sam's reddened face was a picture. He knew he'd suffer.

'Well,' Ian said, 'we'll have to be on our way. Have a good time.' He sounded thoroughly grown-up, versed in social management.

The boys swooped off. One minute half a dozen bright faces confronted the old people,

217

and the next the youngsters turned their backs, ducked, and were swiftly out of the kitchen.

'The energy,' Thelma said.

'The little monkeys,' Sarah echoed.

'I think it's very good,' Jack Lang spoke in a meditative drawl, 'that they bother to come and say hello to us. They've been really well brought up. I don't think at that age I'd have gone out of my way to seek my grandparents out.'

'Not at any age,' Sarah said, ambiguously. The others did not know where the fault lay, with grandparents or the young Jack Lang. 'Get me another drink, Jack, would you?' She passed her glass across. He moved round the table.

'Anyone else?' he called back from a few steps away.

'It worries him,' Sarah said. 'Not only the domestic trouble, but the possibility of Fran's firm going under. He doesn't sleep properly, and that's unusual for him. I'd have said that if he'd have been woken up and told that nuclear missiles had been launched at him and he'd four minutes left to live he'd have nodded, turned over and dropped off again.'

'We never hear anything about that famous four minutes now,' Thelma said.

'Francesca was his favourite?'

'Yes. And she was always less trouble than anybody else's children. I think he thought he'd begotten the perfect daughter. And now this.'

'Is he well?'

They looked over at him as he queued for his wife's punch. His face was unlined, and his back straight. He kept closing his eyes as if to ward off some sight he detested. His suit, plain navy-blue tie gave an impression of quiet conformity. His expression was pleasant, but distanced from this company in casuals, these untidy mops, these skin-head hair cuts. One guessed that his shoes, in spite of the mud outdoors, would be the only pair in the place giving evidence of having been polished.

'Yes,' Sarah said, 'he's well enough. Blood pressure up just a bit. Touch of arthritis in the hips. But, yes, he's fit.'

'Does he enjoy his job?' Frank asked.

'He complains more than he did. He'll have another seven years to do if he goes on until he's sixty-five.'

'Is that what you expected?'

'Yes, I did. Or I did until recently. I'm not so sure now. His department's big, and seems to be very successful. These outside reports, inspectors' assessments, you know, place it in the highest category. There's plenty of research going on. He's a good picker, Jack is. He's got some really really clever young men.'

'No women?'

'Yes, there is at least one young woman and she's a top-class theoretical flier. "Wasted on this place," he says. But they're mostly men.'

'And he doesn't feel threatened by these

219

young Turks?'

'He doesn't say so. He knows what he's doing, and if he differs in his ideas from them, well, he and they expect it. And he carries the top cards. He can recommend promotion for them, I expect. But since this Francesca business it's knocked the life out of him.'

'Sssh,' Thelma whispered.

They saw Jack returning with his wife's glass of steaming punch. He made his way neatly through the crush, smiling at them from the start of the return journey.

'I bet you were talking about me behind my back,' he said, setting down the drink.

'Nothing but compliments,' Thelma answered.

'You should have waited till I could hear them.'

A quarter of an hour later the two grandfathers sat outside on a plank seat idly watching the bonfire roaring upwards. They were yards back, but the heat powerfully brushed their faces.

'Some size, this,' Frank said. 'It's a good job we're well away from any buildings.' They followed the volcanic upsurge of smoke and sparks, the ferocious crackling of the wood. One or two adult males with forks kept the inferno within bounds and replenished. 'Talk about pollution.'

Face fire-red, handsome, Lang stared into the heart of the blaze.

'This Francesca business has troubled me,' he said. He did not speak clearly, but muttered into his hand or the darkness beyond the fire, hoping perhaps his partner would ignore him.

'Yes,' Frank answered. 'You feel so helpless.'

'She's clever. A much better mathematician than ever I was. And I used to think, when Ian and Hugh were babies that there she was cooped up in a house, and what a waste it was. And then she signed on for EMEG, and showed her mettle. She shot up like a rocket, and was taken on the board after three years. I was proud, I can tell you. She'd now done both things: been a mother and begun a glittering career. Then . . .' The word fell like lead among the shouts and the explosions. The two men, a foot between them, sadly weighed down, glowered in the excitement.

'I know,' Frank said.

'First this matrimonial breakdown.' Lang paused as if to allow his companion a moment to appreciate the formality of his language. 'That's enough for anybody. Especially when you consider how well suited they seemed, and how nicely the boys were getting on.'

'I wouldn't want to defend Stuart,' Frank offered.

'We don't know. It seems he's the one chasing off after a new partner, but Francesca may have been neglecting him. Sexually, socially, domestically. We don't know. And then on top of it all EMEG begins to totter. If

221

only they could fetch in for themselves a couple of years' solid work, that would keep the plant and work-force fully employed, then the firm would have time to sort itself out. They're basically a strong concern, not only with outstanding products, but able to change, to swap about. And fairly quickly at that. Fran has a big hand in that.'

'Why has this Far Eastern project come to grief?'

'These deals are often tricky. People need a quid pro quo. I'm not saying it's all palm-grease, because it isn't, but their negotiators try to see to it that they are making the most of their opportunities, squeezing the last advantage to themselves out of the rival firms which are tendering.'

'Were there many others?'

'Oh, surely. European, American and, from what I hear, Asian. And the longer they stay at this stage, the longer the auction will go on.'

'But new rolling stock won't be forthcoming?'

'I don't think,' Lang said, 'that will bother them much. Put the whole shoot back a year, so what? It's worth it if they're saving large amounts or getting a better deal. They'll manage with the old carriages and trucks. They're getting their money's worth out of them.'

'But if the system breaks down?'

'It won't. Or not any more than usual.

They'll patch up and stitch up and keep the railway trundling on. And the curious thing is that often it doesn't matter how much money, capital they have. They're like millionaires saving sixpence on some minor job. There are some in this country who organize their business on just such lines.'

'And it's not sensible?'

'Not if you need new plant, or whatever, quickly to increase your business. But this new railway, well. It won't make a great deal of difference to the balance of their economy.'

'Why are they doing it, then?'

'They'll have to make a change sometime. Railways are necessary to them, just about, and rolling-stock does drop to bits. Now they've got oil money they'll use it. But the old suspicions lurk. "Uttermost farthing" is the motto.'

Again the two crouched in silence, neither concentrating in spite of the intensity of their gaze at the bonfire. Lang clasped fingers between his knees, wrestling himself out of misery.

'Surely,' Frank asked, 'Francesca will be able to find another job, with her qualifications and experience?'

'I don't doubt it. But not at board level. And having reached there, and deservedly, it'll be a tremendous disappointment to her not to continue with work of that sort. Oh, she'll get jobs. I could wangle her into my own department, and shall certainly do so if it

223

comes to the worst. She won't be able to move, you see, because of the boys. The scales are weighed against her. I don't think it's at all likely that she'll get anywhere near her present level of salary locally. If she were a man she'd be off. But she's tied.'

'I see. Stuart could offer her work, he says.'

Lang ignored that.

'You hear government ministers telling us that in future we'll, people will, have to change careers two or three times in our working lives. How can a woman do that?'

'The husbands may have to take second place.'

'Can you see Stuart doing that?'

'No.'

A rocket swished soaring into the sky, clean above the smoke, and burst into round stars, exploding with ferocity.

'I could do with another bun,' Lang said.

'Good idea.'

The two rose and walked towards the house, stumbling slightly.

'We're getting old,' Jack Lang ventured. 'And tonight it feels like it.'

CHAPTER FOURTEEN

Frank delivered Francesca and her sons to the East Midlands airport where Stuart was already waiting. He had been into the office that morning and still retained the worried scowl of a responsible man.

'Have you packed everything?' he asked his wife.

'No,' she answered shortly.

'Enjoy yourselves,' grandfather encouraged the boys.

'We'll try to ring you,' Ian said. 'We did telephone Australia and it was clear. Slightly late. You had to wait just a fraction of a second.'

'It was by the satellite,' Hugh interrupted.

'But the reception was perfect. Now what we want to see is what it's like somewhere out in the country in Italy. That's the test.'

On the way back Frank said to Thelma how grown-up the boys seemed.

'They talk to you like equals sometimes,' he said.

'Is that good?' Thelma asked.

'It is. More than good.'

'I love that pair,' Thelma murmured, to herself. Frank took his left hand from the wheel to pat her arm.

They received cards from the boys, one of San Miniato, one of the statue of Neptune in the Piazza della Signoria. 'Mum says this is awful, but we quite like it. Ian and Hugh.' In the first postal delivery after the New Year there was a letter from Francesca, which said how much they were enjoying themselves. They'd been to a bingo session in the village on

Christmas Eve and then to midnight mass. Ian had won a prize; neither of the boys had any difficulty with the Italian numbers. For her and Stuart the caller had translated into English, though 'I couldn't understand that, either.' All four had visited the Uffizi museum in Florence. 'I thought the boys would be bored stiff, but they found all sorts of things that interested them. It's been a good idea to take them abroad, because it gives me insights into their thinking that so far I've missed . . .' The weather had been kind with two days of flawless skies. They wouldn't be back until the weekend before the boys started school. Stuart was already home, and Francesca guessed they would have seen him. This had been the best holiday they had ever had.

Stuart had not contacted them, to his mother's disgust.

'That son of yours is a rum body,' Thelma grumbled. 'Do you think he's come back to . . .'

'. . . dally . . . '

'. . . with his Clare Cooke?'

'Well, even if he has, it doesn't stop him from contacting us, does it?'

'I'd think not,' Thelma answered carefully. 'But he might think we'll interfere in some way.'

'How could we?'

'It's his guilty conscience.'

Frank suspected that his son had returned early to get back to ruling the roost in his office.

226

He thought that at one time he might well have acted similarly. He said nothing of this to his wife. Thelma phoned Sarah Lang who had been away in Gloucester over Christmas. Sarah had received a letter that morning from Fran, still delighted with her vacation. Though Stuart had returned now she had kept the hired car and had been to Siena, a beautiful hill-city where the winds had roughed them up. 'But it was beautiful. Ian took photographs by the dozen, and Hugh said he wished he lived there. That really surprised me. But they're changed, developed enormously, the pair of them. In some ways they're exciting strangers to me, and I guess this is my fault. I've been too busy to notice, but I'm making up for it every blessed minute. Any time now they'll have grown beyond me, so I'm revelling in this holiday. It's the best, the happiest I've had for years.'

Thelma read her letter from Italy to Sarah. Both women sounded joyously youthful. Sarah said that usually during the younger Stapletons' holidays all she received was a card with a comment on the weather and the comfort and convenience of the hotel. If the family had formerly visited some place of historic or aesthetic interest, a brief half-sentence sufficed. Last year, for instance, from Spain came 'Visited Alhambra. Good.' This year Francesca wrote in greater, gentler length because the boys now reacted more like adults, and Fran felt herself involved. Before she had

227

been responsible for the administration of the holidays, the smooth organization of laundry or excursions. This year she and the boys shared the excitement.

'She hardly says a word about Stuart,' Sarah ventured.

'No.'

'Do you think he took part in these trips and expeditions?'

'I took it that he did. And while we're talking of that young man,' Thelma's exasperation shook her voice, 'have you heard anything of him since he came back?'

'Not a word.'

'Neither have we. I don't know what's wrong with him. I'll get Frank to ring him at his office. He won't want to do it. "Oh, leave him alone," he says, "He'll get in touch when he sees fit." I despair sometimes. How's Jack?'

'He's away on a conference again.'

'Does he like that?'

'I can't make out. I think he has to go. He always says, "It's a good job I got into the habit of working hard when I was young. Otherwise I wouldn't get anything done now. Even so, this everlasting round of meetings stops me doing anything very serious."'

'Does he pick up ideas at these conferences?'

'He says not.'

The two arranged to meet to continue mining this rich vein of inadequacy amongst partners.

Thelma pressed Frank who twice 'phoned his son's office. On the first occasion Stuart was out, and on the second engaged with an important client, but the secretary promised she'd ask the boss to ring his father the moment he was free. No 'phone call followed. Thelma sounded off furiously, at such length and volume that her husband dodged out of her way in the late winter afternoon for a walk he did not want.

He set off, crossed a park, then wound his way through shops and houses, hounded by traffic noise. The day had been bright and even now at four o'clock the sunshine, low in the west, spread shallowly dazzling. He walked more quickly for now that the sunlight was no longer directly on the streets one could feel the ice in the wind. He continued towards the crown of a hill covered completely by decent houses, mostly semi-detached, privately owned, with squares of front gardens, well-kept but stereotyped. He had come further than he intended, but slightly elated had already decided on his roundabout way back home. It would take almost an hour and he'd end the walk in darkness. He stopped and looked along the road, now increasingly steep, down towards the dual carriage-way in the valley and then up again across a slightly rising landscape amongst houses and two factory chimneys. When he had reached the wide ring-road below, hidden as yet by the precipitous slope, he'd turn right on that and begin the dull haul home.

Frank stopped. Over the other side he could see the horizon, perhaps three miles away, a flattish range of low hills towards which the land between rose gradually from the valley. To the north-west, strings of lights stretched along streets lost in the blue-grey of darkness, most in short, straight, broken lines, whilst a few swept wide in curves like gorgeous scars across the landscape. On the rim of the land as far as his eyes could see between the houses close to him a line of clouds massed, grey and continuous, without breaks of tone, the top rising and falling in peaks against the green-grey sky above. These had the exact appearance of a range of distant mountains, and the illusion was strengthened by the clear towering of skies, pale, fading pastel green and blue, but without a blemish, a rag of cloud. He might well be looking at the hills of Tuscany; in this evening light his airy fantasy and remembered Italian solid rock seemed indistinguishable.

Frank stopped for a moment, for he had been walking at speed and his breath came short. He leaned on the concrete post of a gate to examine the small garden which he could still make out in the gathering darkness. A privet hedge cut it off from its neighbour and the north winds, and within its confined space it held three promises of Spring: a tall lilac near the pavement extruding awkwardly over a stone wall, a low forsythia by the drive and in the middle of a dull lawn a small magnolia soulangiana. All were leafless, apart from a few tatters; the trunks and branches glistened with damp; the rusty ruin of two of last year's blossoms clung to the lilac. All seemed bedraggled, unpruned, but he rejoiced in their potential. He felt a sudden, useless affection for them and the sparsely-berried cotoneaster and the winter jasmine. Francesca and her boys looking out on real Italian hills on this same evening would not have these close-to-hand comforts. Florence had disappointed him by its lack of gardens; the great villas and palazzi doubtless possessed them, hidden broad acres behind high walls, out of view of the plebeian pedestrians, the man on the lorry or the velo. Here an unexceptional suburban street had raised the spirits, his hopes in the evening. He thought of Francesca and Ian and Hugh, and his imagination built a solidity of successful content for him, heart's ease. He remembered Thelma at home, worrying about Stuart, wishing that her husband could drum up the son and a credible explanation from the telephone. Thelma was a good woman, unreasonable, talkative, but thrice his moral size.

He marched off down the last of the hill, steeper at each step.

The traffic along the valley road clashed noisily; lines of cars queued at the islands;

impatient drivers hooted; petrol fumes polluted the air. Frank went at it hard, elbows working, steel-tipped heels clacking on the pavement. As he and a bunch of pedestrians crossed by a Belisha beacon, a gaffer drove into them. A squeal of brakes and the car stopped at forty-five degrees to the direction of the road. People skipped clear; the car had touched no-one, by a miracle. A young man, banging on the car windows abused the driver. Traffic massed impatiently behind. The car sheepishly drew away, and Frank reached safety. The young man, in full raucous obscurity harangued two or three of the bystanders with time to spare or shock to clear on the far pavement.

When he reached home, Thelma had the kettle on.

'You're late.'

'I got carried away,' Frank answered.

'Sarah Lang's been on the 'phone. Could we go over this evening, not for anything formal, just for a drink or a cup of coffee?'

'Yes.'

'I told her we would.' Thelma smirked. 'If you wouldn't go, I'd go myself.'

'What's all this in aid of?'

'I don't know. Perhaps she's reluctant to let the Christmas spirit evaporate, or she's so pleased with Francesca's letters from Italy, or she wants to quiz you about Stuart's silence. Oh, Jack's just back home, a day early from his conference. He couldn't stand it any longer.'

They arrived at seven-thirty, were seated by Sarah in the best chairs, were surrounded by trays of savoury delicacies. Both visitors refused alcohol, so that Jack was despatched immediately to the kitchen to make coffee.

'He loves messing about with the percolator,' Sarah said. 'And adding refinements of his own.'

'Such as?' Thelma, entering into the gaiety of the evening.

'Oh, he'll put a touch of Mocha in with the Kenya, or a pinch of salt, or bicarbonate of soda, for all I know.'

'And does all this make a difference?' Thelma asked.

'I'll say this for him: he can make a good cup. Whether it's because he measures things out carefully, or it's all his fancy touches, I wouldn't like to say. Perhaps it's because he goes out to make it while I can sit here with my feet up. Maybe that's the magic ingredient.'

Jack took long enough over his brewing but he finally brought the coffee in on a huge tray, with bone-china cups, two sorts of sugar, milk and cream.

'Black or white, Thelma?' he asked.

'As it comes,' she said. He frowned, staggered back as if mortally offended.

'Half and half,' she amended, stoutly.

'Sarah?' He poured with considerable skill.

'You know how I like it.'

'Now then, Frank?'

'Oughtn't I to have it black, so as not to ruin the taste?'

'You like milk in it?'

'Usually.'

'Well, that's how you shall have it. It will taste differently, of course. More bland. But there'll be something radically wrong with your taste buds if you can't appreciate the coffee itself. I'll make it for you as I make it for myself.'

'And what more could I ask?' Frank said.

They relished the moment with Jack presiding, sipping appreciatively, smiling at each other. Jack spoke about the local football teams, said that Stuart had season-tickets and took his sons down to the home matches. This arrangement had been slightly spoilt because Hugh had to turn out for school rugby some Saturday afternoons, but the Premiership team played as often as not now on Sunday or on a week-night.

'Does Stuart enjoy it?' Frank asked.

'From what the boys say. We've not seen anything of him for weeks.' Sarah.

'I guess it brings something out of the children that Stuart knew nothing about,' Jack glossed. 'It'll be rather like Fran and this Italian holiday.'

'What impressed me about that,' Thelma said, 'was that she suddenly discovered they were intelligent, and growing up, and could

234

share things equally with her.'

'I don't remember that happening with Stuart when he was their age,' Frank said.

'Was that our fault or his?' Thelma probed.

'I'd blame myself. I was too busy to take him to football matches. I'd have bought him a ticket, if he'd shown any interest, but to the best of my recollection he didn't. But credit where credit's due, he takes them down, even if he's still no interest.'

'Is it worth it?' Sarah asked.

'How do you mean?'

'Well, if he took them to classical concerts or good plays you might think he was doing them more good. It would be educational, not just kicking a ball around.'

Jack Lang intervened.

'I think,' he said, 'that they're joining in with the middle of the road people. I know we hear a lot about football hooligans and the rest, but most of the people down there are decent citizens expending a fair amount of their spare money to watch a match, and let steam off.'

'Do they understand the game?' Frank argued. 'The impression I get is they want something or somebody to support. They aren't there, most of them, to judge the skills of the best footballers in the country, but to watch their team win. And they don't mind if it's done by talent or luck as long as it *is* done.'

'You don't know anything about it,' Thelma said. 'You've never been to watch them.'

235

'And there your expert stands condemned.'

'Have you ever been down?' Thelma asked Jack.

'Not with Stuart and the boys. Once or twice on my own.'

'What was it like?'

'It's quite exciting. I got quite carried away. I felt like shouting.'

'Did you go with him?' Thelma asked Sarah.

'No fear. I've something better to do with my time. And money. It's as expensive as opera.'

Jack Lang talked at length about the conference he'd attended. He spoke rather more quietly than usual as if by keeping his voice low he did not betray his colleagues with his strictures. There had been virtually nothing at the meetings he'd chosen to attend which had caught his interest. 'Francesca would have been more at home with it than I was,' he confessed. The young men performing had been clever and ambitious, but they'd seemed thoroughly theoretical. 'When I started my academic career you'd find a good number of the speakers at conferences, and there weren't nearly as many then as now, were men who actually worked as engineers on site, had even started as apprentices, and they concentrated on how they'd got the piers of a bridge to stand on shifting surfaces or how they'd made sure an explosion half-way up a high-rise block wouldn't bring the whole building down or what was the cheapest way to build safe hotels and dwelling-houses in an area prone to earthquakes.'

'Don't they do such things now?' Frank asked.

'Of course. But in my day I used to think that the problems were thrown up in situ. For instance, what different sorts of concrete would be necessary in the building of a nuclear power-station? The use of computers has made an enormous difference. You can try models out in a way we couldn't.'

'Isn't *that* interesting?' Frank again.

'Oh, yes, could be, but I went to one talk on materials needed for use in the exploration of space and the speaker, not so young either, was trying to think what would be required in a hundred years' time, let's say, for the probes they'd be sending up. But he fell between all the stools. There was nothing very new to me. It was rather like a lecture to first year undergraduates making sure they'd a respectable grasp of the basic knowledge, the ground work. And it was either that or some young high-flier talking right above our heads about the mathematics of shape. I went to hear one topologist, and for all I could make out he might well have been lecturing in Mandarin Chinese. I can only stand a certain amount of frustration and so I offered my excuses and came away early. I'd made all the contacts I'd wanted to.' Lang laughed, shamefacedly. 'Sarah says it's my own fault. I've thought about it since I've been back home, and I think she's right.'

'Have an engineer's problems changed all that much?'

'No. There are all kinds of developments we need to investigate still, but I have the impression that my sort of approach is slow and lumbering, and in any case will only come up with half an answer, instead of dozens of extra new, investigable solutions.'

'Wouldn't that make a good lecture?' Frank asked.

'Oh, we always have long sessions on the education of engineers. And the branches of engineering are so many these days that there's always argument as to the basic requirements of engineering students.'

'But if there are so many new developments, doesn't that make for interesting exchanges?'

'It ought to. But it didn't. I went to one on acoustics. The ideas were interesting, but the man lectured to fellow experts, who probably didn't need the thing, anyway, who had read it up in the journals.'

'No new state-of-the-art stuff, then?'

'I suppose so. But I'm not expert enough to know what's been done and what's about to happen. It's the same with all sciences; we know our own little corners, and not much else. Even with practical subjects like mine.'

'Is acoustics about making concert halls sympathetic to all sorts of sounds, solo voices, symphony orchestras, amplified pop-groups?' Thelma asked.

'Yes. And keeping noise out or in. If you live near an airport or a motorway how do you protect yourself? And how do you do it economically? There are hundreds of necessary adjustments to be made in all sorts of fields these days.'

'Do they overlap?'

'Of course. If you're designing a dam, you need to know about, let's say, materials and building—as well as water-engineering. They'll employ experts in each speciality, but one must surely understand a fair amount about the others' lines. Or pick them up pretty quick.'

'And you came away early?' Sarah chided.

'Yes. I'd had enough. A good many of my age and status didn't even go.'

'But you did?' Frank asked.

'I'm optimistic. I live in hope of something catching my eye. To tell you the honest truth I don't always understand what the young men back here in my department are after. They work hard, and publish, and privately look on me as somebody who helped Noah build the Ark. I've heard them lecture.'

'But they respect you?' Sarah said, emphatically.

'Yes. As somebody who organizes a department worth working in, and who'll be required to support them when they come to apply for chairs and all the rest. But as an engineer? I doubt it. I still carry on my research. I still edit, together with two really clever young Americans, an influential journal. I'm not nobody to them, no. But I'm an anomaly, a left-over, or a historian of the subject. I'm like a professor of Greek. What I know is interesting, and might even be useful now and then to those just starting the subject, but as a practitioner, well, I'm as much use as a classicist to a modern novelist. Less so.'

'You sound more like eighty-eight than fifty-eight,' Thelma said.

'My subject's on the move. When I started most universities in this part of the world had professors of mining, or mining and metallurgy. It's not so now. The world needs mining engineers, but the need is smaller. There are more departments of aeronautical engineering than naval or marine engineering these days. And that's as it should be.'

Sarah stood up.

'My poor old husband has worn himself out with all this confession, and so, in my humble opinion, we'd better eat something. I hope you're hungry, Frank.'

'It'll be mere greed.'

Sarah and her battered husband cleared the coffee pot and cups and bustled out, warning their guests to sit still since no help was required. All was prepared.

'He's an interesting man, Jack Lang,' Thelma said, in a whisper.

240

'Yes. And not so far behind fashion as he makes out. I was talking the other day to Tom King, his vice-chancellor, and I had the impression that Tom greatly respects him. He's stuck to engineering, made one or two real advances, keeps this journal he edits up to date and relevant, and is apparently highly regarded. And he had not, Tom said, "disappeared into administration", which he easily could have done. "I'm the man on the coal-face," Jack tells them, "and if now I feel more like the man in the lamp-cabin that's still useful and necessary".'

'Except that mines are closing. That's what he thought.'

'I guess that's why he chose the metaphor. He'd be ironical at his own expense.'

'I like him.'

'Oh, so do I. He knows what he's about. Sarah, now, she's different. She's tactless, and is likely to blurt out the first thing that comes into her head. I suppose that if Stuart and Francesca divorce then we shan't have much to do with them.'

'I don't want that, Frank.'

'No. Nor I.'

'But we've got to the age,' she said, 'where we have to put up with what comes our way and that's that.'

A rattle outside the door changed the glum expression on Thelma's face to one of social well-being. Sarah entered followed by Jack.

Both pushed trolleys, laden with dishes. Both host and hostess beamed like actors at curtain-call; they did not bow, but such action seemed not unlikely.

'Look at that,' Frank whistled. 'What a spread.'

Plates were issued, and they took portions that suited for size. Sarah clearly had excelled herself, so that Frank who had intended to eat next to nothing took a second slice of a delectable cheese quiche.

'Melts in your mouth,' he said.

They did not talk much while they ate. Both Thelma and Frank refused wine, and Jack was therefore ordered out for a bottle of a non-alcoholic beverage, of Sarah's concoction. This was sweet, slightly herby and fizzed, setting off her savoury delicacies to advantage.

'There's something almost religious about eating food as good as this,' Frank said.

'It still puts weight on,' Sarah warned.

'How does Jack manage to keep so slim?' Thelma asked.

'He's always running about attending this meeting and that. And when he's at the university he doesn't sit down to meals, just swills black coffee.'

'Of his own making?'

'It's instant, believe it or not.' She smiled. 'He's always been thin.'

This led Sarah to reminisce about the first time she had seen Jack. As a second year

242

student she'd accompanied a friend down to watch one of the many university teams play soccer. Jean's latest boy-friend, a ginger youth who careered up and down the left wing, was the attraction. Sarah had watched one of the defence, a lanky young man, with nicely-shaped legs, who seemed to govern his game with his head, issued orders with a quiet voice amongst all the shouting, or with a pointing hand. At the end of the match it happened that Copper-knob had walked out, by chance, from the pavilion with the leggy defender, and introductions were made.

'And that was it?' Thelma asked.

'Oh, no. Not for some time. We ran across each other on a few occasions and just said hello before he finally asked me out.'

'And you knew this was the right man?' Frank demanded.

Sarah screwed her face comically as if trying to wring out from her memory some suitable answer.

'Well, he seemed a serious sort. He was a couple of years older than me, had a first, and was doing research.'

'What she means,' Jack interrupted, 'is that I was keener than she was.'

'And how did you get her round to your way of thinking?'

'I was always there. And we were both looking for jobs together after I finished my Ph.D. I found one in South Wales, and she

applied to teach down there, and so we got
engaged, and then married, and we had Fran
and then John pretty quickly.'

'So you gave up teaching?' Frank asked
Sarah.

'Yes. And we moved back up here to a job at
Loughborough. And two years later Jack's old
prof wanted him back in the department, so we
shifted over to Beechnall when he went to the
university again.'

'How long had you been in industry?'

'Five years. Two only teaching at
Loughborough. But my prof, Jimmy Evans,
thought that was an advantage for the young
men in his department. I was taken on
temporarily for a start just in case I didn't suit
them, but it worked out well enough. Jim and I
agreed on a line of research that really did us a
power of good, both of us. That was partly
luck.'

'Or good judgement,' Sarah said.

'My position was made permanent, and
there I stuck till I moved to the headship of
department at the Poly. And there I've been
ever since.'

'A shining light,' Frank said.

'An example to us all,' Sarah added.

They laughed and slapped their knees, not
quite knowing why.

'And it fulfilled your ambition?' Frank asked
seriously.

'Well, I suppose . . .'

'No,' Sarah said. 'No, it didn't. He made a name with his research. He took off like a rocket. He could easily have had a chair, two at least were there for the taking by the time he was thirty-six. But he's a bit of a stick-in-the-mud. He didn't want to move to the Poly, the North Midland. He thought it was a come-down. Now he knows he's done a great deal for the department there, and so that it gives Beechnall University a run for its money as far as reputation goes.'

'Well,' Jack drawled doubt.

'They've tried very recently to tempt him back,' Sarah said. 'In fact they want him to go now. Not the first time. At the age of fifty-eight. It's unusual.'

'And will you go?'

'I don't suppose so. I'm thinking about it. Sarah would like me to move. She tells me that Beechnall University sounds better than the University of the North Midlands (Beechnall), but I don't honestly know.'

'It's your own university. And mine,' Sarah said. 'And time was when you'd have given anything to be the Head of Department there.'

'Yes,' Jack said. 'Y-e-e-s. I shall have to make my mind up in the next week or two.'

'And what's your present position?' Thelma asked tactlessly.

'Don't know. Why should I up-sticks at fifty-eight, nine by the time I get there? What good can I do in the half-dozen years I'd have left?'

'Get you out of a rut,' Sarah said sharply.
'And into another.'

'They obviously don't think so,' she replied, 'or they wouldn't be putting such pressure on you to move.'

They let the subject drop. Jack waved the non-alcoholic bottle above their glasses, benignly. He appeared to be thinking of something other than the welfare of his guests. A half-smile played round his mouth, but his expression was distant, that of a man listening to great, much revered music.

Sarah and Thelma between them revived conversation again, this time discussing future holidays.

'There's a brochure through the letter box at every post,' Thelma complained. 'And the Sunday Magazines.'

'Do you read them, though?' her husband asked.

'I know *you* don't.'

Sarah said that Francesca's enthusiasm for Tuscany had revived hers. 'But it will have to be early because I don't want to be there in the summer. It's too hot. And if Jack's moving jobs then he won't want to be too far away.'

'How men's minds are made up,' Jack murmured.

'If I go early, Easter-time, perhaps I can persuade Thelma to come with me. The weather can be superb then.'

'What about Frank?' Jack again, gently.

246

'He's capable. He can look after himself. Or the pair of you can go out for meals together. Anyhow, he can come to Italy. You're going to spend some time there, my lad.'

'I am, am I?'

'Yes. I'm not having you back here on your own worrying yourself to death.'

'About what?'

'Whatever it is you men do worry about.'

The telephone rang in a room outside.

'You go,' Sarah ordered Jack.

'Ten past ten,' he said. 'I wonder who that would be at this time of the night.'

'Go and find out.'

He made for the door.

'It's probably Francesca,' Sarah said, 'ringing to say they've arrived safely.'

'It's a bit late.'

'She's probably waited until the boys are out of the way in bed.'

Sarah rose to serve them, again imploring Thelma to consider seriously an Italian trip. 'I love going abroad, but I like to guarantee I've got a friend there whose company I'll enjoy. You might by chance find somebody, but it is a chance, and one I don't like to risk.' Thelma said she would discuss it with her husband, but Frank granted her his permission immediately.

'There you are then,' Sarah said.

'I'll have to consult my big diary back home. That will have the final say. Though I must admit I'm very tempted. I'll let you know

247

before the weekend.'

Frank tried to describe his ideal holiday. He would take it in a part of the world that was, if not new to him, at least very different from the place where he lived.

'Somewhere exotic?' Sarah asked.

'Not really. Exotic means distant and hot to us English and I dislike that. There'd be dust and flies.'

'Wouldn't the Antarctic count?' Sarah continued.

'I suppose so. But that if anything would be worse. I demand a temperate climate for my holiday.'

This led Sarah to begin on a story of how her luggage went astray on a flight to New York, and then to theft, robberies, muggings in England.

'Have you been broken into?' Thelma asked Sarah.

'Twice in the last five years. And we have all the proper alarms and lights and the locks and bolts they recommend.'

'How did they get in then?' Frank.

'Oh, broke a window, double-glazed at that. And during the day.'

'Didn't the alarm go off?'

'Yes. But nobody took much notice. One neighbour was away on holiday, and the other couldn't get into our back, unlike the burglars. He rang Jack at work, and the police, but by the time anybody arrived it was all over. They'd

248

gone over the garden wall with such bits and pieces they'd stolen. My neighbours saw them go. Three of them. But there was nothing he could do. He'd rung the police.'

'And where were you?' Frank asked.

'Sybil Martin and I had gone out for lunch. We do sometimes: trip round a garden-centre and then into a pub for a bite.'

'Perhaps it was as well,' Thelma said. 'They might have harmed you.'

'I don't know. I don't think they try to break in, at least in day-time, if they're sure somebody's at home. These muggers pick on old ladies, or old men sometimes, who live alone in little flats with no telephone, and neighbours who don't hear or care what's going on, because such people often have cash about the house. They don't use plastic money.'

'Did you lose much?'

'A few pounds, a bit of paste-jewellery. The video was away for repair. In any case, they seemed on foot so they couldn't take anything too bulky. But I suppose we were lucky.'

'In some places,' Thelma said, 'these burglars are drugged up to the eyes and don't know what they're doing. I guess they'd kill you as soon as rob you.'

Sarah nodded, and still encouraging them to eat said that society had changed. Nowadays, she argued, we lived much closer to death than we did fifty years ago just after the War. In the middle of the complaint she suddenly stopped,

249

listened, as if she'd heard sounds of another break-in. She seemed rapt, mouth slightly open, eyes wide, hand held ready to fly upwards to stifle a scream. After a minute or two, as her guests watched, she suddenly remembered them and said, in an ordinary enough voice, 'Jack's a long time on that phone. I wonder who he's talking to.'

The Stapletons had no answer.

'He's usually short with people. He's like a lot of these scientists, he doesn't care for modern inventions that break into his privacy. D'you know what he says? "We quickened all the means of communication up when it would do us a lot more good to have to sit and wait".' Sarah sighed, not exactly troubled, but put out by something she could not easily explain to herself. She continued to frown, even when they resumed pleasant conversation, this time at Thelma's instigation, on nursery-men, catalogues, gardening magazines and offers.

The door quietly opened and Jack returned.

Frank looked up at his host whose face was set and pale. Jack's body, it seemed, had shrunk in a moment inside his suit; his left hand, like a blind man's, felt for the back of his chair, though he remained standing. He did not speak; his mouth gaped slightly perhaps to gulp for air. His features offered no message, pale, handsome, intelligent, but revealing nothing, giving nothing away. Only the slackness of his clothes and the groping fingers, not yet still, on the chairback showed unease. Thelma smiled at Jack in welcome. Sarah did not give him as much as a glance, but continued bending over one of the trolleys, intent on a plate, doiley-covered, of home-made chocolates, each in its coloured paper-case.

'Who was that then?' she asked, still not looking up.

Jack did not reply immediately, grasping his chair, working his lips. Now Sarah straightened, stared.

'George Buckley.'

His wife made a kind of interrogative whine.

'He's the man who loaned his villa to Francesca.'

'What did he want?' Sarah showed her exasperation at his niggardly speech.

'He wanted to know if she'd arrived.'

Jack dropped his chin to his chest as if he'd exhausted himself.

'He'd tried to get through to Stuart, but he's not at home. He's tried three times.'

'What did he want her for?'

Sarah was now upright, alert, aggressively so. Jack did not lift his head, stood shamefaced, a delinquent schoolboy outside the head's study. His mouth opened wider, and they could hear his breathing.

'He said he didn't want to alarm us.'

Again the awkward pause, the failure to catch the eyes of the others.

'Yes?' Sarah's one word smashed into the

silence. She stared, seated now.

'There's been an accident in Italy, a bad road accident, on the way to Pisa.' Jack pawed the air. 'I couldn't make out how they'd got to know. Either his wife listens to Italian radio or somebody in Italy had rung her up. It was a dreadful pile-up. And an English woman and two boys were involved. She thought they were killed.'

'Francesca,' Sarah said, faint expulsion of breath.

'No names were mentioned. But Maria, his wife, thought that it was today Francesca was travelling back. She'd go by Pisa airport. So she wondered.'

Again the awkward, tortured silence. Jack writhed, forcing himself to speak again.

'Buckley said he tried several times to get hold of Stuart, but there was nobody in. He'd rung the police, and they suggested trying to contact the Italian embassy. Buckley knew their number. I guess his wife is Italian from what he said. She tried them.'

They sat, not looking about, choked on anxiety.

'He didn't want to, to upset Stuart or us, so he'd left it until he thought some news may have come through, to see if he could be of any assistance.'

Sarah was crying now, tears dripping off her cheeks. She made no noise, sat straight-backed, not covering her face, a statue weeping.

Thelma crouched, as against a blow.

'He hoped it was nothing to do with our family, but he was sure, or his wife was, that today was when they were to travel. I told him we didn't know.'

'What did he say to that?' Sarah asked, and having spoken began to sob.

'Nothing. He didn't comment.' Lang's voice wasted so that the last word was a hoarse whisper. 'He kept repeating things. It appeared that Maria had gone somewhere so he couldn't question her now. She was staying the night with a friend. He was in a hotel. He had to ring her later to let her know anything he'd learnt.'

'It's not . . .' Sarah began, and stopped.

'He kept stressing,' Jack whispered, unconvincingly, 'that there was nothing to connect Francesca with the accident, that he'd never forgive himself if he'd come out with this story to us and there was nothing in it. Maria had apparently done the telephoning to the Italian embassy in London. They knew nothing, but they promised to make inquiries, took her 'phone number, and said they'd ring back as soon as they heard anything. She gave them Francesca's name and Ian's and Hugh's. But they hadn't rung back so far.'

'Is that a good sign?' Thelma asked.

'I've no idea.' Despair emptied his voice.

Again they sat. Sarah sobbed, not noisily; Thelma had moved across to hold her hand. Lang still stood behind his chair.

'What's the best thing we could do?' Thelma asked her husband. The question caused Frank to jerk his head.

'I tell you what,' he said, clearing his throat. 'I'll go and try to contact Stuart, if I may.'

Lang waved a limp hand towards the door.

'Just outside,' he said.

Frank rose. Suddenly his legs shook so that he thought he'd collapse. He leaned, after one step, on the table, his hands by a quiche with a clean-cut sector removed. He heaved himself up, shuffled towards the door, looking at no-one.

'The numbers are on the phone-table,' Lang said.

Outside Frank stood with the list. His legs lacked strength still. He panted as if he'd been bending or running. He found Stuart's number; he knew it already, but he did not trust himself. Steadying himself, he dialled. The ringing tone sounded clear, strong, disturbing the air, but unanswered. No-one picked up the phone. In his daze Frank listened, sure now that his son's house stood empty. Once, twice, three, four, five times he gave it three more rings, but without hope. Finally he carefully recradled the phone. He shuddered, fiddled with cold, damp fingers at the door handle, crept in with the others.

Their heads lifted.

'No. Nothing. Nobody's there.' His voice sounded normal, at least to himself. Sarah let out a whoop of a sob, a short hiccough of grief. Her husband now sat by her; his arm circled her shoulder and her face shone with tears.

'Is there anything we can do? Thelma asked her husband.

'No, I don't think so.' He looked across at Jack. 'Buckley said he had given the police our addresses. Stuart's address would be in the car.'

'The accident was some time this morning,' Jack said. 'You would have thought they'd be through to us now.'

'They'd get in touch with Stuart first,' Frank answered.

'And for all we know,' Thelma said, 'he's gone chasing out to Italy.'

'He would have let us know.'

'He'd be in shock,' Thelma answered her husband. 'You never know what he'd do.'

Frank had not sat down. He stood in the middle of the room, incapable of consecutive, rational thought, his body leaden-heavy with grief.

'We'd better get back home, Thelma,' he said. He never called his wife by her christian name. He squinted at the carpet round his feet. 'We'll give Sarah and Jack a hand to clear away and wash up.'

Jack Lang gently disengaged himself from his wife's arm and rose. He groaned, but the noise was involuntary; he did not realize that he had made it. He staggered a step, knees bent, then held himself upright.

'It's all right, Frank,' he said. 'We can manage.' Then rather pathetically. 'It'll give us something to do.' His eyes glistened.

Both Sarah and Thelma had struggled up from their chairs, and Thelma had taken her friend into her arms. Two well-dressed women, verging on the elderly, hugged in a small, uncertain stasis, snatching at a curt stoppage of grief. The men did not interrupt but waited in silence for their parting.

The Langs did not accompany Thelma and Frank beyond the door to their car. The east wind blew cuttingly through a sky almost clear of cloud, sparkling with dim stars.

Within ten minutes they had reached home.

CHAPTER FIFTEEN

Frank put the car away and locked the garage.

Thelma had switched on more lights, but had not left the hall where she stood, still in her outdoor clothes. The front door hung half open.

'Oh, Frank,' she said.

He put his arms around her and they swayed together. Swaddled in top-coats and scarves they lacked both balance and human touch. Face barely made contact with face. They found no comfort. Thelma's hat rolled from her head to the floor. She must have decided on a social effort to wear the thing, but he had not noticed; old people rarely looked at each other except in the most cursory way. They know what is there, what's to be seen, to be expected.

Thelma broke away from his ungainly embrace.

'I can't breathe,' she said. She took a step backwards, bent without trouble to retrieve her fallen hat. She was crying, but uncertainly as if she had lost control over herself, her natural functions, her personality, her poise. Frank patted then stroked her arm, but without conviction. They had nothing within at this dark moment to protect or console each the other. They knew the weight of grief without remedy.

Thelma recovered first, hung her hat crookedly on a peg and said, voice commonplace, unaffected by weeping, 'I'll put the kettle on. You go upstairs and see to the electric blankets.'

She walked out to the kitchen. There the bar-lights spluttered then shone steadily.

He stumbled towards the stairs, where he could only make progress by heaving his feet heavily from tread to tread. Six steps up breathlessness halted him so that he had to lean forward, throat blocked, his eyes spilling tears. He did not know how long he held his position on all fours. He pulled himself up by the stair-rail and finally reached the landing. In their bedroom the curtains had been drawn.

He switched on the blankets without thinking, then unable to recall what he had done, checked the controls. HI, he read. He groaned out loud, and made his pained way downstairs, knees aching, shoulder to the supporting wall.

Once in the kitchen Thelma ordered him to take his overcoat off, saying that the house was warm. He obeyed, turning about, settling the garment neatly on a hanger.

'What will you have?' Thelma called from the kitchen. To make up his mind was a major, unsurmountable difficulty.

'Tea,' he said. He did not mind. It was the shortest word. 'Weak, please.' The decision to qualify the first decision had steadied him. If not his own man, he was at least his own shadow.

'We'll have it in here,' she said.

He shuffled forward into the clean brightness of the kitchen. She was already pouring.

'Get yourself a stool,' she ordered. He took his cup from her and set it down on a formica surface. He stared, but did not sit; he searched for a voice.

'I think,' he said, 'I think I'll just try Stuart's number again.'

She watched him, slowly shaking her head, signifying that he would waste his time, turn bad to worse. She dredged for words.

'That's a good idea,' she said.

He did not believe his ears.

Back in the hall he dialled Stuart's number, checking it as a huge shudder raked his back. Throat tight, mouth gaping he listened to the dialling tone.

The 'phone was lifted.

'Hello.'

He did not recognise the voice, nor believe in it. Silence engulfed both ends of the wire.

'Hello,' he said. 'Who is it?'

'Ian.'

Clear. Two small syllables of paradise.

'This is Grandpa. Grandpa Frank.' The boy made no reply. 'You're up very late.'

'We've only just this minute come in.'

'Are you all back? All four.'

'Yes.'

'Hang on a tick.' He answered boyish voice with boyish sentence. 'Thelma,' he shouted. 'Thelma. It's Ian on the 'phone. They're all back.'

He heard her struggling in from the kitchen.

'It's Grandpa Frank. He's just ringing to see if we're home.' Ian's explanatory sentences. 'It's Dad, Grandpa. He'll talk to you. 'Bye for now. 'Bye, 'bye.'

A low muttered colloquy in the background, presumably Stuart issuing orders to his son with a hand over the mouthpiece.

'Hello. Stuart here.'

'You're back?'

'Yes.'

'You're very late. We've been trying to get

259

you all night.'

'We changed plans. They flew from Florence to Stansted, and I picked them up there, and then we called in at the Stirlands' in Cambridge.'

'Who?'

'John Stirland. You remember him. He was at school with me. He runs some sort of light engineering concern down there. Just a minute.' Stuart began to bawl out at his sons ordering them to get ready for bed and to stop fooling round. Thelma now stood by Frank's elbow, panting, her face ugly with joy. 'Bloody kids.' Frank laughed aloud.

'Just have a word with your mother, will you?'

He handed the 'phone to Thelma who asked a tremulous question or two about the holiday and Francesca's journey and then, out of character, suddenly pushed the 'phone back towards her husband. He took it, surprised. She backed away.

'You're all all right then, Stuart?'

'Yes. Fine.'

'Good. Good. I'll ring off now, because I want to give the Langs a call. They'll be very relieved to hear you're back.'

'Uh?' Not very interested.

'We'll tell you all about it when we've got a bit more time.'

'Very good.' Matter-of-fact.

They made their goodbyes at speed. Frank

turned to Thelma, put a hand gently on her shoulder, shaking his head. Tears shone on her face still. He kissed her mouth, hugged her, spirit dancing, but sedately.

'Do *you* want to ring the Langs?' he asked. He thought that it would strengthen her to be the bearer of good news. She shook her head.

'No. You.' Two weak syllables and tears gushed again.

'They're back,' he said, gruffly. 'Back. Nothing to cry about.'

'Oh, Frank.'

'I know,' he said, 'I know.'

She wagged an admonitory finger at him, at the 'phone, as if she couldn't get the words out.

'Ring them,' she managed at last. 'Ring them.'

Now the finger pointed imperiously and he obeyed.

He had to wait for an answer. Surely they had a 'phone upstairs? Why don't they get a move on? Here I am with what they most want to hear in the wide world, and they can't even hurry themselves to pick the 'phone up. Perhaps they're afraid. This is the police with confirmation of the tragedy. Frank breathed deeply, made slight signs of frustration in the direction of his wife, who stood unmoving and amazed, fazed with joy.

At last Jack Lang lifted his 'phone.

'It's Frank Stapleton, Jack. They're home. Safe.'

'Francesca?'

'Yes. And the boys. They didn't come via Pisa. Stuart picked them up at Stansted.' He gave the story.

'One minute. I'll just shout up to Sarah.'

The clatter of the 'phone, the call upstairs, Frank's telling Thelma in a whisper, Jack enlightening Sarah with shouts. Finally Jack picked up the 'phone again.

'And they're all quite all right?'

'Yes. And if you hurry up and ring Francesca she'll still be up and about.'

'Yes. Thanks, Frank. Isn't it marvellous? I don't know what to say.'

'It's wonderful. And incredible. I don't know why we deserve it.'

'I'm sure you do.'

'The accident,' Frank said, 'presumably took place.' His voice creaked solemnly. 'And it means bad news for somebody, if not for us. A woman with two small boys ... they were killed. If that man Buckley had it right.'

'Why was he ringing?' Jack asked. 'With only half a tale? Some people haven't the sense they're born with.' He sounded angry. Frank let it pass.

'You call Francesca,' he ordered.

'I will. I can't tell you how thankful I am. Oh, here's Sarah. Do you want a word with Frank?'

'Not now.'

Sarah spoke nevertheless, if still uncertain. He told her what he knew, and said she should ring her daughter at once.

'You told Stuart what Mr Buckley said?' she asked.

'No. He didn't seem very interested, and my priority was to let you know as soon as I could. Good news can't wait.'

'Frank. You're an angel.'

'Right. I'll fold my wings.'

He and Thelma made their way upstairs. Neither could sleep. They made love, unusual these days, gently, and then his wife crept down to the kitchen for more tea. He had dropped off before she returned, and was glad to be woken to a consciousness so replete with pleasure.

'It's a marvel,' he said. 'A miracle.' Sipping, upright.

'You were convinced it was Francesca?'

'I was.'

'And it seemed,' Thelma continued, 'so wrong that Hughie should recover from meningitis only to be killed in a car.'

'We shall never be the same again,' he said.

She stroked his face, looking hard at him, lined and radiant.

*   *   *

To their surprise they heard nothing from Francesca and Stuart, nor from the Langs in the next few days. Though Frank held his peace, Thelma remarked on the silence. They received a delayed post-card from Italy: The Palio in the Piazza del Campo, Siena. The inscription was by Hugh. 'We didn't see this horse-race which takes place in the summer. Mum said you wouldn't like it, but it's world-famous. Love. Hugh, Ian, Mum.'

'I'd have thought one or the other of them would have come round,' Thelma said.

'The boys will be back at school.'

'I know.'

'And the weather's cold and nasty.'

'Frank, saintly demeanour doesn't suit you.'

He crossed his hands on his chest and closed his eyes.

'You clown.'

'I'd guess that they've no idea how upset we were.'

'Sarah would have let them know, even if Jack chose to keep quiet.'

'They're busy.'

'I hope so, but that's still no reason for not getting in touch.'

Half-way into January Frank received an invitation from his son's secretary to undertake 'a small but tricky piece of work'. He made his way down to the offices of Bell and Stapleton and was granted a five minute interview with the principal.

Stuart asked after his parents' health, and barely waiting for an answer handed Frank his brief and gave a two-sentence explanation why he had been brought in, and why tact was

264

necessary. His secretary would fill in relevant detail.

Frank was equally curt.

'You're still alive?' he asked.

'What do you mean?' Stuart had assumed the face for his next piece of business and had already rung for his secretary.

'We've seen nothing of you since your Italian holiday. Neither of you, nor Francesca, nor the boys.'

'You surprise me. I thought Miriam had brought the boys round. I'll look into it.'

'Sometimes I think you're living in some other world.'

The meaning only slowly penetrated Stuart's consciousness and then to his expression. His secretary entered the room.

'Right,' Stuart said. 'Mrs Shipley will clear up any difficulties. The brief's as clear as we can make it. The M.D., Harry Thorpe, will be there to see you.'

'Ah, sweet mystery of life,' Frank said to the secretary who looked uncomprehendingly at him. 'Are you busy these days?'

'We're worked off our feet. Mr Stapleton hardly knows which way to turn.'

'I can believe that.'

At the weekend Mrs Daley brought the boys round to the Stapletons'. They were full of their Italian holiday, and Hugh claimed he'd like to live there permanently.

'I wouldn't mind learning Italian at school,'

265

Ian said.

'Is that possible?' Frank asked.

'No. They don't teach it.'

'If you could learn it, what would you drop?'

'Latin.'

'Won't that help you with your Italian?'

'It might,' Ian answered, 'if I knew it in the first place.'

'You're just like your father.'

'Who is?' Thelma asked.

'Ian. The pragmatist.'

'What's that mean, Grandpa?' Hugh inquired.

'The practical man. One who deals with things as they are.' He coughed. 'There are other meanings.'

'Our Ian,' Hugh said, and laughed, as if he'd learned something.

Miriam Daley had clearly questioned the boys closely about their Italian stay, and filled in detail for the grandparents. The boys had enjoyed the change, the new world, but now it was all back in its place, the memory, and school, rugby, the Forest took priority. Hugh's form-master, 'Old Palmer', was about to get married.

'Old?' Frank inquired. 'How old is he then?'

'Fifty.' Hugh guessed.

'Forty-five at most,' his brother corrected, rather pedantically. 'He's marrying Mrs Hilary Thomas, a divorcee.'

'How does it happen that you're so well-

266

informed?'

'One of her sons is in my class.'

'Poor old Tommo,' Hugh commiserated.

I don't know. Palmer's not so bad.'

'Has he been married before?' Thelma demanded.

'I've never asked him,' Hugh said, cheekily.

'Hugh,' Mrs Daley warned.

'Sorry, Gran,' the boy answered. 'I just don't know.'

The grandparents enjoyed this question and answer session. The boys chattered without much inhibition, and nearly emptied the biscuit-barrel. They burst with energy, and yet maintained a marvellously old-fashioned politeness, even when the questioners exceeded decorum.

'What had the girl-friends to say about your being away over Christmas?' Thelma asked.

'They managed,' Hugh offered.

'They hadn't gone off with somebody else?'

'They didn't say so.'

'So they were pleased to see you back?'

'Delighted,' Ian answered. Without irony. They all laughed.

Both Thelma and Frank tried to prise information out of Mrs Daley about the present relationship between Stuart and Francesca. She gave nothing away, either purposely misunderstanding their questions or answering blandly. Both parents were exceptionally busy, she said, but the whole family took their evening meal together at least four or five times a week. Stuart was to accompany his wife on a business trip to London on behalf of her firm. Miriam had no idea of the nature of the business. How the two behaved at home in private Mrs Daley did not know, and any subtleties of approach to find out, as attempted by Thelma, were wasted. The younger Stapletons were like dozens of other ambitious professional people, driving themselves hard at all hours, but coming home, watching television, eating meals, going late to bed, dashing off early next morning, monitoring the progress of their children.

'She's not giving much away,' Thelma complained, after Miriam had taken her charges back home. 'Do you think she honestly doesn't notice what's happening?'

'Nothing may be happening,' Frank replied.

'You don't believe that, now, do you?'

When Frank had finished the 'little job' at Thorpe's for his son, he dropped a memo, with a caution or two for future dealings with the firm, in at Stuart's secretary's office.

'Would you like to give it him yourself?' Mrs Shipley asked pleasantly. 'He's free now, and I'm sure he'll want to have a word with you.'

Stuart was all smiles before an empty desk.

'Sit down,' he invited. 'Coffee? Tea?'

'No thanks. They fed and watered me downstairs.'

Frank then said a few explanatory words

268

about his memo. Stuart listened, benevolence in his face, every muscle at ease.

'No,' Stuart said. 'They're a careless lot one way or the other. But I like Harry Thorpe, and I'll drop him a word of warning.'

'Will he pay attention, though?'

'I'd guess so. He's had it easy so far. Now things have become tight again, he's tried to cut corners. But basically he's sensible, and he'll see to it that he follows your advice. Oh, he'll understand it, never you fear. And his business is sound enough.'

Stuart had both hands flat on his desk, his head back, like an old-fashioned family doctor giving good news, but warning the patient not to run unnecessary risks. Frank could not help being impressed, for his son's manner had, or aped, a magnificence of ease that demonstrated the head of a vastly successful organization.

'And how are things at home?' Frank asked, grimly enough.

'Oh, pretty well, really.'

'Between you and Francesca?'

The younger man looked pensive, drummed pianissimo with his right hand on the desk top.

'We can't grumble.'

'Look, Stuart,' Frank spoke with a painful, pseudo-reluctance, 'when I get home and tell your mother that I've had a chat with you, the first thing she'll ask me is how things stand between you and Francesca. You know that.'

269

'Don't blame her.' Amusement twisted Stuart's mouth. 'You've some interest, surely? Yourself?'

'Never mind the debating points, just answer my question.'

'Put it to me again, so that there can't be any possible doubt of just what it is you want me to answer.'

Frank could not be sure whether his son asked in earnest for information or was merely trying to rile his father. The young man's expression seemed open, and his posture friendly.

'We were led to believe,' Frank began slowly, 'that you and your wife were on the point of parting, were seriously consulting solicitors about divorce proceedings.'

'Yes,' Stuart said. 'That was so.'

'But is it so now?'

'Ah.' Stuart writhed in his chair after the long monosyllable. 'The situation is not now so clear cut.'

Frank sat silent, refusing to be goaded into another question, staring straight into his son's eyes.

'Is that good enough?' Stuart affected rationality.

'No. As well you know.'

The son leaned back, locked his fingers together, blew out a whimsical breath.

'We went on holiday together in Tuscany during the Christmas period. We enjoyed

270

ourselves. We live together. Still. We go, for example, together to functions at the boys' school. We discuss problems amongst ourselves.' Again the mocking, quizzical smile. 'As far as the solicitors are concerned, matters are in abeyance.'

'There's been a reconciliation?'

'You could say so, though I don't know that I'd put it so strongly.'

'Have you been to counselling? Relate, for example?'

'No. It didn't seem altogether necessary or meaningful. Whatever advance has been made we have made ourselves.'

'Can I be blunt?' Frank's anger sparked.

'I can't stop you.'

'People told us that you were having an affair. They named the woman. A Mrs Clare Cooke. We, in fact, met her, at an EMEG dinner where she sat at our table.'

'Yes. She told me. You made a favourable impression on her.'

'Is the affair still going on?'

'I wouldn't quite put the question like that. We occasionally see each other.'

'What does that mean?'

'Exactly what it says. We go, and I stress it's not often, to a concert together. She's keen on music. But you know that. And she sees me as a brand to be plucked from the burning. Her husband, Trevor, has other interests, so I accompany her.'

271

'That's dangerous.'

Stuart shook his head.

'One thing leads to another. Or gives rise to talk which makes bad worse. What does Francesca say about it?'

'I don't think she minds.' Stuart bit his lower lip, as if in appreciation of her attitude. 'Now I'll be frank with you. Frank.' He grinned at his awkward repetition. He never called his father by his first name, so that the word-play was deliberate. What it showed, Stuart's embarrassment or his present state of contentment, his father could not guess. 'In the first place the attraction was sexual.'

'You mean you committed adultery?'

'Yes. You could put it like that.'

'And?'

'We did think, and very seriously, about leaving home and living together. Both Trevor, her husband, and Francesca knew about this. But otherwise we were discreet. We didn't make a public song-and-dance about it. But it was touch and go. The wronged parties, if you'll allow the expression, were not prepared to be very forgiving. I don't blame them. And it was made worse in Fran's case because things weren't going well for her at EMEG. She must have lived in hell.'

The sentence surprised Frank.

Stuart rose to his feet, and stood, swaying almost gracefully, behind his desk.

'That will have to do for this morning,' he

272

said. 'I have a new client, Lord Felstead, in ten minutes. But I felt I owed you, and Mum, an explanation. It's only half a tale as yet, but there you are. . .'

'You're not thinking of parting? Is that the present situation?'

'One doesn't know. Fran's been badly knocked about, not only by this, so she's not very forthcoming about her future plans.' He ushered his father towards the door. 'I tell you what. I'll arrange for you and Mum, and the Langs, if that seems sensible, to come up to dinner in the near future, and then you can see for yourself how things stand.'

Stuart patted his father's arm, shook hands with manly firmness, and had his father outside in no time.'

'Is Lord Felstead here?' he asked his secretary. 'No? Well, I'll go and spruce my appearance up.' This to his father. 'Show Mr Stapleton out, will you, Caroline?'

'I know my way.'

Mrs Shipley accompanied him downstairs to the foyer.

'We like to do things properly here,' she said. 'And now to meet his lordship.'

'When's he due?'

'Eleven-fifteen. Ten minutes.'

Out in the cold street Frank found himself standing quite still, considering his interview. He could not shake off his impression that Stuart had been enjoying himself. Perhaps it

273

was not quite at his father's expense, but the son must have been pleased with himself for some reason. He should have been more circumspect, more pessimistic: the marriage was by no means safe. And yet, yet. Frank had always regarded his son as a man in love with change, a good fault sometimes. For that reason the father had left Luke Brailsford in charge, a real conservative, opposed to any sort of alteration, to give Stuart the opportunity during Brailsford's two years' interregnum to be held back. As he'd explained to Thelma, time and again, when she savaged him for not making their son head of the firm, 'There's nothing to be said in favour of change for change's sake.' She'd argued, classed him, with Luke, amongst the stick-in-the-muds, and he'd admired her energetic defence of her son, and admitted to himself that she was twenty per cent in the right.

He grinned to himself, straightened his gloves and examined his reflection in a plate-glass window. Upright still, smartly-dressed, hatless, but wearing glasses now, he did not look his age. He'd have no difficulty completing a full day's work at Bell and Stapleton, though he did not want to do any such thing. He wondered what Felstead was after. He did not know him personally, but the man had made a large name in the manufacture of telephone and satellite equipment. Stuart must have chased him, unless the visit was for some charitable purpose. Frank did not connect Stuart with charities; doubtless he handed money out to proper and deserving causes, but it would be all thought out carefully, nothing spontaneous, no digging into his trouser-pockets to hand change to a beggar or a busker.

Frank stopped and looked at radios, CD and cassette players and videos, plain black boxes of marvellous potential, in a shop where he had just recently replaced his own not very ancient equipment. He loved such magic. All his life he had been able to switch on and hear speech and music from first the old wireless in his father's house, an art déco cabinet, later replaced by a gramophone and radio in a piece of substantial furniture, not altogether dwarfed by the side board. All the up-and-coming had them, radiograms; like the fur-coat and the grand piano in his youth they represented arrival, success, but sometimes nemesis was signalled by the removal of the same piano. He had never seen it actually happen, but he pictured it vividly; the busy workmen, not too used to this kind of labour, and the long faces of the ex-owners, their fate sealed as the instrument rattled on its trolley towards the pantechnicon.

'Don't tell me you're buying more equipment.'

This female voice excited him. Francesca.

'No. Just window-shopping.'

'Good.'

She looked bright, dressed smartly and yet in sober colours. One expected a large limousine, preferably black, at the call of such a person.

'What are you doing here?' he asked. 'At this time of the morning?'

'Calling in on my solicitor,' she said. His heart dropped.

'Jenny Townley?'

'No. It's not my personal one; it's the firm's.'

'Are you well?'

'Yes. I can't stop. I've got two minutes before I'm due there.' She pointed to the offices of Dodsley, Kemp in lavish Victorian brick at the top of the street.

'I've just been to see your husband. He seemed very pleased with himself.'

'Oh, good. I'm glad.'

'Are you well?'

'Perfect.'

'I know that.'

'Flatterer.'

She was already moving elegantly along the road away from him. He watched her progress with pleasure. She did not look back, small valise under her arm, a determined woman.

CHAPTER SIXTEEN

The dinner party did not take place until the end of February and, moreover, at the Langs' house. The arrangements had been

276

complicated enough, involving two cancellations, but Sarah and Thelma had enjoyed themselves. 'Born administrators, the pair of you,' Frank had declared, delighted. Finally they had fixed the date: the last Monday of the month.

'Why have they chosen a Monday?' Lang asked Frank.

'To cheer up people like you, who have to work.'

'These things should take place at the weekend,' Lang grumbled, 'but I don't suppose the young people are willing to waste good Saturdays on the likes of us.'

When Frank reported this conversation, from a chance meeting in the street to his wife, Thelma answered that according to Sarah Lang it was well nigh impossible to get more than five minutes from either Stuart or Francesca on the 'phone because they were so busy.

'Francesca?' he inquired.

'She's more pushed for time than Stuart.'

In the middle of the month, Mrs Jordan, Sarah's mother had died, unexpectedly in the nursing home. One day she had refused to eat, shutting her mouth in defiance of all blandishments and then the next morning as breakfast was being prepared had died.

'Well, Mrs Jordan,' the girl, who had helped her dress and led her to her chair, had said cheerfully, 'I hope you're going to make a good start today. There aren't any lumps in the porridge this morning. It's just as you like it. I helped make it myself.'

She had tucked the napkin into the old lady's collar and fixed up her tray-holder.

'I'll be back in five minutes.'

'No, thank you.'

Mrs Jordan had spoken with a peculiar clarity. With none of her usual mumbling. She had even lifted her chin from her chest, demonstrating a strength or challenge that caused the girl to ask,

'Are you all right?'

'Thank you.'

Again the clear enunciation. The face, though, the girl remembered, had been expressionless. Ten minutes later, returning with the porridge, she had found the old lady dead. She had made no sound, as far as they could ascertain from the other inmates or the auxiliaries at work in the room. Her position had not changed; her hands were placidly in her lap, her head forward as if she had nodded gently off.

'It was utterly, utterly peaceful,' the matron solemnly informed Sarah Lang. 'If one has to go, that's the best of all ways to do it. It was so easy. She just gave up the ghost.'

Both Stuart and Francesca attended the funeral, as did Frank and Thelma. The boys were dispatched to school as usual. Sarah reported that she had ten minutes of serious talk with her daughter at her house afterwards.

278

Fran, she declared, seemed healthy, optimistic and sensible.

'Did she know her grandmother well?' Thelma asked.

'Oh, yes. They were great friends. "My grandma says" was Fran's favourite conversational gambit when she was little.'

'So she was upset?'

'No, I don't think so. That wouldn't be like her. She came to terms with my mother's condition when we first had to put her into a nursing home.'

'Did she visit her?'

'Once or twice for a start. But when she became certain her grandmother didn't recognise her, that was it. I used to argue with her that perhaps it stimulated Mother to have a visit from a young, well-dressed woman, even if she hadn't much idea who the visitor was. But it didn't cut much ice with Fran. She didn't see herself as a possible carer for the aged. Hugh's illness may have altered her attitude, but I don't even know about that.'

'Did she say anything about Stuart? How they were getting on?'

'Not really. She certainly mentioned him, but said nothing about any divorce.'

'She was cheerful?'

'Well, it was a funeral. And she's a bit like her dad: she suits her mood to the occasion.'

'I've been at funerals,' Thelma said, 'that have been more like parties. And not on account of alcohol, either. Some people laugh and joke and sing and shout, because they're still alive.'

'They're not Francescas. That's for certain. She always has a sense of occasion. Even as a child. She insisted Jack wore a dark suit and I silk tights and an expensive dress, or expensive-looking, if ever we appeared at a school function.'

Hearing this Frank inquired what he should wear for the dinner party. Thelma chose suit, shirt, tie, cuff-links, socks, for him.

'You'll leave me to clean my shoes for myself, will you?' he asked.

'You invited me to choose for you.'

'I'm very grateful.'

Jack also wore sub-fusc and a sombre silk tie over a dazzling white shirt which suited his neat thickness of grey hair. Stuart sported light grey with a cheerfully patterned tie and a purple-striped shirt. He looked rubicund, well-to-do and appeared to be putting on weight, although he claimed that he played badminton twice a week.

'Does Francesca?' his mother asked.

'She's too busy just now. She might later.'

'Doing what?'

'Work. What else?'

They ate traditionally at the Langs' candle-lit table, carrot soup, roast beef, trifle, cheese. Frank who had a slight cold and would rather have been at home enjoyed every mouthful.

280

Stuart and Francesca spoke marvellously friendly to each other. He ribbed her, with a sort of tactful love, when she asserted that she could easily become a vegetarian, especially when she thought about the slaughter of animals.

'Just slip your beef on my plate if your conscience troubles you too much,' Stuart said.

'They're such beautiful creatures.'

This led to discussion about Creutzfeldt-Jacob Disease, not altogether polite, Frank thought, to the hostess and her choice. Lang, however, proffered his opinions with a strong conviction. It could not harm. Stuart argued against him just for the devil of it, out of joie-de-vivre. His father-in-law laughed quietly deep in his throat.

'Will you two stop arguing and get on with your meal,' Sarah ordered.

'It's the talk that makes meals memorable,' Jack said.

'It makes us sit here waiting for you two to finish.'

'Think what you're learning,' Stuart said.

'I'll tell you what I've learnt,' Sarah answered. 'That men talk a lot more than women.'

'We knew that already,' Thelma backed her up.

Jack and Stuart pulled comical faces, husbands driven mad with surprise at the irrationality of women. Frank asked Francesca about her work, and was rewarded at once by fat smiles from Stuart and his wife. She was busy as ever as she had been, and enjoying every minute.

'And coining money,' Stuart boasted.

The part-time work she had taken on had doubled, so that she had seriously considered going freelance, but just as she was discussing it with her partners and husband, Italian State Railways had appeared with an order that would keep EMEG at full pressure for at least eighteen months. And more to come.

'Not this Thailand contract, then, if that's what it was?' Frank pressed.

'No. That's still hanging on. I guess the Italian people had been let down by a firm in their own country, or one in the EEC, (I know now they had), and then, for whatever reason, had turned to us in desperation. And it so happened we could do it. That was lucky.'

'Why luck?' Frank again.

'You can't just set a work-floor up to do some absolutely new thing in ten minutes. That's the snag. But this job seemed ideally suited to what we could do. The alterations were minimal. That's why I say it's luck. And probably why we got the job. We could hardly believe it. I mean we're used to killing ourselves with unnatural changes to get new orders in, and here, lo and behold, here's somebody asking us to do something we're exactly prepared to do.'

282

'They believe in Santa Claus now up at EMEG,' Stuart said.

'And there's plenty in it for you? Personally?' Frank asked. 'For you and your computers?'

'Oh, yes. There's always work for me these days. It's the nature of the business. Our business. There I am with my models dazzling the eyes of all and sundry.'

There followed a conversation between Francesca and Professor Lang about the Italian contract. It was technical, not always understandable by Frank, but enjoyable to the protagonists, he could see. The daughter's knowledge of engineering and technical processes seemed equal to the father's, and both were delighted. They spoke without speed or force, but Fran cleared the ground to the complete satisfaction of the professor. The two appreciated each other, and to such an extent that they seemed to forget the rest, and yet, as Thelma said to Sarah in the kitchen where she and Frank had helped clear plates, 'I don't know half of what they're on about, but I could listen to them all night.'

'Do they often talk together like this?' Frank asked Sarah.

'I've never heard them before in my life. They used to argue at one time.'

'It's all very technical,' Thelma said, 'but to me it's like a love duet. I'm talking daft, aren't I?'

Sarah laid a heavy kiss on Thelma's cheek,

283

and then stepped round her to kiss Frank.
'Goings-on at the kitchen sink,' he said.

When they returned with the cheese-board, Jack and Francesca were still at it, explaining apparently why one method had been chosen rather than another, and Stuart, chairman or ringmaster, watched them, knowing that for the moment his office was superfluous so that he could enjoy the performances without any intervention on his part.

'We've bored you all stiff,' Jack said, last to help himself to the cheese. White Stilton was his choice. He, Sarah and Stuart toyed with glasses of port. The table shone tranquil under the chandeliers. Replete, hosts and guests cultivated a silence of satisfaction.

In the end it was Jack Lang who spoke. He coughed deep in his lungs as a preliminary to speech, then methodically cleared his throat. Frank noticed that his wife and daughter both watched this prelude with affection.

'I hope,' he said finally, still unready, 'that I'm not going to say something out of place.'

'Impossible,' Stuart murmured, richly.

'This has been a marvellous meal, but that's what I expect from my wife. None the less I thank her. From the bottom of my heart. It has put us all in a cheerful mood.' He seemed now slightly embarrassed by the formality of his expression, as if he thought he should have been standing to voice such opinions. 'Or perhaps my stomach.' He made no attempt to

284

lighten the tone. No applause rewarded him. 'And you've appreciated it and made your pleasure known, palpable.' He added the last word with defiance, as if he expected them to complain about its aptness, or accuracy. He raised his glass, moistened his lips, looked round. Later, on the way home Thelma had offered a comment which surprised her husband. 'Do you know, Frank, even Jack's ears seemed to be intelligent.'

Now Lang pulled himself tidier, tapped the table to collect his wits.

'This is not the time for speech-making. Nor is this a speech, especially in the sense that it's not prepared. It's extempore.' He looked about.

'From the bottom of the heart,' Stuart said, not without sarcasm. Nobody in any way encouraged him further.

'It won't be news to anybody that we,' he indicated by a wave, 'the older generation, have been for some time worried,' he frowned again at his own word, 'at the state,' another grimace, 'of the marriage of Stuart and our daughter Francesca.' He stopped again, to scratch his forehead with the nail of the fourth finger of his right hand. His difficulties had become obvious. Frank guessed that Sarah had nagged a promise out of him to say something if the younger couple were not themselves forthcoming, and now Jack, against the run of his own personal wishes, grimly kept his word.

285

'I don't know if this is a good time or a poor, but we've all looked on the wine when it was red.' He raised his glass to stare into the port, a pathetic gesture of illustration. 'I haven't found it easier on that account, that I must admit, and I don't know whether it will have made, their, well, confessions, that is, if they care to give them, any simpler.' Now he lifted his glass again, and returned it slowly, hoping that Stuart or Fran might intervene with an answer to put him out of his embarrassment. 'I have a grave suspicion that this speech might be turning bad to worse.' He sniffed.

'Rubbish,' Sarah said, quite violently.

'Well, in for a penny, in for a pound.' He paused again. 'It would have suited my book much better if either Fran or Stuart had volunteered information in the course of our prandial conversation, but they haven't. So it's left to me to blunder in. I can only hope they don't mind, though I know if I were in their place, I would.' He touched, then cleared his throat. 'I'm quite prepared to be told to mind my own business. But there we are. I've put my cards on the table.'

Lang was holding his glass up to the light, and squinting at it as though the rest were not there.

Sarah looked up, agitated, holding herself back, both fists on the table.

Francesca spoke, after a silence, in a voice clear as a running stream.

'Thanks, Dad,' she said. Then no more. Nothing further.

'Well?' Jack pursued it.

'We're doing rather better.'

'Good. Good.'

Francesca looked towards her husband, and spread out a hand, granting him opportunity.

'That's about it,' Stuart said. 'We're doing better. Since before Christmas, November say, when we fixed up the holiday in Tuscany. It began to go more easily.'

'What do you mean?' Sarah could not contain herself.

'Exactly what I say. I know it seems improbable. For something like two years we'd been at loggerheads; at the very best, uncomfortable. In my case, and I speak only for myself, it did vary. When I was busy, I'd no time for introversion, and so I wasn't much bothering myself how we were making out. When I think about that now, it speaks for itself, but I didn't see it so at the time. But that was at its most quiet. Again, I can only tell you what I felt.'

'Have you explained all this to Francesca?' Thelma asked.

'Yes, he has. We've discussed it.' Francesca answered for herself.

'But there was worse than that. Sometimes I felt so worked up, so stressed that the mere sight of Fran left me angry or resentful. She'd only to say "Please" or "Thank you" and I glowered at her. I was sure she was getting at me in some way. It was, I suppose, guilt on my part.'

'On account of this Mrs Cooke?' Sarah snapped.

'No. That was never serious. I know I used to consider how much better it would be if I were married to Clare. But that's typical of me. I didn't see things straight. When I look back now I can't imagine how much, how often I got it wrong. I can still feel the hurt and annoyance, even now, but not the reason. I just didn't see eye to eye with Fran, not about anything. Even when I took the firm over, when Luke Brailsford had to pack it in, you'd have thought that would have changed things, but it didn't. I hated Francesca, her successes and all she stood for.'

'What about the children?' Thelma asked.

'I would have seen to it that they were well looked after. And Fran, for that matter. She could have kept on with Miriam, so she could continue to work. And the house. And don't think I was being generous. I was only too willing to buy myself out.'

'You could have afforded this Clare Cooke?' Sarah, rushing injudiciously in.

'She had a job. But in any case she wasn't willing to leave Trevor. So any thoughts of marriage there would quickly have come to nothing.'

'And you realized this at the time?'

'Yes. I did. I think I did.' Stuart threw his head about, publicly exhibiting his troubles for the first time. 'I often wonder what I did realize.'

'And there was six of one to half-a-dozen of the other?' Thelma asked judicially.

'Yes,' said Francesca.

'No,' Stuart answered. 'I was the cause. Fran was fed up with me, from time to time. But I made a meal of it. I was most to blame. The majority of people just manage these blank periods, get on with something else and keep home-life bland, quiet, pacific. It may not be marvellous, but it's better than nothing, and it's imperative if there are children to be considered. I understand that now. I didn't then.'

'You were too churned up?' Sarah asked.

'Exactly.'

Francesca intervened. They could see she would, as she drew herself slowly upright, making them wait on her. A remarkable woman, she outclassed them all, even in her silence. When she spoke her voice sounded low, without harmonics, easy, soothing.

'I was as bad as he was. He couldn't do right for me.' She turned towards Thelma. 'One of you advised me to think what it was like when we first met. I did. I could. And it made no difference. He could do nothing for me.' She sighed unselfconsciously as if her memory had undermined her self-possession. 'When I

289

thought of the boys I was convinced that they'd be better off if we separated.' She shook her head, appalled perhaps at her own foolishness. 'Did Hugh's illness make any difference?' 'No. I don't think so. When something like that happens, you do your best to cope with it. It was the same with Clio Pugh. With Hughie, my own child, I had to put a lot more time in. And he recovered. Remarkably quickly, all things considered. One just does what's to be done. With Hugh it was a full-time occupation, at least for a short period. With Clio, it meant a visit or two a week. Both had to be fitted in, with no argument. But at the time it did nothing to alter my feelings against Stuart. Perhaps I didn't brood on them so often, since I'd other things to do. It's amazing to me now, that when Clio became so ill, I never compared my troubles with hers, or realized, assessed my advantages. She was a talented, beautiful woman, as full of life and plans as I was, and now was marked to die, painfully, without all this dignity they talk about, whereas I had a home, a job, two marvellous children, help, money, prospects, good health. True, I didn't want my husband. I remember Clio saying once that her death was like a husband, always there, on hand. I thought that was a bit dramatic, she always was an actress, but it didn't ring any bells with me. Stuart keeps saying that he can't explain now why he felt as he did. Neither can I. And we're both intelligent, middle-aged people, I'm thirty-five, now, but we were caught up in this aggression and hate. They're strong words, and wrong words really, but they give you the impact. We weren't rational people, I can tell you.'

'And what caused the change?' Jack Lang asked the question for them all.

'God knows,' Stuart said.

'I can't account for it, but I think we both gradually are beginning to understand the advantages of staying together. But that wouldn't have happened unless there had been a lessening of the tensions and angers between us. Why that came about I can't explain. I can guess, but it is only guesswork. Perhaps, as you suggested, it was Hughie's illness. He was precious to both of us: we thought we were going to lose him, and then suddenly he was given back to us. Miraculously. I don't suppose either of us put the two events consciously together.' She looked round the table, like a satisfied headmistress with her prize pupils on distribution day. When nobody offered to speak she set off again. 'I have wondered if it was perhaps our relative positions at work. Stuart was now where he wanted to be, at the head of his firm and beginning to set in place all the changes he felt necessary to bring it right up to date. At the same time I wasn't doing so brilliantly. Stuart knew it wasn't my fault, and perhaps felt sorry for me.'

'Well.' Sarah sniffed disapproval. 'I don't

know about that.'

'There's nothing wrong with it,' Francesca answered pacifically. 'If we're doing nicely, we're a bit more inclined to be generous. Or at least I am.'

'Have you heard this before?' Sarah asked aggressively of Stuart.

He inclined his head in assent, unwilling to interrupt his wife.

'We've discussed this,' Francesca said. 'I've said all this, and more to Stuart. We didn't argue, or not much. Neither of us has any idea how important it is, or was. Perhaps we've changed physically, shed all the cells or hormones or outgrown whatever it was that caused our animosity, our estrangement. I don't know if that's even medically possible. I doubt it. But it's certain that when I was offered the chance of this Italian holiday at Christmas and put it to Stuart I found I could talk to him without this seething of dislike and anger.'

'Were you surprised?' Frank asked.

'Yes. In a way. I could hardly believe it. And I couldn't think it was a permanent condition. I was very doubtful about putting the Buckleys offer of their home to Stuart in the first place. I expected him to dismiss it out of hand. We hardly knew the Buckleys. What were they up to? It wouldn't be fair to the boys to take them out of England at Christmas. He didn't want to go; he was far too busy. I can tell you I was hesitant about broaching it at all. But when I did, he listened, asked a question or two, and said it sounded quite an idea. He asked me to look into exact dates and put it to the boys. He seemed pleased in a mild sort of way. He raised the matter the next day, told me when he'd be free, and asked me if I wanted to arrange it, or was he to do it? All very quiet, very friendly, rational.'

'But how did you feel?' Frank asked.

'A bit suspicious. I wondered what he was up to, whether he'd let me fix it up, and then withdraw at the last minute. But that didn't seem to be the case. He was nice. That's about the word for it. Ordinary. Plain. Unexaggerated. Normal as we had not been. He seemed nice.'

Fran stopped, to smile.

'I didn't expect too much. I didn't think there was an imminent big change. I thought perhaps he was doing it, accepting the holiday for the sake of the boys.' She touched her face, in puzzlement. 'But I enjoyed talking something over with him without hassle or hostility. It was good. But I wasn't building any hopes on it. I never even thought there were any. It was something for the moment. After the trouble we'd been in you don't, in my view, find yourself suddenly, miraculously reconciled. It was for the minute only. The speed of the whole change had been too great.'

'And in Tuscany?' her father asked.

'We enjoyed it, did things together as we hadn't for long enough.'

Francesca sat back, contentedly pushing a biscuit-crumb round her plate. She was ready to field the next question. It came from Frank.

'What is it like now?'

She waited, examining the small plate, face pensive.

'We're suspicious. I am. I guess Stuart's the same. He'll tell you for himself.' She thoughtfully bit on the forefinger of her left hand. 'We can't quite believe it. There'd been so much pain and torment and trouble. My view was, is, and I don't know how much worth you can attach to it, is that once relationships are as deep in hurt as ours was then they can only get worse. That's how ours developed. The sting didn't disappear, the wound never healed. We were in such emotional chaos that anything we did, however sensible or advantageous, only made things worse. Moreover, I'd have sworn that the only sensible action was to separate and put an end to it all. Best for us, for the boys, for everybody.'

Now Francesca looked seriously round the table.

'That's why when you ask us you get this grudging little answer: "We think we're doing better." We can hardly believe what's happened. We've discussed it at length, at least twice. That in itself is a marvel. Six months ago we'd have been scratching each other's eyes

294

out.'

'Has there been physical violence between you?' Jack asked.

'No. Not really. And what bit there has been was on my part.'

'I see.'

'So we're understating it all. Now, I mean. What's happened now.'

'Is that because you're afraid,' Thelma asked, 'that one or the other will say or do something out of place, and you'll be back to square one?'

'Exactly.'

The table had grown silent, without a movement from anyone. Jack Lang, rousing himself as chairman, posed a question.

'Is that right, Stuart?'

Stuart shrugged, breathed deeply, noisily through his nostrils. He appeared to disapprove, but of what they were uncertain. He rolled in his chair, then straightened his back.

'You heard what the lady said.' He spoke steadily, at ease, superior, the managing director. 'Fran has given a very clear account of how she thinks things stand. I'd say she's caught it exactly right.' He paused. 'I wasn't altogether convinced that we should explain anything to you. You'll recognize why that is. You can interfere with the best will in the world and the results prove catastrophic. We're not altogether certain. Yet. The change is there all right. Make no mistake about that. But we're a suspicious pair. We're not prepared to take it for granted. We've had two, more perhaps, desperate years, and here we are hand in hand.' He grinned at his expression. 'We're not prepared to let go, but we aren't dancing in the streets. We hope. Yes, we hope. I hope. Fran said there had been no hope for her. But there's a bit now. As far as I'm concerned.' He breathed deeply, filling his broad chest. 'There's one more thing I want to say, and then we'd do best to drop the subject, at least for the present.' He pursed his lips, waiting perhaps for approval. 'I want to thank you all. It's one of the reasons why we're come together. Fran didn't mention it, but we've talked together about it, and I think she's deliberately left me to say this. We knew all the time how worried you were. We didn't want to hurt you.'

Francesca made as if to speak. Stuart indicated her turn by a movement of the hand. She sounded severe.

'When we were so badly at loggerheads, and when I was certain that there was nothing for it but to part, I used to think to myself that I should never be able to drop in on Thelma and Frank, that I shouldn't be their daughter any more. I hated that. I know I don't see you very regularly now that we've Miriam to bring the boys over, but in my mind I belonged in your house as I belonged in my mother and father's. It seemed to make no difference when we were

296

quarrelling most fiercely. It stood separate. Small. Something that could not alter anything. I regretted that this would be a consequence of our divorce, and regret appeared weak compared with the ferocity, the conflagration between Stu and me at our worst. But now I'm not so sure. Perhaps when we were at our most lunatic it didn't count for much, but once there was a half-chance of recovery, it seemed more important, a kind of prop, a buttress, a foundation even.' She smiled beautifully warm, both at the four and her metaphors. 'And so we do thank you. You're a bonus to us, a prize.'

'And thank you,' Jack said.

'Amen,' said Thelma out of the blue.

Stuart stood and shook hands with them all, then walked round the table to kiss mother-in-law, mother, wife.

Frank applauded.

The talk lasted for perhaps another hour. Nobody drank a great deal. Frank enjoyed a discussion about the options the boys could choose at their school. Francesca and Stuart did not always see eye-to-eye, he noticed, but could discuss their differences without animosity. Ian, the elder boy would be a scientist. There seemed no doubt about that.

'They ought to be good at maths with all you lot about,' Sarah said.

'Oh, they are, they are, but Hughie seems to enjoy languages. Though I was amazed how quickly they both picked up Italian words.

297

Amazing.'

Jack spoke of retirement; they'd never heard him mention it before. He was not going to the University. He'd decided.

'Have you had enough?' Thelma inquired.

'You'd think so to hear him sometimes,' Sarah answered for him.

'Not really. I can still do a bit on the research side. It's the meetings, the paper-work that get me down. But I'll doddle on till I'm sixty-one, and see then how I feel about it.'

All six then talked wildly, ignorantly about the pleasures of retirement.

'The snag is the grave's getting close,' Frank said, grinning.

'We don't know that, thank God.' Thelma.

'Do you ever think about dying?' Sarah asked Frank.

'Yes, I do. But not seriously. When some dire illness hits me then perhaps I'll give it serious thought.'

This sobered then slightly left them at a loss so that Francesca ordered her father to put some music on.

'What do you want?' he asked.

'Something cheerful but serious.'

'Like us,' Thelma intervened. 'But not too difficult. Simple, in fact.'

'Like us,' Frank said.

Lang thought.

'I know,' he said, and went straight to his chosen CD 'Listen to this.'

298

A violin rang out, strong, broad, formal, climbing and dipping. Frank knew the piece, but could not put a name to it. He imagined the marvellous right arm of the soloist building these magnificent sounds with masterful strokes of his bow. The whole room shook with the power, the demand, the haughty beauty. Once the breadth of the opening pages was done the fiddle tripped, danced, skeetered into ordered joy. The six did not move; Lang and Frank seemed taken out of themselves, caught up, entranced. Thelma smiled at the pleasure of others. Stuart sat still, but his mind was elsewhere, not on the music. Sarah looked at her husband with admiring candour, delighted to be associated with a man who could make such a choice without hesitation. Francesca held herself upright, hands on the chair-arms, but was changed, her face calm, waxy, frozen into loveliness by the miracle of the music.

As soon as the quick movement had ended, broadly, but without fuss, as if the composer refused to lengthen their pleasure one note beyond reason, Jack Lang leaned forward, touched the 'off' button. Small lights flashed; silence replaced sound.

'What was that?' Francesca asked. 'I know it as well as anything.' She retained her still beauty, but whistled the opening of the second, quick movement.

'Praeludium and Allegro in the style of Pugnani by Fritz Kreisler,' Lang said slowly, relishing the opportunity.

'Why did you choose that?' Sarah asked.

'I used to try to play it myself when I was a boy. It was never anything approaching that, but I knew what it should sound like.'

'Perfect,' Francesca said. 'I wonder why.'

It took a long time for the party to break up. Frank and Thelma severally claimed at intervals that it was getting late, that they should go, but they delayed, hesitated, tacked on some further snippet of conversation. They had no more music. It seemed that this meeting, these exchanges, carried for all six an emotional charge of inestimable value, so that in some way by remaining in company, however trivially, they strengthened the marriage-ties between the young people. All would have denied this, so baldly stated, but the confessions, the wine, Kreisler's pastiche had put them beyond logic, left them a willing prey to their feelings, and momentarily the better for it.

When Frank and Thelma finally left, the others crowded to the hall to help them on with outdoor clothes. Kissing prevailed and quietly-muttered thanks. Time for talk was over. Thelma had never been so happy, and said so. Sarah spilt a few tears, and clung to her friend's lapels. Only Stuart seemed unaffected; he was cheerful, hugged his mother and Sarah, but Frank thought, based his behaviour on that of the others rather than from inner compulsion.

The one man out. Did he like his son? Frank dismissed the suspicion, only for it to reappear immediately. Was he jealous of the boy? Of his success? Of the length of the triumphs yet to come? He thought not, but he was not sure. He shook his son's hand for the third time.

'Go carefully,' Stuart warned.

'Thelma will see to that.'

They prolonged the parting, less noisy than revellers on the pavement outside a pub at closing-time or a winning football team on the pavilion steps, but as intense.

'Open up, Jack,' Thelma said, 'or we'll be here all night.'

'It'll be freezing the other side of that door,' he answered.

'We can stand it.'

The night struck cloudlessly cold, but they did not care under the stars. Just before they began to drive down hill towards the main road, Thelma touched Frank's arm and ordered him to stop.

'Let's look about us,' she said.

Delighted, they stared out, at the lacing branches of the forest trees planted a hundred years earlier by the roadside, and beyond them to the straight lines and curves of the distant street lamps, cicatrices of light, and then up to the fragile blue of the moon-touched arch of the sky and the faint stars.

They stared, still, saying nothing, drinking in the beauty they had earned.

'It's good,' she said.

'We've healed a small hole in creation,' he answered.

She stared uncomprehending, and then fell into the comfort of silence.

Thelma spoke first, ordering him home.

'Sailor will wonder where we've got to,' she said.

We hope you have enjoyed this Large Print book. Other Chivers Press or Thorndike Press Large Print books are available at your library or directly from the publishers.

For more information about current and forthcoming titles, please call or write, without obligation, to:

Chivers Press Limited
Windsor Bridge Road
Bath BA2 3AX
England
Tel. (01225) 335336

OR

Thorndike Press
P.O. Box 159
Thorndike, Maine 04986
USA
Tel. (800) 223-2336

All our Large Print titles are designed for easy reading, and all our books are made to last.